"Can we still have ~~t~~ **love best about Ch** ~~~~

Amos wrapped his arms around his father's waist. "Nellie said we could only get mistletoe if you agree."

"Mistletoe? Why are you so insistent on mistletoe?" Luke looked down at his son.

"Because!" A wide grin split Amos's face. "Everyone kisses and hugs, and they're all happy. We need more happiness in our house. And maybe, if Nellie kisses you, then you would be happy, too."

"Nellie can't kiss Papa!" Ruby declared, shaking her head furiously. "It's not right."

A lump formed in Nellie's throat. Apparently, there were limits to the changes Ruby would approve of. Even Luke looked mildly stricken at the thought.

Would she and Luke ever kiss? Sometimes Nellie hoped so. But then she thought about how it would merely be a platonic kiss to Luke, but if Nellie kissed him, she'd be doing it with all her heart.

A difference that would absolutely destroy her.

Danica Favorite loves the adventure of living a creative life. She loves to explore the depths of human nature and follow people on the journey to happily-ever-after. Though the journey is often bumpy, those bumps refine imperfect characters as they live the life God created them for. Oops, that just spoiled the ending of Danica's stories. Then again, getting there is all the fun. Find her at danicafavorite.com.

Books by Danica Favorite

Love Inspired Historical

Rocky Mountain Dreams
The Lawman's Redemption
Shotgun Marriage
The Nanny's Little Matchmakers
For the Sake of the Children
An Unlikely Mother
Mistletoe Mommy

DANICA FAVORITE

Mistletoe Mommy

HARLEQUIN® LOVE INSPIRED® HISTORICAL

Recycling programs
for this product may
not exist in your area.

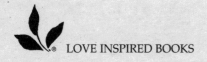

LOVE INSPIRED BOOKS

ISBN-13: 978-0-373-42544-0

Mistletoe Mommy

Copyright © 2017 by Danica Favorite

This edition published by arrangement with Love Inspired Books.

® and TM are trademarks of Love Inspired Books, used under license.
Trademarks indicated with ® are registered in the United States Patent
and Trademark Office, the Canadian Intellectual Property Office and in
other countries.

www.Harlequin.com

Printed in U.S.A.

Do not store up for yourselves treasures on earth, where moths and vermin destroy, and where thieves break in and steal. But store up for yourselves treasures in heaven, where moths and vermin do not destroy, and where thieves do not break in and steal.
—*Matthew* 6:19–20

For the real Ruby, Charlie, Maeve, Amos, Ruth, Ely and Lydia, may you continue to grow in God's love under the guidance of your amazing parents. I'm so proud to call them my friends, and I'm grateful I get to be a part of your lives.

Chapter One

Denver, Colorado, 1883

Luke Jeffries twisted his hat in his hands as the woman stared at him from behind her desk. Like he was an errant schoolboy facing the teacher for his misdeeds. But he hadn't done anything wrong. At least not in the way most people considered something to be wrong. He hadn't hurt anyone or broken any laws, and yet standing in front of a strange woman, begging her to find him a mail-order bride, felt more wrong than anything the worst of sinners could do.

"Please, ma'am," he said again, swallowing the guilt in his throat. "I'm not asking for me. But you see, my children…" Luke shook his head. Took a deep breath. "Without their mother, things have been hard for them. I've got to work."

Some folks might say he didn't. The mining company gave him a nice payout after Diana's death. But he couldn't accept their blood money. It just sat there in the bank, taunting him, telling him what they thought a woman's life was worth. But none of that would bring back the woman he loved. A dollar couldn't tuck in the children at night.

Which was the greater sin? Going to some agency to find himself a bride he could never love? Or spending money that could never replace what had been taken from him?

Luke straightened his shoulders. "I'll provide my wife with a good home. Plenty of food, and the children are well behaved. It's a good life for a decent woman."

"And what about you, Mr. Jeffries?" Mrs. Heatherington, who ran the mail-order-bride agency, stood, leaning over her desk to stare at him even harder. "What do you have to offer of yourself?"

It was the very reason he'd come here. Nothing. Absolutely nothing. "I will be kind to my new wife, if that's what you're asking. I'm not a violent man. I don't drink. I don't gamble. I go to work every day at the smelter, then come home to spend the evening with my family."

"What of love?" the woman asked quietly, almost too quietly, but his heart heard. And wept.

"I can offer her the love of a friend or a brother. I have no expectations of my future wife to be anything more."

Luke stared down at his hat, knowing he wasn't doing it any favors with the way he was twisting it, but right now the feel of the material gave him some comfort, like it was his only friend.

"It seems to me that you need a nanny or a housekeeper, not a wife," Mrs. Heatherington said, sitting back down and jotting a few notes on a piece of paper. "I can give some recommendations of a few agencies that might help you."

"No. I appreciate that, but I do need a wife. I can't afford to pay someone, and to be honest, my living situation…" Luke shook his head again. "It wouldn't be proper, having a woman come and stay with us if we weren't married. Housing in Leadville is hard to come by, and our little house is but one room, with a tiny loft for sleeping."

Mrs. Heatherington looked up at him over her glasses. "But you aren't going to love her?"

It was obvious what she was asking, and yet such things weren't spoken of, not in polite society, not with a respectable woman like Mrs. Heatherington. Then again, Luke wasn't sure that asking someone to find him a wife was something a person did in polite society, either.

"With all due respect, ma'am, I think I understand what you're asking. And let me assure you that I have no desire to have…" Luke paused and drew in a breath. "Any sort of…relations…with my new bride. Our marriage is to be in name only."

And yet his words only served to make the woman stare at him like he was a criminal.

"Just what exactly do you think you're offering? What would induce any woman to marry a man who only wants her to be a housekeeper or nanny without pay, and without the benefit of someone to love her? Someone to care about her?"

Luke shifted uneasily as she rose from her chair yet again.

"Please, ma'am. I just thought that maybe there was a woman out there, someone who doesn't have all those romantic notions. A widow, maybe. Someone who needs a good home, children to raise. Women dream of that, don't they?"

He looked at her, hoping she could see the earnest desire in his heart to find a situation that would work for not just him, but for a woman who wanted a similar situation.

"Women dream of being loved, Mr. Jeffries. They dream of being more than someone's domestic servant."

Shaking his head, he said slowly, "I don't intend for her to be my servant. We'd be partners. Working together for the good of our family."

Mrs. Heatherington glared at him.

"This isn't just about me. My children need a good woman to guide them. My daughter Ruby, she's…" Luke hesitated, trying to find polite words to describe the situation he found himself in. "Things are changing in her, and she needs a woman to help her."

Once again, he stared at the floor, anything to avoid meeting the gaze of the woman who stood on the other side of the desk, judging him. Making him wish he hadn't seen the ad in the paper promising to find men good wives. Easier than Taking a Mail-Order-Bride Ad Yourself, it claimed. We Do the Work for You. And since he'd tried finding a mail-order bride, with no answers to his ads, this seemed to be his last option.

"Surely a woman from your church could discuss

those things with your daughter," Mrs. Heatherington said kindly. "I understand it would be difficult for a man, but—"

"I won't have anything to do with the church," Luke said, his attention snapping back up at her. "That's the whole reason we're in this mess. As far I'm concerned, the church killed my wife. Even if they could help, I wouldn't take it."

With a pang, Luke thought of the many meals the ladies had brought over for his family when Diana had been killed. He hadn't wanted to take them, hadn't wanted to eat the food, but the children had been so hungry, and Luke's efforts at preparing anything edible hadn't gone over well. Every bite had made him feel sick, and he'd been grateful when ten-year-old Ruby had calmly told him that her mother had taught her to prepare some basic things, and she'd taken over the cooking.

But it wasn't Ruby's place to prepare the meals, do her mother's chores and take care of her siblings. Especially now that the woman Luke had hired to watch Maeve, the youngest, who wasn't yet in school, had quit. Maureen's note to him saying she was leaving had somehow gone awry, and Luke found out that Ruby was skipping school to do the job herself. She deserved to have her childhood back, which was one more reason Luke had to find a wife. Clearly hired help couldn't be counted on, and Luke still didn't understand how it had taken him nearly a week to find out that Ruby had taken over. Since then, he'd relied on the generosity of neighbors, but Luke had to find a more permanent solution.

It didn't feel right to take a wife not six months after Diana's death, but Luke was out of options.

"I'm sorry, Mr. Jeffries. I can't help you," Mrs. Heatherington said, coming around to the side of her desk. "We are a Christian organization, and it's my obligation to bring together men and women of faith to create a loving home."

She shook her head as she looked at him with sympathy. "I am truly sorry for your loss, and I can't imagine how difficult it must be for you to have lost a wife, and for your children to not have a mother. But this goes against everything I believe in. Too many women come out here as part of mail-order-bride schemes, thinking they're going to end up with a wonderful life. All too often, they end up in terrible situations, some even being sold to houses of ill repute."

"I would never—"

Mrs. Heatherington shook her head slowly. "Perhaps not. But what happens to this bride of yours when the children are grown and you have no need of free labor? Or one of you realizes that you do, in fact, need someone to love in your life?"

Before Luke could answer, a voice called out from behind him. "I'll do it."

Luke turned to see a woman standing in the doorway. Though her clothes seemed to have once been of fine quality, they were now threadbare and worn. Her dark hair was piled on top of her head in a simple yet elegant style, and she bore herself like a lady of means. The lines at the corners of her deep brown eyes indicated a weariness of the world matching his own. Yet her face seemed to have a strength to it that said she was not going to let any of her hardships get her down.

"And you are?" Mrs. Heatherington stepped past him to approach the woman.

"Nellie McClain," she said, entering the room. "I've come to see if you'd find me a husband."

Nellie looked around the room, then her gaze settled on Luke. "He'll do just fine."

He'll do just fine. Not exactly the words of love and devotion one would expect to come from a bride, but Luke wasn't looking for love and devotion. Still, he knew nothing of this woman, and it seemed odd that she'd jump right in and offer to marry him.

"But you know nothing about him," Mrs. Heatherington said. "And we haven't… That is to say, I don't know who you are, and we haven't gone through the interview process."

"It doesn't matter," she said. "You won't help him, but I can."

"What do you mean, you can?" Luke said.

"I need a husband," she said, turning her attention to him. "Based on what you said, I think you're exactly what I'm looking for. I don't want a man to make promises with his fancy words. I don't want some notion of romance. All I want is someone who is decent, hardworking, and knows how to treat people right. I know it's wrong to eavesdrop, but based on what I heard in here, it seems to me that you have the qualities I seek."

Her words might not sound like what a man hoped to hear from a prospective bride. But they were music to Luke's ears, given that it seemed like they wanted the same thing.

"But what of love?" Mrs. Heatherington asked. "You seem like a nice young lady. Surely you want better for yourself."

"With all due respect," Nellie said, "I'm a widow. I know what it's like to marry over some foolish notion like what a person thinks might be love. A woman like me needs nothing more than the protection of a good man and a family to care for. To be able to raise children is a pleasure I dared not hope for, but I would be extremely grateful for the opportunity."

She stepped farther into the room and looked at Luke, and for the first time, he was able to examine her features and see that while it was easy to mistake her for a young lady in the marriage mart, her bearing bore the strain of someone who had seen far too much pain in so short a life. A widow. This woman knew what it was like to love and lose, and it was obvious she wasn't willing to take the risk again. A perfect match for him.

"I'm sorry for your loss," Luke said. "What makes you want to marry?"

Nellie hesitated. A dark look flashed across her face, and Luke wished he could ask her about it. But he barely knew this woman, and it didn't seem right to dig into her pain.

"I suppose it sounds selfish for me to say that I wish to be cared for. A woman in my position finds herself taken advantage of and placed in bad situations because she is alone. There is little a respectable woman can do on her own, and she is often faced with challenges simply because of her circumstances. I've had enough struggle and hardship, and all I really want is to live life in peace."

She looked up at him with such sadness in her eyes that even if he hadn't already decided to marry her, Luke would have found some way of helping her. He couldn't disagree with her words. Though he had nothing but respect for women, he had also seen how many other men mistreated them. A woman on her own was a target for all sorts of vile deeds. Based on the expression on Nellie's face, Luke would guess that something terrible indeed had happened to her.

"I can't promise you that a life with me will be easy," Luke said. "I live in Leadville, a mining town in the mountains that boasts of luxuries and society rivaling that of Denver. However, Leadville also has a dark side, an uncivilized side, and the best I can offer you is a tiny cabin on a dirty street in the midst of it. We've plenty enough to eat, clothes on our backs, and as long as you don't require anything fancy, you'll have what you need."

"But what of love?" Mrs. Heatherington asked again, looking distraught and wringing her hands as she came forward. "The two of you sound like you're planning a business deal. But marriage is so much more than that. What happens when the children are grown? What happens when you can't bear the sight of each other?"

Luke took another look at Nellie. It wouldn't be proper of him to say, but Nellie's eyes were not her only attraction. The light shone on her dark hair in a way that made it sparkle. Being able to bear looking at her wasn't the problem. He was more worried that he would like looking at her a little too much.

Nellie smiled at her, a gentle expression that made Luke want to know her better. "There are different kinds of love. Romantic love is something I want nothing to do with. It is a whimsical notion that makes fools of too many men and women. But there is also the love of a mother, father, brother, sister, and what I hope to develop with my future husband, that of a friend."

Then Nellie turned her gaze on Luke, smiling at him. If only Mrs. Heatherington hadn't made him consider her beauty. Her warm, gentle smile made him feel more at ease than he'd been since he'd stepped foot into this room. She was lovely indeed.

"Can we agree to become friends?" Nellie inquired. "Surely it isn't too much to ask. After all, it would be best for the children to have the example of the adults in their lives trying to get along. And, as Mrs. Heatherington said, once the children leave, it would be nice to spend the rest of my life with a friend."

Friends. He'd come here looking for a wife, and it seemed almost unbelievable that he might be leaving with something more. If he and God were on speaking terms, he might even thank the man upstairs for such an unexpected blessing.

Luke turned to Nellie. "For you, the possibility of a child was more than you could hope for. I hadn't even been thinking about gaining a friend. But it would be mighty nice to have someone to talk to and a companion for my life. It would be my honor to be your friend. And I hope you will do me the honor of becoming my wife."

Another smile lit up Nellie's face. "I would be delighted," she said.

Had Nellie really just accepted a proposal of marriage? It shouldn't be a surprise; after all, that was why she'd come. But it seemed almost too good to be true to have a husband fall into her lap.

"I cannot countenance such a thing," Mrs. Heatherington said. "My matches come from careful consideration and selection. This could ruin my business."

Nellie turned and looked at the older woman. "I do apologize. Fortunately for you, your business had nothing to do with this match. You'd already told Mr. Jeffries that you can't help him. I hadn't yet put in my application with you. Therefore, you aren't liable for anything that happens between us. We are merely two parties who happened to meet at your place of business and came to an agreement on our own. Thank you for allowing us to have this conversation in your parlor. We shan't trouble you further. Good day to you, Mrs. Heatherington. I appreciate your thoughtful contributions to this matter."

"You would really marry a stranger?" Mrs. Heatherington looked shocked, like she'd never heard such a thing.

"How is this any different from what you do?" Nellie stared at the woman for a moment.

Mrs. Heatherington met her gaze. "I have a long questionnaire that I use to determine whether or not a couple is suited for one another. I compare their likes, interests, temperament and values, and bring together compatible people to share each other's lives. But you're right. You made this decision on your own. As long as you do not hold me responsible, then I suppose I have nothing more to say on the matter."

Mr. Jeffries stepped forward. "Thank you for your time, Mrs. Heatherington. I greatly appreciate the careful thought and consideration you gave to my situation. I can see that you care deeply for doing right by your clients, and even by strangers. It's commendable, and though we did not use your services, I will always speak very highly of you and your business."

Then Mr. Jeffries held his hand out to Nellie. "I believe there is a restaurant down the street. Will you join me for an early supper so we can discuss the terms of our marriage?"

Leaving Mrs. Heatherington looking rather like she'd been through a terrible, unexpected storm, Nellie took his arm and exited the building.

The air was crisp, and the scent of burning wood from people's fireplaces, along with the unmistakable heavy clouds in the distance, told her that deep winter would soon be upon them. All the better to have this matter settled so quickly and easily, then. A few more weeks, days even, and the weather might have made things more difficult.

Once they'd gotten about halfway down the block, Nellie looked up at Mr. Jeffries. The previous scene echoed in her mind like a strange dream. And though it seemed completely out of place, Nellie chuckled softly.

Mr. Jeffries stared at her. "What's so funny?"

"Did you see the look on Mrs. Heatherington's face? I thought she was going to die of apoplexy. What kind of person marries a complete stranger?"

She shook her head, marveling at herself. Nellie wasn't normally so quick in her decisions, but as she'd heard Mr. Jeffries pleading his case with the woman, she knew she had to help him. Who could refuse a man who needed that kind of help?

Besides, she needed his help, as well.

"Us, I suppose." Then Mr. Jeffries frowned, making him look considerably older than he seemed to be. His blond hair held no flecks of gray, and his face was unmarred by wrinkles. A young man, bearing the burden of a much older one. "That seems incredibly irresponsible, doesn't it?" Then he sighed. "I don't know what else to do. It's been so hard since my wife died, and I'm out of options. I've been told I have good instincts for people, and I feel like I can trust you. Plus, it seems as though we are of similar mind, which seems the same as the shared values Mrs. Heatherington spoke of. I must admit, though, what interested me the most in you was your happiness about the children. You don't mind not having children of your own?"

There was no judgment in Mr. Jeffries's words. Too many people saw Nellie's childless state and treated her as though she had some kind of defect.

"I cannot have children," she said quietly. Shame ate at the pit of her stomach at the admission. Her lack of fertility was one of the reasons Ernest had been disappointed in her as a wife. She hadn't been able to give him the son he'd wanted, and for that he'd made sure she was punished.

Mr. Jeffries slipped his hand into hers. "Then you shall gain three," he said, giving her hand a squeeze. "Ruby is ten, Amos is seven, and Maeve is two."

Tears filled Nellie's eyes. Mr. Jeffries hadn't hesitated when she admitted her infertility. Though she had spent her whole life wanting nothing more than to be someone's mother, she'd always considered it a blessing that she and Ernest had never had children. She couldn't imagine submitting a child to his cruelty.

Some might think her foolish for wanting another husband, considering how Ernest had treated her, but Nellie had to hope that this time she had chosen better. When she'd married Ernest, she hadn't yet learned to recognize the cruel glint of a man's eyes that said he cared only for himself. She hadn't known the reddish tinge to the end of a man's nose and the sour smell that came with the overfondness of drink. Back then, Nellie loved the flowery phrases used to beguile because she thought them romantic, not realizing that poetry held little truth and deception was easily hidden behind pretty words.

There was comfort in Mr. Jeffries's frank speech. He held no air of pretense, and there was no sign in him of the kind of man she'd learned to fear. She'd been honest when she'd told Mrs. Heatherington that a woman like her could not get by without the protection of a husband.

Before she'd come to Colorado, she'd found more than her share of challenges simply because she was a woman alone. People wanted to deal with her husband or her father, not a young widow. Marriage offered her the chance to live without having to continually justify her situation.

But as she looked up at Mr. Jeffries and his gentle gaze, she wondered if he'd have much sympathy if he knew her full story. Knew the horror her marriage had been the last few months, and what Ernest had done. One would think that his death would have brought her freedom, but...

Nellie shook her head. She was free now. In a new part of the country, with a new last name, thanks to her soon-to-be husband, they wouldn't be able to find her. A man's debts weren't supposed to pass on to his wife. Then again, most men didn't sell their wives to cover their debts. Slavery might have been abolished, but it didn't stop men from making backroom deals to hand over their wives for financial compensation.

Married to a man who'd had no part in the arrangement, Nellie would be protected from them coming after her. She'd run away when Ernest died, but they'd found her at her sister's and dragged her back to the horrible place they'd been keeping her.

Where she'd seen cruelty in the faces of other men, she saw a kindness in Mr. Jeffries, a gentleness, and a deep sadness at having lost his wife. She didn't expect him to love her in that way, but knowing that this man had a heart made it seem safer somehow to trust him. Even though there was still so much to learn about him.

Glancing up at Mr. Jeffries, she smiled. "Since we're to be married, might I trouble you for your name? I heard Mrs. Heatherington refer to you as Mr. Jeffries, but we should discuss what I am to call you."

"Luke." He smiled back at her and squeezed her hand. "And I hope you will allow me to call you Nellie."

"Of course." She returned his smile, though part of her wished she hadn't made the effort. Luke had a pleasantness of manner, and the way he looked at her almost made her feel like a schoolgirl.

But she'd long ago lost any of those schoolgirl dreams.

Nellie hated the thought that she needed a man. But the police only shook their heads pityingly and told her they couldn't help her when she'd gone to them to escape the men who'd bought her.

"Go to your husband or father," they'd said. What was a woman without either to do? Especially since one of the men Ernest sold her to had claimed he was her father, and at that point no one would listen to her story. A father had the right to do what he wanted with his errant daughter. A husband could force his wife into unspeakable things, and no one would lift a hand to help her. Nellie's only chance was to find a good man who would give her the protection of his name.

As they crossed the street and headed toward the restaurant Nellie remembered passing on the way here, she stole a glance at Luke. He didn't seem the sort to hurt a woman. Though Mrs. Heatherington's words might have provoked a lesser man, he'd remained calm and polite, and Nellie hadn't seen any signs of a temper.

Still, when she found herself seated across from Luke at a table, she had to wonder whether she could really trust him. He'd been a man looking to get what he wanted; therefore, he'd shown only his most pleasing side.

When the waiter came and poured her a cup of tea, Nellie couldn't help herself.

"What do you think of the roast beef?" she asked, pointing at the menu but leaning forward enough to spill the tea. All over Luke.

"Oh!" He jumped, but his gaze immediately went to Nellie. "You didn't burn yourself, did you?"

She stared at him for a moment. She'd spilled the tea on him. On purpose. Well, not so he would know she'd done it on purpose. But when she'd accidentally spilled things at home, Ernest would yell at her, call her obscene names, and sometimes...

Nellie shook her head. "No. I'm terribly sorry. I was so engrossed in the menu, I'd forgotten the tea was there. I didn't mean to be so careless."

Kind eyes looked back at her. "Accidents happen. You'll find, in a house full of children, we have our share of spills." He dabbed at the mess with his napkin. "And it's only tea. Easy enough to get out in the wash."

The waiter rushed over with more tea and napkins.

"I do apologize," Nellie told him. "I'm usually not so clumsy."

With a smile, the waiter said, "It's all right, miss. Happens all the time."

"That's just what I was telling her." Luke sent another warm look her way. "I believe she's a little nervous, as she's just accepted my proposal of marriage."

A broad smile lit up the waiter's face. "Congratulations to you both."

"Thank you," Nellie said, feeling some of the heaviness leave her chest.

As soon as the waiter left, Luke leaned in. "I hope it's all right that I said that. It occurred to me that you might be nervous about marrying me, which accounts for your accident. I know we're strangers, but I hope that over the next couple of days, you can get to know me and feel more comfortable with your decision."

His words already made her feel better about marrying him. After all, Ernest had wooed her with sweet words about her beauty and how much he loved her. Luke was more focused on making her feel at ease with him and the situation. Nellie couldn't recall a time when Ernest had done the same. Even in public, he would have said something to belittle her.

"I appreciate that," she said, smiling. "I hope I can do the same for you."

He nodded slowly. "I just need to know you'll be good to my children. Love them like your own. Keep the household running smoothly."

Luke paused, looking around the room before bringing his attention back to her. "And I hope it's not too much to ask, but I would dearly love a clean house. I hate to speak ill of the dead, but Diana was not much of a housekeeper."

For a moment, Nellie looked at him, unsure what to make of the twinkle in his blue eyes. "What do you mean by not much of a housekeeper? My late husband was most particular, and I—"

Nellie gave an involuntary shudder, hating the memories that came to her, unbidden.

Luke leaned forward and placed his hands over hers. "We'll come to an agreement, don't you worry. I learned to do the dishes Diana left in the sink because she'd gotten carried away with visiting her friends, and I imagine if you can't do things to my liking, I can do it myself. That's what marriage is about. Finding ways to compromise and figuring out what's most important."

He gave her hands a squeeze, then leaned back in his chair. "The world didn't end because the dishes didn't get done in a timely manner. And now that Diana's gone, I'm grateful her friends got that extra time with her. When you lose someone you love, you figure out that the battle you thought worth fighting shouldn't have been fought at all. I'd do the dishes every single day if it meant having her back."

With a slight shake of his head, Luke continued. "No disrespect to you, of course. I'm just saying that you don't have to bend over backward to please me. All I ask is you do your best, and I promise to do the same for you."

Tears filled Nellie's eyes. She'd thought herself immune to a man's sweet words. But these words held a different kind of sweetness—the hope that not all men were monsters. And perhaps even an answer to all the prayers she'd said on this journey. That she'd find someone who would be kind to her.

Chapter Two

When they'd finished their meal, Luke escorted Nellie across town to the hotel where she'd been staying. Because she was a woman traveling alone, the respectable establishments had turned her away. Too many women of ill repute came under the guise of being a widow. Luke glanced at Nellie as she avoided a puddle. He couldn't imagine anyone thinking so poorly of her, a genteel woman who'd clearly hit on hard times. The place she'd found was not in the best part of town, and Luke would feel better having her in his own hotel—in separate rooms, of course.

Though their conversation over dinner had turned to easier topics, Luke couldn't get Nellie's earlier reactions out of his head. She acted almost afraid, like she thought he might hurt her. He'd answered her questions about the house and the children, his expectations thereof. Almost like a job interview. But not.

Underlying it all was the tension of knowing he would be married to this woman, sharing his life with her. He and Diana had not spoken of these things prior to marriage. They'd flirted, talked about the weather, and when her parents weren't looking, stolen a few kisses.

In his head, he'd firmly told himself he would not be kissing Nellie McClain. But every once in a while, he found his mind drifting.

Like now. Luke shook his head. "I'm sorry, could you please repeat that? I got distracted."

"I was asking how you discipline the children."

Luke followed her gaze to the entrance of a store, where a mother stood, scolding her child harshly. Even at a distance, Luke could see the fury in the woman's eyes, her face red, as the child practically cowered before her. The little boy looked to be slightly older than his youngest, Maeve, and he seemed too young to have done anything so terrible.

Luke took a deep breath and let it out slowly. He hadn't given his expectations of discipline much thought, but now that Nellie was asking, he realized he should have. How could he have thought to bring a woman into their lives without knowing how she'd treat them?

"I know conventional wisdom is that to spare the rod is to spoil the child, but I don't believe in striking a child. I don't know what that child did, and it's not my place to judge, so perhaps I shouldn't say anything, but I prefer to use other methods with my own children." He glanced in the direction of the mother and child as they continued on their way.

Nellie nodded. "I agree with you on that. Corporal punishment only serves to create fear, and I wish for the children to learn about love."

Clearly they agreed on parenting, but the tone in Nellie's voice made Luke wonder if there wasn't more to her words than what she was saying. Once again, Luke found himself wanting to ask Nellie more personal questions, to learn about this fear that seemed to be lurking underneath. Because she was afraid. What had her husband been like? Something deep inside Luke told him that he'd hurt her. Badly.

"You never said—how did your husband die?"

He watched as Nellie drew in a breath that caused her shoulders to shake slightly. How easily he'd strayed to a personal subject, even though he'd been doing his best not to.

"I'm sorry," Luke said. "I shouldn't have asked."

She shook her head. "It's all right. If we're to be married, we should be able to answer one another's questions."

Looking as though she had to steel herself for the topic, Nellie straightened. "He was shot in a saloon for cheating at cards."

What kind of man would do that to his wife? Luke's stomach churned. "That must have been difficult for you. I'm sorry for your loss."

"I'm not," Nellie said quietly. "I didn't approve of his lifestyle, and it caused me nothing but grief. Which is why I apologize if any of my questions seem impertinent, but had I known certain things about Ernest beforehand, I would have never married him."

None of the reasons Luke previously had for wanting to marry Nellie seemed to matter now. Next to him was a deeply wounded woman, and his heart cried out for her. He wanted to help her. To heal her. He couldn't give her his love, no, that would be too much for him. But he would show her that the things she hinted at, the things that lay beneath the surface of every line on her face, they were not true of every man.

"You can ask me all you want. I promise to give honest answers." Luke sighed. "Though I suppose if your late husband cheated at cards, you probably have no reason to believe me."

A tiny smile turned the corners of Nellie's lips. "I've gotten good at telling when a man is lying. And I believe you."

"Thank you." Luke wasn't sure why it mattered so much, but it felt good to know Nellie believed him.

"Might I ask how your wife died?"

He should have expected the question, but her words were like a shotgun blast to the chest.

Fighting the nausea that always came when he spoke of it, Luke took a deep breath as he looked at Nellie.

"She was serving with the church ministry to the miners. There was an explosion at the mine, and she was killed by falling rocks." He shook his head, trying to banish the image of his wife's lifeless body.

Nellie gave his arm a squeeze. "I'm so sorry for your loss. I heard you say at Mrs. Heatherington's that you are angry with the church because of her death. I can understand why."

"Thank you. I shouldn't be bitter, but it's hard. And it's even harder walking through those doors and having everyone try to make up for something that can never be replaced. They say what I suppose are all the right things, but nothing can be said to erase the pain in my heart. All their words about God's love— if God loved us so much, why would He have taken her from us?"

His voice shook as it always did when he spoke of Diana's death, and Luke looked away, but Nellie held his arm tight. Hopefully she wouldn't question him further on the topic or try to convince him that he needed to let go of his grief. People didn't understand. He couldn't… He just couldn't.

It seemed wrong to talk about his late wife to the woman who would soon be his next wife. Especially when he knew that he would never be able to share the kind of love with Nellie that he had once had with Diana.

Even now, he couldn't help but hate himself a little at the thought of marrying so soon after Diana's death. It seemed an insult to her memory. But what other choice did he have?

Nellie gave his arm another squeeze. He was grateful for the convention of her taking his arm to be escorted through town, even if she held him a little too tight to be acceptable. Though he normally didn't enjoy the comfort others offered, the genuine compassion Nellie showed him felt almost like a lifeline.

"Grief is a personal thing," she said. "You need to mourn your wife in the way that is best for you. Sometimes I feel guilty for not mourning my husband, but that is my burden. I respect your need to deal with your wife's death in your own way."

He turned his attention back to her, noticing the

tenderness in her eyes. Her response confirmed his belief that marrying Nellie was the right thing to do. Luke was tired of everyone telling him how to act after his loss. None of them knew what he was feeling. Even Pastor Lassiter, who had lost his own wife years ago, could not possibly understand the unbearable weight in Luke's heart. Nellie was the first person who didn't pretend to know what he was going through.

"Thank you," he said. "I appreciate your understanding. I won't ask the details of your marriage. I suspect you were not as blessed as I was, and for that I am truly sorry. Your late husband was a fool. Which is a pity, because even in the brief time I have known you, I can see that you are a wise and loving woman who deserved better."

Luke placed his free hand over hers and gave her a squeeze. It felt nice to have another loving human touch that asked nothing of him and only sought to give.

A hint of pink tinged her cheeks, and she looked away briefly.

"Don't do that," Luke said. "You have nothing to be embarrassed about. I know there is not love between us, at least not the romantic kind. But even now, I care for you as a friend. As your friend, I don't judge you for your lack of grief. Instead, I praise you for finding the strength to carry on and being willing to open your heart to me and my family."

With a gentle smile, Nellie turned her attention back to him. "I consider you a friend, as well. Thank you for understanding my situation and being willing to accept what I have to give."

"No thanks are needed. After all, you are doing me just as great a service. I believe we will get on together well."

If Nellie needed any other convincing that marrying Luke was the right thing to do, this conversation had done the trick. He was a man with a good, loving heart. Luke deeply grieved his wife, and for that Nellie was thankful. It seemed odd to be thankful for a man's grief, but it was an indication that he cared for others. What Nellie needed most was someone with strong compassion, someone who had the capability to love.

Not that Nellie desired love for herself, but if a man could love, he could be kind. In fact, it was a relief to know that Luke had buried his heart with his wife. He'd already loved someone, which meant he wouldn't be falling in love with Nellie, and there would be no danger of her falling in love with him. A perfect match.

Or at least as perfect as Nellie could expect from a stranger. She could hear her mother's voice in the back of her head, cautioning her that a man who didn't love the Lord with all his heart was no man at all. But what did she know of Luke's heart? Or of any man's heart, for that matter? In the early years of their marriage, Ernest had been a churchgoing man, respected in their community. It wasn't until the drinking and gambling had gotten out of hand that things started falling apart.

She should count it a blessing that Luke was honest about his relationship with God.

If only it wasn't for the sinking feeling in her stomach telling her she shouldn't settle for so little.

Nellie fought the urge to laugh at such ridiculousness. So little? She'd been offered the world with her first marriage. Everyone thought she'd done so well in marrying Ernest McClain. Look where that had gotten her.

Which left her here, walking through town with a stranger willing to marry her, because like Nellie, he was out of options. And as if Nellie needed any other reminders, they walked past a house of ill repute. Though it was too cold out for the ladies to be sitting on the porch, beckoning men to sample their wares, it was obvious they were inside, waiting.

Nellie shuddered. She'd been kept in a place like that. And she was never going back.

Luke pulled her closer to him. "I'm sorry we have to go past those places. You'll find we have similar parts of town in Leadville, but our home is in a decent area where you won't be bothered by the likes of them."

Closing her eyes briefly, Nellie sent a silent prayer, thanking God for a husband who wanted a marriage in name only, but also asking Him to help keep her secret. She hadn't been in that place willingly, but most people didn't seem to understand that.

"On to more pleasant things," Luke said, patting her hand. "How do you envision our wedding?"

As Nellie smiled back, she was grateful for the way Luke took her feelings into consideration. Though her late mother would have argued that Luke's estrangement from the church was a large matter, each of these small kindnesses he continued showing her added up to be far more than any measurement Nellie could have given. Even before things got bad, Ernest had never been so considerate of Nellie. Her world had revolved around pleasing him—or facing the consequences.

Just because Luke struggled with his faith didn't mean Nellie had to give up hers. Besides, it wasn't as though she'd been a regular churchgoer herself. Ernest had forbidden her from going after they threw him out for showing up to service drunk, and Nellie had learned to observe her faith in her own quiet way.

Nothing would change in her faith if she married Luke.

Except she'd promised herself that when she finally found freedom, she'd throw herself into a church community and participate in every activity that had been denied her so long.

Would he make her break that promise?

"You do still want to marry me," Luke said, looking down at her, "don't you?"

Nellie met his gaze. "Of course I do. I was just thinking…"

Did she dare ask him about her reservations? They'd talked about everything else, and her faith was no small thing.

But she'd seen the flash in his eyes when he spoke of his anger at God. Everything else she'd done to test his character, to see if she could push him into the kind of rage she'd seen in Ernest…was it all to be for nothing if she didn't pursue his potentially negative feelings now?

"I was just thinking about God. And church," Nellie said firmly, looking him in the eye. They had paused in front of a church, and Nellie took that as a sign that they needed to have this conversation.

Luke didn't flinch. "You're worried my anger at God would prevent you from going?"

Nellie seemed hardly able to draw a breath. It was as though he could read her thoughts.

She nodded slowly, her eyes searching his, looking for a hint of the rage she so feared. Had she provoked him this time? Better now than after the wedding, when she wouldn't be able to undo her mistake.

If marrying Luke was a mistake, she'd figure that out before they went through with it. Never again would she endure the pain she'd suffered during her marriage to Ernest. The coins she'd sewn in the waistband of her skirt and hidden in the toe of her shoe didn't amount to much, but it would give her enough. Nellie had learned a few tricks of her own from Earnest's vile friends. Never put all your coins in one place. She would always be able to escape.

If Luke revealed a temper, best to end things now.

"My quarrel is with God alone," Luke said slowly. "I do not fault others for not sharing my anger. I would not ask anyone to bear the burden I carry. You're free to worship as you choose." His face darkened slightly as he took a deep breath. "Though I would ask it not include me. Save your sermons and conversion speeches for those who need it. I am not among them."

As Nellie searched his expression, she could find no hint of violence, no sign that he would hurt her if she disobeyed him.

"All right," she said quietly. "I can agree to that."

Luke let out a long sigh as he turned toward the church. "I suppose you'll want a church wedding."

"No," Nellie said. "I would be happy visiting a justice of the peace. But there is your family to consider. What would be best for them?"

Luke frowned, as if he had already thought that far ahead and was troubled by the answer. "I don't know. Ruby will be angry, because she feels as though she has taken her mother's place. I told her I was considering taking another wife, and she doesn't believe it's necessary. She thinks she is running the household just fine."

As Luke shook his head, Nellie gave his arm another squeeze. It seemed slightly inappropriate that they were behaving in so familiar a manner so soon. Yet Nellie found great comfort in a man's gentle touch, a touch void of violence and with no expectation other than that of being a friend.

"Ruby is but a child. It's not right to ask her to give up her childhood. She disagrees, but that belief comes from a child's mind. The others..." Luke shook his head again. "Amos seems content enough. He fights with his sister because he doesn't like her bossing him around. And he has a point. She oversteps, but there is no one else to be in that place. I keep thinking if they had a mother, they could return to being siblings, and maybe even friends."

Luke looked at her and smiled. "Maeve is a delight. Sometimes it's frustrating that she has no memory of her mother. But she needs one, desperately. She needs a woman's gentle touch. A grown woman, not her sister, because a sister is not like a mother, and Maeve needs both."

Clearly Luke had given this matter a great deal of thought. He cared for his children and wanted only the very best for them. Though Nellie's reasons for marrying him were selfish, she could at least do some good here.

"I'm grateful to be allowed the chance to give your children the mother they need. It won't be easy, because I'm sure the older two miss their mother dearly. But I hope you'll aid me in keeping her memory alive for them and letting them know that a person's heart is big enough to allow two mothers to love a child."

"That is exactly how I feel," Luke said. "But my children will take some convincing. Which is why I like your idea of simply going to see the justice of the peace. I don't have any family to invite to a wedding, other than the children. I think the gesture will be lost on them."

Then he turned his gaze to her, his face full of thoughts she hadn't yet learned how to decipher.

"What about your family? Will they be disappointed at you not having a wedding?"

With a sigh, Nellie thought briefly about her sister. "My parents are dead. All I have is my sister, Mabel. But she is too far away to come for a wedding, and after my last marriage, I can't see her appreciating our circumstances."

That, and letting Mabel know where to find Nellie could put Mabel's family in danger. When Nellie had gone to Mabel for help after Ernest's death, Ernest's men told Mabel that if she ever helped Nellie again, they would harm Mabel's family. Given that they had already burned down Mabel's barn, Nellie knew these were not idle threats. When Nellie escaped to come West, she promised herself that she would never again put her sister at risk. Though Nellie longed to see her sister again, she had no idea whether or not those men would go back to Mabel looking for Nellie. If Mabel knew nothing, she would be safe.

"If she ever wants to visit, your sister would be most welcome. Once our family is firmly established, perhaps we can go see her."

Tears filled Nellie's eyes. It seemed like such a small gesture, yet Luke's willingness to include her family was almost a dream come true. Ernest had discouraged Nellie from spending much time with her sister. Even though they lived in nearby neighborhoods in St. Louis, Ernest always found excuses for the families not to get together. Granted, Mabel lived on a farm at the edge of town, but it was an easy ride and not too difficult a walk to the neighborhood where Nellie had lived.

Once again, Luke gave Nellie a tender look. "I know how hard it is to be so far from family. Even worse when your family does not understand your choices. Neither of our families approved when Diana and I chose to move West. But it was what we had to do."

Luke appeared lost in memories of Diana for a moment. Nellie was struck again by the deep love Luke had for his late wife. But this wasn't just about what Luke had lost. It was about how much more he was still willing to give.

"So it's settled, then," Nellie said, smiling at him, turning her back on the quaint little church. "We shall visit the justice of the peace and be married. Then we can return to your home with me as your wife, and I will care for your children."

Luke looked at her. "Is it really that simple?"

"It does seem odd, doesn't it?"

Though many people would make the argument that Luke and Nellie didn't know each other nearly long enough to marry, sometimes time wasn't what was needed. Ernest had courted Nellie for nearly a year, yet she hadn't known all the reasons not to marry him. In these few short hours of knowing Luke, Nellie had never been more certain of a person's character. With their hasty marriage, it gave Nellie a way to hide, but also a second chance at a life she'd always dreamed of living—that of a wife and mother.

When Nellie had come up with her plan, she felt guilty at the thought of attaching herself to a man who might someday fall in love with her. The place in her heart that allowed a person to fall in love was so firmly locked tight, it would never open. But with Luke, she had no reason to feel guilty. His heart was in no danger of becoming entangled with hers.

Briefly, Nellie thought about the men who were after her. She'd done so much to protect Mabel. Though Nellie was reasonably certain that they would leave her alone if she was married, part of her wondered, was she putting Luke and his children in danger?

Nellie shook her head. She hadn't come straight to Denver from St. Louis. She'd traveled to several places looking for a fresh start. And then she'd seen it. The ad for Mrs. Heatherington's Matchmaking Service. She'd liked Mrs. Heatherington's descriptions of mail-order matches gone wrong. It was easy enough to lie over letters, claiming to be of greater beauty than one had, to possess qualities or characteristics that didn't exist, and to so completely miserably represent oneself as to be perpetuating a lie. It had given Nellie comfort to think that someone would examine a potential match and weed out men who would not be a good choice.

And so, Nellie had boarded the train to Denver. She'd been careful in all her journeys, giving false names, wearing clothes that would make her appear completely unremarkable and even going so far as to purchase tickets under her own name for destinations she had no intention of ever visiting. Yes, it had cost her nearly all that remained of the meager funds she'd squirreled away and hidden in the hollow of a tree at the back of her former property. The house had to be sold once Ernest died. Or at least that was what the men had told her. When she'd finally escaped, the house appeared unoccupied. But she knew they would look for her there. However, the money had still been where she'd hidden it. So she'd taken her money and run.

None of the men would suspect that Nellie had the means for so much travel. But she'd been careful anyway. There was no reason she should ever be found.

Luke took a step forward. "We need to continue on," he said. "I'm not very familiar with Denver, and I have no idea where we would go to be married. If we were in Leadville, I suppose I should ask Pastor Lassiter to marry us. But I cannot, will not, bring myself to ask for his help. I know he wants to, and I know he means well. Many say that he genuinely cares about my circumstances. But I also can't help but wonder if he's trying to help me out of his own feelings of guilt. He made the decision to send the ladies to the mine to serve the miners."

Nellie squeezed his arm and smiled. "I do not know the man, so I cannot say. I hope you don't mind, but I believe I will leave my judgment of the pastor until I have met him myself. I know you are not comfortable with the church, but it would be good for the children if you allowed me to bring them."

A sad smile found its way onto Luke's face. "Of course. I have been neglecting their spiritual education. Diana's friends have asked me if I might allow them to bring the children to church."

Luke's shoulders sagged as he shook his head. "I know my children need to go to church. But if I allow them to go, people will see that their clothes need mending, and though I am not ashamed of my children, they will feel compelled to once again step in and help me. I cannot bear such a thing. I don't want to hear how my home needs a woman's touch. Or that this is no life for a child. I don't want people questioning my decisions, telling me how I ought to be raising my children. Nor do I want their charity. Most of all, I cannot bear the weight of any more of their pity."

How interesting that Luke was a man of such pride. Though pride was a sin, and Nellie often thought it to be a terrible flaw in a man, something about the wounds in Luke's pride made Nellie want to hold him tight and tell him everything would be all right. Unlike Ernest, who had reacted with his fists when his pride was wounded, Luke seemed to withdraw into the shame and do everything he could to make things right on his own.

None of this was Luke's fault. He'd lost his wife, and in some ways, lost his way. The grief would have to be worked out on its own. But Nellie could help with the other things. Their home would once again have a woman's touch. The children would go back to wearing clean, neat clothing. They would be well fed and well kept, and everyone who saw them would see that the Jeffries family was doing very well indeed.

"You don't have to bear that weight alone. I promise to do my very best to make sure there is no reason for such pity to be bestowed upon us. In the eyes of everyone else, you are moving on with your life. You've given your children a mother to care for them, and I promise to take that duty seriously."

Luke let out a long sigh as they crossed the street. "Do you know how frustrating it is to be mad at God, to be so angry with Him, and yet want to thank Him for how wonderfully He is arranging matters for your family?" Then Luke shook his head again. "But if it were not for God taking my wife away from me, He would not need to be providing for us now. So how am I supposed to feel? It is still God's fault that all of this has happened to us. I am still so angry, so hurt, and it seems almost an insult that He's choosing to remember our family now."

Anger vibrated out from Luke's body. Of all the men she'd known with the right to be angry, Luke had the greatest. But in his expression of anger, he did not raise his voice. He did not get violent. Rather, he seemed to be filled with such a profound sadness that only the weight of his bones was keeping him upright.

"I can't pretend to understand your level of anger at God. But I agree with you—it seems terribly unfair. I won't always understand how your children feel, but I will offer to them the same compassion I'm giving to you."

Luke nodded slowly. "I have never known such compassion. You do not understand what a gift it is to be allowed to feel what you feel. You're the only person who hasn't tried talking me out of my anger at God. I suppose some might see that as a lack of faith. But I think you know that this is between me and God. It is something I must work out on my own."

He lifted her hand to his lips and kissed it. Gently. Not like a lover's kiss, or even that of a dashing suitor. But something that reminded her of the warm kiss of her sister's greetings. Comforting. Safe.

"Thank you," Luke said. "Most of the time, I feel as though I am suffocating from the weight of all that I must deal with. Everyone wants to take it away and make it disappear, but it's not that simple. You seem to know that. Instead, you are offering me a lifeline, choosing to walk alongside me and giving me what I need without lectures or judgment."

"I am not one to judge," Nellie said quietly. After all, hadn't she done many things others would judge her for? Even as she stole a glance at the man who was to be her husband, her stomach churned at the thought of him finding out all of her secrets. Though she reminded herself that he'd been firm in saying he wanted a marriage in name only, the uneasy feeling didn't go away. There was no reason for him to know everything.

But as they passed another place that looked a little too much like where Ernest's creditors had kept her, Nellie couldn't help but think herself a terrible person for hiding so much from him.

Chapter Three

They took the train to Leadville a couple days later, man and wife. Such an odd thing, how quickly it had all happened. Just a few days ago he'd been a total stranger. But wasn't that what they'd both sought? Mail-order spouses were also strangers, and Nellie would like tò think that at least she and Luke had come to respect one another prior to their marriage.

Had she made the right decision? Nellie stole a glance at Luke, who seemed to be engrossed in reading his paper. Was he really the kind man she thought him to be, or had she misinterpreted the situation? Nellie pressed her hand against the waistband of her dress, where she'd sewn her coins. Though some had told her to sew money into the hem of her skirt, it was more comforting to be able to feel her money close to her. As she wiggled her toes, she felt the other coins, a secondary source of protection. If Luke was not as he seemed, she at least had enough for train fare. Where she would go, she did not know. But at least this time, she had a way out.

Was it wrong for her to have a plan in case things didn't work out the way they'd hoped? Most people didn't get married with such a plan. But most people hadn't been married to Ernest.

Luke patted her leg. Then he pointed out the window. "Look! Leadville is just ahead."

He craned forward, and if he could have stuck his head out the window, he probably would have. For the first time since they'd gotten on the train, a wide smile filled his face. Though she'd always believed in the saying "Handsome is as handsome does," she couldn't help but think he looked handsome, with his blond hair, blue eyes and infectious smile. Fortunately, his looks were not nearly as important as the other things that had drawn her to him. She knew better than to be swayed by a pleasant smile.

"I'm so excited for you to meet the children. I can't believe I've been gone so long. Until this trip to Denver, I haven't been away from them overnight." With a sigh, Luke shook his head. "At least not since Diana died. Before she died, before we came to Leadville, I was often away, trying to find work to support my family. This job in Leadville gave me the chance to come home to my family every night. I can't tell you how much it means to me to see my children every day."

This man couldn't possibly be a charlatan. Nellie smoothed the top of her bodice over her skirt, grateful the material was thick enough to hide the outlines of the coins. Hopefully she would never have to use them. Funny how life turned out. The whole reason she'd been saving this money to begin with had been to leave Ernest. But she hadn't gotten the chance before he'd sold her. And then he died.

At least now, Nellie knew how little she could survive on. If things with Luke got bad, she wouldn't stay as long as she had with Ernest. But as Luke waved out the window at a woman standing with three children, Nellie prayed she would never have to leave. Watching the mutual delight on the faces of father and children, part of her felt as though she'd finally come home.

"I assume those are your children there," she said. "Who is the woman with them?"

Luke turned to Nellie. "That's Myrna Fitzgerald, our neighbor. Her daughter, Ellen, was good friends with Diana. Ellen was injured in the mine accident. I suppose it sounds odd, but I feel more comfortable asking the Fitzgeralds for help, considering they, too, suffered. Myrna's husband, Seamus, is my boss. In many ways, the Fitzgeralds are like a surrogate family. Our daughter Maeve is named for Myrna, whose middle name is Maeve. She assisted Diana greatly when we first came here."

Then Luke let out a long sigh as he gestured for Nellie to stand. "I hope it doesn't make me sound ungrateful, not letting them do more. They often ask, but they have their own family, their own lives. I do not wish to impose. Still, I hope you will look to them as friends. They've been in Leadville for a long time and can teach you much of what you need to know."

As Nellie stood, she smiled up at him. "I will be

grateful for their assistance. But don't worry, I also don't like to overstay my welcome. I'm sure it will all work out just fine."

Though lines still creased Luke's forehead, he smiled and nodded. "I'm glad. Seamus thought me foolish in my pursuit of a mail-order bride. The Fitzgeralds want me to find love again, but they don't understand. No one does."

Nellie grasped Luke's hand and squeezed. "It's all right. None of that matters now. You don't need to feel the pressure of trying to attain something that is not possible. We know where we stand with each other, and it's enough."

But as they exited the train, and Luke let go of her hand before they came into view of his family, insecurity thrummed at her insides. Of course he wouldn't want his family to see him holding a strange woman's hand. It was ridiculous of her to worry about such a small gesture. And yet, losing the warmth of his touch made Nellie feel more alone than she could have imagined.

She fell in step behind him, noting his quick pace. Indeed, the closer he came to his family, the lighter his steps seemed to be.

Nellie watched as Luke scooped up a little girl into his arms. That must be Maeve. Two other children, presumably Ruby and Amos, wrapped their arms around him. Contentment filled Nellie as she saw the genuine affection between father and children. A man who raised his fists to others could not possibly incite such warmth upon his return.

After a few minutes, Luke released the older children and shifted Maeve to his hip. "Thank you," he said to Mrs. Fitzgerald. "My trip was a success."

Then Luke stepped aside and, for the first time, gestured toward Nellie. "There is someone I would like you to meet."

"I told you we didn't need a nanny." Ruby stamped her foot and glared at Nellie.

"She's not a nanny," Luke said. "This is my wife, Nellie."

The two older children frowned, and Maeve merely looked confused. Nellie stepped forward, trying to quell the butterflies in her stomach as she smoothed her bodice over her skirt once more.

"It is a pleasure to meet you. Your father has told me many wonderful things about you. I'm looking forward to getting to know you better."

Ruby's scowl deepened. Her glare burned hotter than any fire Nellie had ever seen. "I can't say the same for you," she said. "I know I'm supposed to be polite, but it's even more wrong to lie. We don't want you here. We don't need you here. It would be better for all of us if you just got back on the train and went home."

A child's words weren't supposed to sting, and Nellie should have been prepared for the immediate rejection. But something cold twisted in Nellie's insides at the way Ruby looked at her.

"Ruby!" Luke admonished his daughter. "Nellie is my wife. She's not going anywhere. And I will not have you talking to her like that. She's a fine woman and will take good care of you all. This is for the benefit of our family."

"Have you forgotten Mama? How could you try to replace her?" Tears filled Ruby's eyes as she stepped right up to Nellie. "I hate you, and you will never be my mother."

Before Nellie could answer, Ruby turned and ran through the crowd. She should have known this wasn't going to be easy. Nellie took a step forward, but Luke held out his free hand. "No," he said. "I should go."

He held out Maeve to Nellie. "Maevey, Papa will be back soon. Be a good girl for Nellie."

As Nellie took the little girl, Luke turned his attention to Amos. "Please be good for Nellie."

The little boy nodded but did not speak.

"Myrna, could you please show Nellie to our house? Help her get settled?"

With a sigh, Luke turned his attention to Nellie. "I'm sorry, I didn't know she would react this way. I'll be home as soon as I can."

Before either Nellie or Mrs. Fitzgerald could answer, Luke was gone. Nellie didn't blame him. The worry for his daughter's safety was written all over his face. Though many of the new arrivals on the train had already left the station, several people still milled about, and this was no place for a child on her own. Even one who thought she was an adult.

"Well," Mrs. Fitzgerald said. "Isn't this a fine pickle we're all in?"

"I'm so sorry for the trouble," Nellie said. "I would greatly appreciate any assistance you can give."

Mrs. Fitzgerald nodded slowly. "I suppose this wasn't quite the situation advertised. It never is. But I do hope you'll give it a chance before getting back on the train."

"Who said I was leaving? I know we didn't do it right and proper in a church, but I am legally Luke's wife. I have the papers in my bag to prove it." Nellie gestured to the bag one of the porters had set beside her. "Which means I made a promise. And you don't break a promise simply because a child doesn't like it."

Adjusting Maeve on her hip, Nellie bent in front of Amos. "I know I am not your mother, but I promised your father I would help him, and that I would look after you. So let's get to know one another and see if we can't find a way to someday be friends."

Bright blue eyes that matched his father's looked up at Nellie. "Do I have to call you mama?"

"You may call me Nellie, or any other name you choose. As long as it's nice. I know you love your mother very much, and it's all right to miss her. I hope you will teach me some of the traditions she taught you so that we may continue them. I want you to remember her fondly. From what your father tells me, she was a good woman, and you are very blessed to have had her."

Nellie knew her speech was inadequate, given the circumstances, but hopefully it would be enough to earn the boy's trust.

"Can you make chocolate cake?" he asked.

"I can," Nellie said. "I can cook a good many things, and I would be pleased to prepare your favorite meals, if you will tell me what they are." She gave him a smile, hoping he'd see her as someone he could count on, rather than an adversary.

"Anything but eggs," Amos said, sighing. "I sure am tired of eating eggs all the time. That's about all Ruby can cook, and when she tries other things, they're disgusting."

"I'm sure Ruby does her best. You should be grateful for a sister who takes such good care of you. But hopefully, now that I'm here, you two can go back to being friends and playing with each other, and I will take care of the family."

Again, she tried to sound as pleasant as she could. At least he wasn't running away, too.

Amos nodded as he eyed her. "I suppose we can give it a try. So long as we get chocolate cake once in a while. I do like chocolate cake, and the only time I get it is if we go to the Fitzgeralds' house or if there is a special dinner at church. But Papa doesn't let us go to church anymore."

Then he looked up at Mrs. Fitzgerald. "And Papa says it's rude to always ask Mrs. Fitzgerald to make us chocolate cake. So I suppose, if you're Papa's wife, I can ask you."

The little boy looked rather pleased with himself as he came to this conclusion. Nellie smiled. Clearly winning him over wouldn't be as difficult as his older sister. And Maeve was already playing with the locket Nellie wore around her neck.

"How about, once I'm able to assess the situation at the house and find out how much money I'm allowed for groceries, I can make us a nice meal to celebrate our marriage, and we'll have chocolate cake for dessert?"

Mrs. Fitzgerald smiled as she joined the conversation. "I think that sounds like a lovely idea. However, may I suggest that you allow me to prepare a wedding supper for you both and invite our friends and neighbors so they may all meet you? I'm sure you are probably eager to get settled in your own home and prepare your family's meals. However, I think it would be best for you to take the time to get to know your household first."

"I would greatly appreciate it," Nellie said. "But I would like to check with Luke to make sure he has no objection."

This was one more thing they hadn't discussed. What were the rules about entertaining? Did Luke have friends other than the Fitzgeralds and those at church he was currently avoiding? Longing filled Nellie's heart as she remembered how Ernest had cut her off from all social interactions, save for when she was required to serve him and his friends. She'd become a maid rather than a wife.

What role would she play in Luke's home? The children had been expecting a nanny, not a mother, and though Nellie would not expect them to accept her as such so soon, what was she to be to them? A glorified servant? Or something more?

Her stomach twisted again as she realized she did not know the answer.

Fortunately, Mrs. Fitzgerald's smile eased some of Nellie's nervousness. At least to this woman, Nellie was something more than a mere servant. Perhaps in time, they could be friends.

"Absolutely. However, I must insist that you and the family dine with us tonight because I know the state of your kitchen, and it is too much to ask of any woman to come home after such a journey and be expected to prepare a meal."

Nellie smiled at the other woman. "I accept. Thank you for your kindness. Luke has spoken of your friendship, and I can already see why he values you so." Maeve began fussing like she wanted to get down and play. Nellie patted her back gently. "There now, we'll be home soon and then you can be free, and your brother can show me around."

Nellie smiled at Amos. "Will you help show me around until your father gets back?"

"Like I'm the boss?"

Nellie grinned. She supposed it was wrong to capitalize on the fact that Luke had told her Amos resented being bossed around by his older sister. But at least it was a way for Nellie to relate to the boy.

"In a manner, I suppose. We all know that the real boss is your father. And though you're supposed to listen to me, I could use some help. Does that sound good enough to you?"

Amos nodded slowly. "You aren't gonna make me take a bath, are you?"

"Does your father make you take baths?"

"Sometimes," Amos mumbled.

Nellie ruffled the little boy's hair, noting that there didn't appear to be any lice or other creatures of concern, though it could use a good washing. "I'll tell you what," she said. "I do think it's important for people to take baths. And it sounds like your father agrees. But I won't make you take a bath until we've all discussed it as a family and determined what night bath night is."

"Saturday," Amos said, sounding disappointed that he wasn't going to get out of taking a bath, but as he smiled at her, she realized he was also probably relieved that she wasn't going to insist on baths more often.

Though Nellie probably would make changes to the family routine as time went on, for now, her plan was to do her best to keep them all on a comfortable schedule. As they seemed ready to make changes, Nellie would discuss them with Luke, seeking his advice. After all, they were partners. Or would be in time, once they got more comfortable with each other.

Mrs. Fitzgerald tucked her arm into Nellie's free arm. "I'll be honest. I tried talking Luke out of this foolish plan. But now that you've come, and I see that you have the family's best interests at heart, I think this will work out very well. Luke is too proud to ask for help, too proud to accept it." With a grin, Mrs. Fitzgerald gave her a squeeze. "But perhaps a wife is exactly what he needs. Someone to help him, without it feeling like an injury to his pride."

Clearly this other woman understood Nellie's husband very well. And based on Mrs. Fitzgerald's warm welcome, Nellie's nervousness at the family's reactions to her was just silly jitters. She was meant to be here, with this family, and someday they'd find their way together.

Nellie just hoped that despite the rocky start, at least with Ruby, everything would turn out all right. Not that Nellie had expected a warm reception, but as she thought about the hatred in the little girl's eyes, the anger, the fear, Nellie knew that the victories she had so far secured were very small compared to the battles that lay ahead.

Luke had been searching for the better part of an hour, and he still hadn't found Ruby. He'd known that Ruby especially would not immediately welcome Nellie with open arms. But to be so hateful? To run? This was not the daughter he knew and loved.

Had Luke made a mistake in marrying Nellie so quickly?

He thought it best to present them with the deed already done. That way, they would have to accept it. But perhaps he had been wrong. Perhaps he should have given them more time to get used to the idea. Though he'd been telling them for weeks that he was seeking a wife, it still clearly hadn't been enough time.

Luke rounded the corner to the livery. Ruby often came here to pet the horses because they could not afford one of their own. Living in town, within walking distance to everything they needed, it seemed like a wasteful expense. But his daughter dearly loved horses.

"Hello, Wes," Luke said to the proprietor as he entered the stable. "You haven't seen my daughter, have you?"

Wes nodded but put his finger to his lips. "I hear you brought yourself home a wife."

His daughter was here. Luke's shoulders relaxed slightly as he felt his breathing return to normal. And Ruby had at least confided in someone about her pain.

"I did. I'll always love Diana, and we all miss her deeply, but our house needs a woman's touch. I know Ruby says she doesn't mind taking care of the others and the house, but I want more for her. I want her to have the chance to go outside and play with her friends the way her brother does. I want her to go to school and not make up ridiculous excuses about why she needs to stay home for her siblings. And though I know everyone is happy to watch Maeve while I work, I will feel better knowing there is a woman dedicated to her care who is always with her and will watch over her the way I would."

Wes nodded slowly. "And love? Have you thought of that?"

It was the same question Mrs. Heatherington had asked. Luke nodded slowly, remembering Nellie's wisdom. "There are all kinds of love. Just because it doesn't look like what Diana and I shared doesn't mean Nellie and I cannot care for each other in different ways. We are of the same mind, Nellie and I, and I believe we will get on quite well together. She is a very good woman, and I would not trust my children with her otherwise."

"Many a man has married for less," Wes said. "I wish you all the best. Be gentle with Ruby. She doesn't understand the ways of the adults. And she's angry that you would forsake her mother so easily."

Luke's throat tightened. If only he'd had another choice. But he didn't, not if he wanted Ruby to have any kind of decent life. How was he supposed to get his daughter to understand that, when she believed it was her duty to take on her mother's responsibilities?

"I have not forsaken Diana. Some days, I wonder how I can even breathe without her by my side. But she is not here, and I am, so I must make the best decisions I can without her. I believe that Diana would not want our children to muddle through the way they have been."

"You didn't even ask us," Ruby said, coming around from behind the counter. "We didn't want a new mother. We told you not to look for a new wife. I took all those ads you tried to send and burned them in the fire so no one would come. Why didn't you give up?"

At least now Luke knew why no one had ever answered his ads. "What you did was wrong," he said. "You can't meddle with someone's personal correspondence. If you had concerns about my search for a bride, then you should have discussed them with me."

Tears streamed down Ruby's face, leaving little trails in the dust on her cheeks. She must have accumulated it while hiding in the horse stalls. "I did! I told you we didn't need a mother. I was doing fine on my own. I am nearly eleven years old, almost a grown woman. I can do all the things a mother can do."

Luke sighed. His daughter was partially right. But

Ruby didn't understand that a child needed more in a mother than she could provide.

"I know you can do everything around the house," Luke said. "But I want you to have a better life than that. I know you don't like to hear it, but can you try to understand that I only have your best interests at heart?"

Tears filled her eyes again. "But you didn't even let us help you pick her out."

"Well, maybe if you hadn't burned all my letters, we could've read the responses as a family, and I would've allowed you to share your thoughts. But you thought you knew better than your father, and you took matters into your own hands. You don't have the knowledge and experience that I do. That Nellie does. But we can help you, if you let us."

His daughter's face softened, and Luke hoped it was a sign that she was finally beginning to see reason.

Luke held his arms out to her, but Ruby didn't budge. She stood there, tears rolling down her cheeks, sadness in her eyes. His daughter's heart was breaking, and as much as Luke wanted to help, there wasn't anything he could do. Nothing would bring her mother back.

"But we don't need her help. We're doing just fine."

Luke took a step closer to his daughter. "Didn't you just say that it was wrong to lie?"

"We are!" Ruby's voice wavered. "Don't you always say that as long as we have each other, we have enough?"

"And we do. But we also need help. I know you think you can do it all, but you're not ready yet." Luke held his hand out to his daughter again. "I need you to trust me. Have I ever done anything to hurt you?"

Ruby started to shake her head no, but then she nodded. "Yes. You married that woman without telling us."

As if a grown man needed permission to take a wife. Luke sighed. "Other than that? Have I ever done anything else to hurt you?"

"No." Ruby sniffled loudly, then wiped her nose with the back of her sleeve.

"Then let's focus on that. Remember all the times that I've looked out for you. I'm still doing the very best I can to give you and your siblings a good life. Nellie has promised to do the same. I'm just asking you to give it a chance."

Ruby took a step closer to him, coming almost to his arms, but still out of reach. "What if she is not so nice after all?"

Taking a deep breath, Luke considered this. What if Nellie wasn't good for his children? Luke shook his head. Of course she would be.

"We'll find a way to work it out," he said.

"But what if she's really terrible? Will you send her away?"

Luke couldn't imagine making such a decision because he couldn't imagine Nellie doing anything so bad. But the hopeful look in his daughter's eyes made him realize that if she thought there was a chance to get rid of Nellie, she would try. It was a sad thing to acknowledge about one's own daughter, but until Ruby had confessed that she'd burned his letters, he would have never believed her capable of such a thing. Which meant Nellie was in for a far more difficult time than Luke would have imagined.

"I understand what you're trying to say," Luke said slowly. "But that is a decision and a discussion best left to adults. Nellie is here to stay. When you marry someone, you make the promise to stay married until death parts you. I made that promise to Nellie."

Wes stepped around the counter and put his arm around Ruby. It pained Luke to see someone doing for his daughter what he wished he could do himself. But at least Ruby had someone she felt was on her side.

"It's hard losing a parent," Wes said. "But your father's right—nothing's going to bring your mother back. As hard as it is, we have to find a way to keep living the best we can without them. This Nellie woman, I know she's not your mother. But I know your father and I trust his judgment. All he ever thinks about is what's best for you and your brother and sister. If he thinks Nellie will do right by you, I believe him."

Wes squatted so he was eye to eye with Ruby. "But if you run into trouble, you come see me, and I'll do what I can to help."

The glower didn't leave Ruby's face. "I didn't ask for her to come. I don't want her here."

Wes nodded thoughtfully, rubbing his chin. "But she's here. And a lady of the house makes everyone feel welcome, whether they are wanted, needed or asked for. Even the most unwelcome guest deserves to be treated with kindness and respect."

"What's that supposed to mean?" Ruby asked, her voice quivering.

Wes looked at her tenderly. "I think you know what I mean. You haven't even given Nellie a chance. And I'm sure she is feeling pretty terrible right about now."

"Doesn't it matter that I'm feeling pretty terrible?"

The righteous indignation on his daughter's face made Luke want to smile. But that probably wouldn't serve any good purpose.

"Of course it does," Luke said, joining Wes in front of Ruby. "And I truly am sorry that I hurt you. I didn't mean to. But what's done is done, and the best we can do is move forward with grace. And it would mean a lot to me, to our family, if you would at least try."

Ruby nodded, sniffed some more and once again wiped her face with the back of her sleeve. Then she squared her shoulders and looked at her father.

"I won't call her mama. Or mother."

They hadn't discussed what the children were to call Nellie, and though Luke promised her that they would be a team, he hoped she would understand him making this decision without her.

"You can call her Nellie if you like."

Ruby nodded. "I don't want her acting like a mother to me. No kissing, no hugging, no tucking me in at night. I will not treat her like a mother. I will not forget my mother, and nothing you say or do will make me."

Tears stung the backs of Luke's eyes at his daughter's insistence on clinging to her mother. He knew the children missed her, but it hadn't occurred to him that bringing Nellie in would make them think that he wanted to deny their memories of her.

"I'm glad," he said. "I wouldn't ask that of you. Nor would Nellie."

This time, when Luke held out his arms to his daughter, she came. He wrapped his arms around her and held her tight, kissing the top of her head.

"I love you, my sweet Ruby. I know it's hard, and I'm sorry. I miss your mother every day, and I know you do, too. But we need Nellie. You probably don't care about this part, but something tells me that she needs us. So let's all do the best we can to be there for each other, even if it's not the situation we want for ourselves."

Ruby nodded slowly, her tears wetting the front of Luke's shirt. She squeezed him back, and it felt good to be in his daughter's embrace. And he hoped it felt good to her, as well. Even if she didn't realize it now, he would always be there for her, always support her, always love her.

"Do you really miss her?" Big blue eyes like her mother's looked up at him, searching his heart, then breaking it.

"I've told you I do."

"Not very often," she said. "Sometimes I think you don't remember her at all."

Her words turned his insides. Once again, Luke heard Nellie's voice in the back of his head giving him permission to grieve the way he felt he needed to.

"Missing a person looks different to everyone," he said. "I'm sorry that you can't see inside my heart, but the pain of living every day without your mother is there. Nellie isn't meant to take that away. But she can make some of the things that I'm struggling to do on my own a little easier. I need another adult in my life to help me. I know you want to be that person, but it has to be someone else."

"All right," Ruby said, sighing. "I don't like this, not at all."

Luke sighed. Ruby wasn't bending on this point, but at least she'd somewhat agreed to cooperate. He supposed, for today at least, that that was as much of a victory as he could hope for.

Chapter Four

Luke hadn't been exaggerating when he'd said his home was small. The tiny cabin was but one room, containing a small stove in the corner that looked like it was used for both heating and cooking, though Nellie had no idea how anything could be cooked on such a contraption. Shelves along one wall contained what appeared to be the family's meager supplies and very few dishes. A table and chairs sat on one end of the room, awkward and lopsided, like they had been placed there as temporary furnishings, and they'd never gotten around to finding something permanent. The sitting area seemed like another thrown-together spot, with mismatched furniture that appeared to be other people's castoffs. Though Nellie understood why Luke had been hoping for a clean house, she could see the potential in this space to make it a home.

On the far wall, Nellie could see the makeshift ladder built into the wood to gain access to what she imagined must be the sleeping loft. The only other furnishing in the room was an old trunk, probably full of the other household goods. But as Nellie looked around the room, she saw there was no place to put anything else. She glanced at the two bags she'd brought with her. They seemed to eat up the remaining space in the place, and though she'd once lamented the loss of most of her personal belongings, Nellie couldn't help but be grateful now that she'd had to leave almost everything behind. There'd be no place to put it.

"It's not much, I know," Mrs. Fitzgerald said from behind her. "Luke was going to add another room before Diana's passing, but since she's been gone, I think he's lacked the motivation. Perhaps now..."

Her voice trailed off as she probably thought she'd overstepped. Nellie turned to her and smiled.

"It's all right, Mrs. Fitzgerald. I know you mean well. Change will take time, and that's all right. I've been in worse situations, and I know how to make the best of things."

Nellie set Maeve down, and the little girl immediately scrambled up the ladder to the loft. Amos cast a glance at Nellie, then followed his sister.

"Just let them go," Mrs. Fitzgerald said. "And do call me Myrna. We don't stand much on ceremony here."

The older woman looked around the room, then let her gaze rest upon Nellie again. "I apologize that I didn't do more to clean things up in here. It's easier to keep them all at my house when Luke isn't home. I don't know how he manages in such a small space. I tried to sweep, but there's only so much you can do with these little ones running about in here."

Nellie looked down at the dusty floor. "I can imagine." Then she gave Myrna a smile. "I'm sure I'll find a way to manage, just as Diana did."

Myrna pressed her lips together, then looked around the room before pulling Nellie closer to the stove. "Now, I am not saying this to speak ill of the dead, but I think you need to understand a few things about Diana."

Pointing to the stove, Myrna said, "That chocolate cake Amos wants. Do you really think you're going to bake one in this?"

With a sigh, Nellie shook her head. The stove was barely large enough to hold wood for a fire and a kettle on top. She had no idea how she'd make a basic meal on it, let alone a chocolate cake.

"That's right. You're not. Diana was no housekeeper, and she couldn't cook a proper meal to save her life, let alone feed her family. When they first came to Leadville, she and I made a deal. I did all the cooking, and she did all my mending and sewing. I never could sew a straight seam, so it was a good trade for me. I tried explaining to Luke what we'd worked out, but he thought that taking meals from me was accepting charity."

Myrna let out a long sigh. "I don't think he ever knew just how poor a cook Diana was. He knew she wasn't much for housekeeping, but I don't think any of us had the heart to tell him the truth about—"

The door opened, and Luke entered, a sulking Ruby trudging behind him.

"Tell him the truth about what?" he asked, looking confused.

If no one else could bear telling him that his wife couldn't cook, Nellie sure wasn't going to. She smiled at him. "About how difficult it must have been for Diana to cook on your tiny little stove. But just as she managed, so will I."

Nellie gave him a bright smile as she winked at Myrna. They would have to come to some sort of agreement, because Myrna was right. Cooking on this stove, meant as a heating unit, would be near impossible.

If one could look at a woodstove with fondness and love, that was exactly what Luke appeared to do. "The gentleman at the mercantile did say it was impractical, but Diana thought it the sweetest little thing, and she had to have it, so who was I to refuse?"

Then he sobered and turned his attention back to Nellie. "But if this won't suit you, I could see what they'd take for it in trade, and what a different stove would cost. I don't have a lot saved up, but…"

A frown creased Luke's forehead.

"It's all right." Nellie smiled at him. "As I said, I'll manage. You weren't supposed to hear that bit about the stove. It wasn't meant as an insult. Just an observation among women who are accustomed to doing a lot of cooking."

Though Myrna let out an audible sigh of relief, Ruby glared at Nellie. Did the girl, who'd taken on her mother's duties, know about her deal with Myrna? Or did Ruby see this as yet another slight against her departed mother?

Luke nodded slowly. "If you say so. Like I said,

I know it's a hard life. But I do try to make it easier where I can."

He looked around the small room as if observing it through a stranger's eyes. "I didn't exaggerate when I said it wasn't much."

Ruby's glare intensified.

"But it's enough," Nellie said smoothly, smiling as she turned her gaze around the room. "Your family has been very happy here, and I have no doubt that we all will continue to be."

Luke looked up toward the loft. "The others up there?"

Nellie nodded.

"Have you been up yet?"

"No. Myrna had just begun explaining things to me, and we haven't gotten that far."

Her answer didn't seem to please Luke, who only looked more uncomfortable at her words. "Seeing you in here, I hadn't realized…" He shook his head. "It really is a small space, isn't it?"

"We'll manage," Nellie said, reiterating her earlier words.

Luke glanced down at her bags. "There's no place for your things, no privacy for you."

"I guess she'll have to leave, then," Ruby said, the scowl disappearing from her face for the first time since entering the house.

"I'm not leaving," Nellie said, just as Luke said, "She's not leaving."

A small smile turned the corners of Luke's lips as he looked at Nellie. "At least we still agree on that.

But still, I've given no thought to your comfort, and for that I apologize."

"My mother never needed anything more," Ruby snapped, the glare returning to her face.

"Remember your promise," Luke said quietly, looking at his daughter with an expression that spoke of both rebuke and affection at the same time.

Nellie felt her shoulders relax as she examined Luke for any sign of violence. There was none. Just that pervasive sadness that seemed to surround him whenever Diana came up in conversation.

"Well," Myrna said, stepping in to the conversation. "As Nellie and I were discussing just prior to your arrival, I have supper ready for you at my house, and if we don't sit down soon, it's liable to get cold. So let's all head across the alley and we'll get some food in us all."

Nellie was grateful for the sudden ease of tension in the room. Whatever Ruby had promised Luke, she wouldn't have to deliver right away. And the cloud had lifted from Luke's shoulders, a smile filling his face again.

"That sounds wonderful. Thank you for thinking of my wife and realizing that it would be too much to ask of her to prepare supper so soon after her arrival. I'm sure it will make her feel most welcome."

"It does indeed," Nellie said, smiling back at him. Though their words were all polite and proper, things felt strained between them, as if the reality of their arrangement was somehow less satisfactory than it had sounded when they'd first discussed it. Luke continued to seem more ill at ease than happy about her acceptance of the situation.

"I'll just get the children," Nellie said, heading for the ladder. "And have a peek at the loft so I can say I've seen it all. I'm sure it will be just fine."

She could feel Luke's eyes on her as she climbed the ladder. Though it had to be sturdy enough to hold Luke's weight, the way it creaked as she made her way up made her stomach churn. She would get used to this.

The tiny loft was lit by a small window in the eaves, and the space was nothing but wall-to-wall bedding. Which, based on the smell assaulting Nellie's nostrils, hadn't been washed in some time.

Amos looked up from a picture book he'd been showing Maeve. "Is it time for supper?"

When she nodded, he shoved the book under one of the blankets. "I thought I heard you all talking about it being ready. Maevey is almost asleep." Amos nudged his sister, who yawned. "She's not supposed to be up here alone, but I knew she was tired, so I came up to watch her." Then he grinned. "See? I can be a good helper."

"You certainly can." Nellie couldn't help but like the little boy, who seemed so different from his older sister.

"Does that mean there will be chocolate cake tonight?"

Nellie fought back a laugh. Of course it was about the chocolate cake. She should have known that a little boy's heart was closely tied to his stomach.

"I don't know. Mrs. Fitzgerald is taking care of supper tonight."

"I'll find out."

Before Nellie could answer, Amos had sped past her and down the creaking ladder. Maeve let out the soft sigh of a child who'd just lost her battle with sleep. The little girl's lashes were like soot against her porcelain skin. So precious. Nellie brushed Maeve's cheek with the back of her hand. This was such a gift she hadn't been expecting—to have a family of her own to care for.

As Nellie looked out the window to see a few stray snowflakes falling, she realized with a pang that it was nearing Christmas. Why she thought of it now, she didn't know. She'd been pushing aside thoughts of the holiday, one she'd never be able to spend with her sister and her sister's family, for some time now. Ernest had thought it a silly holiday, the merriment ridiculous. She'd hoped that maybe someday, she and her sister...

Nellie shook her head. It didn't matter. She'd given up hope of a future Christmas with Mabel in the interest of keeping her sister safe. Looking down at the sleeping child, Nellie wondered how the Jeffries family celebrated Christmas. She and Luke hadn't spoken of it, but it seemed like there were more and more things they hadn't thought to discuss prior to her coming. Had she made a mistake in jumping into this too soon?

Nellie bent over the sleeping child and began shifting her into her arms. As she did so, she noticed a tattered piece of paper that looked as though it had been torn from a magazine tucked at the edge of the little girl's pillow. It was an advertisement for Christmas toys for children. The well-worn paper had clearly been looked over many times. Christmas was only a month away, and clearly the children had the holiday on their minds.

Nellie replaced the paper where she'd found it. She'd speak to Luke about it later.

Regathering Maeve into her arms, Nellie scooted across the floor to the loft opening. How was she supposed to safely carry the little girl down the rickety ladder?

She peered out through the hole. "Luke?"

Luke appeared at the foot of the ladder. "Is everything all right?"

"Maeve is asleep, and I don't wish to disturb her, but I'm not sure how to safely climb down with her in my arms."

"Hand her to me. I've done this dozens of times." Balancing on the ladder, Luke held his arms out so Nellie could give him the sleeping child.

Fortunately, at two, Maeve wasn't very heavy, so the weight transfer was easy for both Nellie and Luke. She watched as Luke cradled his daughter against him while he made his way down the ladder.

Nellie waited for Luke to fully finish climbing down before making her attempt. She shuddered as she looked through the hole to the floor below.

"Are you all right?" Luke called up to her.

"Fine."

Slowly, she turned around to begin her descent, trying to ignore the way the ladder creaked against her weight. Luke had just done it with a child in his arms; surely Nellie would be fine. It seemed like it took hours for her to finally reach firm ground, and when she did, her whole body was shaking.

"You don't like heights much, do you?" Luke asked quietly.

Nellie shook her head as gently as she could with the room still spinning.

"We'll think of something, then," he told her, putting his arm around her shoulders and giving her a squeeze.

His touch felt comforting, and Nellie wished she could also find comfort in his words. But his tone spoke of so much disappointment that she wondered if he, too, was already wondering if he'd made the right decision in bringing her here.

How had he thought that someone else could be happy in his home? Luke fought discouragement the next morning as he chopped wood behind their house. It had been enough for Diana, their cramped quarters and tiny stove. But as he'd watched Nellie and Myrna discuss the living arrangements, he realized what a poor offering their place was for any woman. He supposed, because he and Diana shared so much love between them, the material things hadn't mattered.

But as he stared at the bare frame that was to have been an extra room added on to their house, a room he'd given up on when Diana died, he wondered if maybe he'd just been lying to himself about that fact, too. Though Diana wasn't afraid of heights the way Nellie appeared to be, she hadn't liked the loft any better. She'd even stayed at the Fitzgeralds' when her time came to birth Maeve because it was easier to have more conveniences available should something go wrong.

He'd buried Diana with a clear conscience, knowing that his wife had been happy in their humble life. But had she really?

She'd nagged him and nagged him about finishing the new room. But he'd always had other things to do, mostly things Diana had wanted him to do, so they seemed just as important.

The wind blew a newspaper in his direction. The air was cold, and judging from the heavy clouds on the mountains, a storm was on its way. He'd best have more wood ready for the weather.

He reached for the paper. Someone else's trash could be useful in their home. But he couldn't resist giving it a quick scan. An advertisement for new woodstoves dominated the front page: Pretty Stoves for Your Parlor. The quaint phrase made him chuckle, except as he looked at the pictures, he could understand the discussion Myrna and Nellie were trying to have without offending him. He'd purchased one of those pretty little parlor stoves—great for heating and conversation, not so great for cooking. A woman who liked to cook needed one of the fancy cooking stoves pictured on the next page.

Luke sighed as he folded the paper and set it under one of the pieces of wood. He wasn't stupid. He'd known that Diana couldn't possibly have done all the cooking she'd claimed to have done. But as he'd overheard the women whispering in the kitchen, he had to wonder if Diana had done any cooking at all.

Of course she had. How many times did he wake in the morning to his beautiful wife standing beside that tiny stove, frying eggs? Every single day. But the top of the stove was only big enough for a single pan. Where had the biscuits and bacon come from?

Luke picked up the ax and swung it above his head. It wasn't his concern anymore. Diana was dead, and there was no sense in resurrecting things best left alone.

Still, as he continued to chop wood and stare at the shell of the room he'd promised her, he couldn't help but feel guilty that he didn't do enough for the woman whom he loved. How was he supposed to make a woman who didn't love him happy enough to stay?

The back door opened, and Nellie peered out. "Breakfast is ready."

Luke put the ax down and grabbed a stack of wood. "Thought I'd replenish your woodpile before heading off to work."

"Thank you. I appreciate it," Nellie said, her voice formal, polite. He couldn't fault her in her speech, but it seemed like she held him at a distance.

When he entered the house, he saw that the table was set and the room already tidied. They'd made a makeshift bed for Nellie on the floor of the main room, and he could see no sign of it now.

What kind of life had he given her? She hadn't signed up to sleep on the floor every night.

"I'll see what I can do about getting you a proper bed," Luke said again. He'd said the same last night, the same when they'd risen, and here he was, once again apologizing for not having thought of her comfort as he should have.

She gave a small smile as she shook her head. "I told you. I've been in far worse accommodations, and to be honest, your floor was far more comfortable than that hotel we stayed at the night before."

"I thought you said you slept fine at the hotel."

Nellie let out a long sigh. "I did, but I found the bed lumpy, so it was nice to have the firmness of the floor last night."

Though Luke nodded, it bothered him that she was so concerned about preserving his feelings that she couldn't be truthful. She could have just told him that she'd found the hotel bed lumpy when he'd asked the first time.

How were they supposed to make a life together when they couldn't be honest with one another?

As the family gathered around the table, Luke noticed the children were all dressed, washed, and had their hair combed. None of the women he'd hired to care for the children ever managed to accomplish so much in so little time.

"What is this?" Ruby asked, her voice full of irritation as she poked at the steaming bowls Nellie placed in front of them.

"Porridge," Nellie said brightly as she sat in her place. "Amos tells me he's tired of eggs, and when I was going through the supplies, I noticed you had a whole tin of it. It was my favorite breakfast growing up, so I thought you'd all appreciate the change."

Ruby scowled and pushed the bowl away. "We hate porridge."

With a look at Ruby meant to remind her about their promise, Luke picked up his spoon. "We haven't had porridge in a long time, so perhaps you'll find that you like it after all."

"Mrs. Fitzgerald makes us eat it at her house all the time," Ruby said, glaring at him.

Even if it was the most horrible thing he'd ever tasted, he would pretend to enjoy it. He sighed. So much for wanting to be more open with his new wife.

Only...he let the porridge roll around in his mouth.

"This is delicious," Luke said, turning toward Nellie.

"Thank you. I found a bit of cinnamon in with the spices, so I added it and just a small amount of sugar. I hope you don't mind, since we're low on sugar. We still haven't discussed the household budget for food and such."

Nellie turned to help Maeve eat her porridge. Something in Luke twisted in a funny way at the simple gesture of watching her feed his daughter. Of caring for a child, living in a situation that couldn't have been what Nellie expected and then having to ask for food money in such a calm way.

He was doing a poor job of being a husband to this woman.

Looking up, Luke realized Ruby was staring at him, her bowl of porridge still untouched, her expression defiant. But she also seemed to be waiting for Luke's response to his wife's query.

He'd given his child too much authority in their home for too long.

"Eat your breakfast, Ruby," he said, giving his daughter another stern look to remind her that she was supposed to be making Nellie feel welcome.

Amos was nearly finished with his, and Luke felt slightly better knowing that not all of his children were taking this change so hard.

"I don't like porridge," Ruby repeated.

"Then you'll go without," Luke told her. He turned his attention to Nellie. "I hope you'll support me in this decision, so please do not give her something else to eat."

"Of course." Nellie inclined her head slightly, then focused her attention back on Maeve, who seemed to be enjoying her meal as much as Amos.

The exchange felt as stiff as it had been with the various women he'd hired to care for the children. He didn't mean to treat Nellie as hired help, yet so far, there was none of the easy banter that had happened between them the first day they'd met.

"That is, unless you had a different idea," Luke said, hoping to bring their conversation back to a more comfortable place.

Nellie finally looked over at him. "No, I think you're correct." She smiled over at Ruby. "You haven't even tried it."

"Fine. I'll starve." Ruby pushed back from the table. "Amos and I have to get to school now."

A glance at the clock told Luke that they would all

be late if they didn't hurry. "And I must get to work. Children, get your coats. I'll walk you."

"Really, Papa?" Amos jumped up from the table and ran to where his school things were kept.

"Really." He smiled in the direction of his son, then turned his gaze toward Ruby. Had he thought to walk his children to school sooner, he'd have known that Ruby hadn't been going at all.

"I should come, too," Nellie said, standing. "Since I'm not familiar with the area, it will be good for me to know where the children's school is, and perhaps along the way, you can point out other items of interest."

Her words were not meant as a rebuke, at least not as far as Luke could tell. As she bundled up both herself and Maeve, Luke couldn't see a hint of annoyance or displeasure on Nellie's face. And yet, he couldn't help but feel disappointment that he hadn't thought of such a simple way to make his new wife feel welcome or help her get to know her new community.

Luke started to clear his plate, but Nellie waved her hand at him. "Don't worry about that. I'll deal with the clearing up once we get everyone off to school. I know you must be anxious to get back to work."

He'd told her that, back when they were in Denver and the conversation flowed freely between them. They'd talked about a lot of things in those few days, which seemed like a lifetime ago. How he liked his job, even with the challenges, and how Seamus counted on him to keep the equipment running smoothly.

Perhaps that was the key to finding an easier way to

converse with his wife—going back to topics that had already been comfortable between them.

"I am, thank you. Seamus was telling me last night that the new equipment he ordered wasn't working properly. I'm eager to take a look and see what can be done."

He was rewarded with a smile. "You enjoy the tinkering, don't you?"

"I do. So many men come here, looking for the riches in silver, but I'm content to make a living doing something I enjoy."

Diana used to harbor dreams that he'd someday decide to stake a claim and find a big vein of silver. But he'd never had interest in such things. He liked, as Nellie said, the tinkering, and finding out how machines worked, then making them work better.

Once again, Luke felt disloyal in making the comparison to Diana, especially since it didn't paint his late wife in such a good light. But Diana had many other fine qualities, and she'd believed in him enough to take a risk and move to Leadville to allow him to work with the machines he loved so much.

What, then, was a man to do? As he pulled on his coat, he could feel the air lighten around him and Nellie, a more comfortable place than where they'd been since arriving in Leadville. Was there a way to get along with Nellie and not be disloyal to Diana? Did he owe any loyalty to a dead woman?

As they walked down the street toward the school, Luke's wife carrying his youngest daughter and holding his son's hand, the picture was almost perfect. A week ago, Luke would have said it was exactly what he wanted. Someone caring for his children and helping to ease his burdens.

But as he felt the weight of the glare of his eldest daughter, Luke wondered if he'd made the wrong bargain.

Once Nellie got the children off to school and Luke to work, she found herself enjoying the peace of her new home. She'd set Maeve to playing with a doll she'd found, and begun the seemingly impossible task of setting the tiny dwelling to rights. She couldn't rightly say the last time anything had been given a good scrubbing. But with the fire crackling, and the little girl singing a little tune as she played, Nellie found she didn't mind the work.

When Luke returned home, he'd find that his dearest wish—a clean house—had come true. At least the main part of it. She couldn't bring herself to make the trek to the loft to clean up there, and with a storm moving in, she couldn't drag the blankets outside for a good cleaning and airing. So that task would remain for another day.

She'd just finished putting the last gleaming dish on the newly cleaned shelf when a knock sounded at her door.

Myrna was there, carrying a large pot of what smelled like stew.

"That smells incredible."

"Old family recipe," Myrna said. "I know we haven't

worked out our arrangement yet, but with the storm coming…"

Then Myrna stopped. And stared. "I've never seen this place looking so fine."

"Just takes a little soap, water and some elbow grease." Nellie smiled and gestured to the table. "Why don't you sit and I'll make us some tea? Then I can put the stew on the stove and hope I'm not tempted to eat it all before supper."

"Ah, there's more where that came from," Myrna said. "And I would be delighted to have some tea. It'll go nicely with these muffins I've baked."

The older woman held up a basket, and Nellie couldn't help the warm feeling that overcame her. It had been so long since she'd enjoyed such female companionship. Ernest had kept her so isolated, and she hadn't had nearly enough time with Mabel before the men came looking for her.

How could all of her dreams suddenly be coming true so easily?

True, the house wasn't much, and she slept on the floor, but she hadn't felt so safe in such a long time. Even Ruby's hostility was a far sight better than the abuse she'd suffered at the hands of Ernest's cronies.

Nellie made the tea, and as she and Myrna chatted, she couldn't help but feel complete and utter joy. There was only one thing missing.

"I understand that Luke has a…difficult…relationship with the church," Nellie said, smiling at Myrna. "But he has given me permission to attend and see to the children's religious education. Do you think you could introduce me to the pastor sometime? Is there a ladies' group, perhaps?" Her voice shook as she made the request, but Myrna didn't appear to notice.

"Praise God!" Myrna said, jumping out of her chair. "We have been praying for someone to come into the children's lives who can show them Christ's love. Luke is just so stubborn, and you…"

The older woman's smile filled her face. "Diana would have hated to see how he's turned against the Lord. And here you are, bringing them back."

Nellie shook her head. "Just the children. I've promised to let Luke resolve things with God in his own way."

"And so he should. But those children…" Myrna looked over at Maeve, who'd been given a muffin and was happily eating it. "They need someone to take them to church and teach them about God's ways. I try, but Luke is afraid he's imposing or taking advantage of me if I do too much."

All things Nellie already knew. "A man has his pride."

"Too much, if you ask me," Myrna agreed.

"I can't say. I hardly know him," Nellie said. "But I can't imagine he'd be happy that we're discussing it so freely."

Myrna leaned forward and put her hands over Nellie's. "You're good for him. I have nothing bad to say about Diana, but he needs a woman like you. People will call you fools for marrying like this. But I know He's brought you to this family for His good purpose."

Nellie would have liked to have said the same thing.

"I hope so. But things have been awkward between us since we've arrived in Leadville. I thought we were building a good friendship, but it seems different now."

"I'll pray for you," Myrna said.

Tears filled Nellie's eyes. She couldn't remember the last time anyone had said they'd be praying for her. That they would take her cares to the Lord.

"There now." Myrna came around the table and put her arms around Nellie. "It's not as bad as all that. You and Luke are going to have a good life together, I just know it."

Nellie nodded as the tears fell. "I know. I just wasn't expecting to find a friend as wonderful as you as part of this new life."

"Just you wait, Nellie Jeffries. You're about to find a whole lot more."

Somehow, that was something too grand to imagine. But as she recalled Luke's description of Leadville as being a dark, cold place, she had to think that he'd gotten it all wrong. Because here, in this tiny kitchen he'd disparaged, Nellie had to think it was something a little like paradise.

Chapter Five

A few days after Nellie's arrival, Luke found himself by the woodpile once again. Only this time, instead of preparing for a storm, he was building that extra room he'd promised Diana. The snow had cleared enough to make the work possible, and it was a far more inviting environment out here than staying cooped up in the house with a sullen daughter and an overly cheerful wife.

Luke's world had never been better. At least not since before it had come crashing down with Diana's death. The house was cleaner than he'd ever seen it, his family was eating three delicious meals a day, and his children seemed almost happy. Except for Ruby, of course, but he knew that would take time. After all, since Ruby was the eldest, she and her mother had been close. But Nellie…well, that was an entirely different story. Things were not tense between them, at least not precisely, but she was so polite to him all the time and he felt like he was walking on eggshells with her.

With a thud, he pounded in the last nail needed to hold the structure steady. The least he could do for this woman, who'd turned his household into a well-oiled machine, was give her a place of her own. It hardly seemed right that she slept on a pallet in the middle of the floor in the main room. Not when she did so much for them. He could give her a proper room, with a proper bed, and maybe a place to put her things.

He'd wanted to build the room for Diana, before Maeve was born, so she could have a comfortable place for her lie-in. But he'd been offered the chance to work extra shifts, and Diana had told him she'd rather have the money, since they were short again.

The back door opened and Nellie stepped out, a smile on her face and a steaming mug in her hand.

"I thought you could use some refreshment." She held the cup out to him.

"Thank you." He drank deeply, appreciating the burn of the hot liquid as it slid down his throat.

Nellie looked around nervously, and Luke tried not to sigh. She always seemed to be nervous about something, worried that she'd anger him in some way. And he, for his part, was always careful to try to make her feel safe. But it didn't seem to do any good.

"I was hoping I could ask a favor," she said.

"Of course."

She shifted her weight, looking at the work he'd been doing. "I know you have your project and all, but I noticed that you don't have a clothesline. I'd like to do some washing, but there isn't a good place to hang anything to dry."

Luke let out a long breath. She never asked for anything for herself, but she did for the household, and it was always done in such an apologetic manner, like she was afraid of angering him.

"That's not a favor," he said, looking around the yard for a suitable spot. "That's necessary for the family. I don't know why you keep acting like you're asking for the moon."

Nellie took a step back. "I'm sorry."

"Stop apologizing!" Luke set the mug she'd given him on a nearby stump. "When are you going to figure out that you don't have to be afraid of upsetting me? You want to know what upsets me? This. You acting like every little thing is going to create a major problem. You need a clothesline? That's fine. We'll make a clothesline."

Luke stomped over to the lean-to, where he kept some rope. After digging through some boxes, he found what he was looking for. He pulled out the rope and tossed it on the ground.

"Where do you want it?"

Wide-eyed, Nellie stared at him. "I didn't mean to make you angry," she said quietly, not moving from the doorway.

He couldn't win. It wasn't that he even wanted to win. He just wanted his wife to not be afraid of him. To come to him without fear or hesitancy.

"I'm not angry," Luke said, taking a step toward her, then realized she had retreated farther into the doorway. Taking a deep breath to calm himself, Luke held out his hands. "All right. I'm frustrated. But you act like I'm going to hurt you or something. I would never—"

The expression on her face told him everything he needed to know. She'd been hurt before. Based on the things she'd told him prior to their marriage, he'd gotten the impression that she hadn't been married to the most upstanding of men. But this level of fear...

What had happened to Nellie?

Luke sat on a log he'd arranged that summer as a seating area. "You don't know me well enough to know that, I suppose. I've never hit a woman, or anyone, for that matter. And even though I know my tone sometimes might sound harsh, I hate raising my voice."

He looked up at her and noticed she'd relaxed slightly, though she hadn't moved from her station at the door.

"I know you're afraid of disappointing me, or not making this what we'd hoped it would be, but you have exceeded my expectations in every way." Luke took a deep breath. No, not every way. And maybe, if he could be honest with her and share his frustrations with her, then they could make progress in their developing relationship.

"My only complaint," he continued, "is that you seem to always be afraid of me. Or of letting me down. We're partners, and I thought we'd agreed to talk about things. You shouldn't be afraid to talk to me or ask me for anything."

Nellie didn't react to his words. Had he done something to hurt her without knowing?

"Unless I did something to make you afraid? In

which case, I'd like you to tell me so I won't do it again."

Finally, Nellie took a step in his direction. "No, you haven't done anything to make me fearful. I just…" She glanced over her shoulder at the house, then at the room he was building.

"Based on what I've seen in the house, and how everyone reacts to what I do, it seems like I do things quite differently from your late wife. I'm constantly upsetting old routines and traditions, and I don't want to make it seem like I'm erasing her memory. Everything I do is wrong, according to Ruby, and I've seen the dark shadows in your eyes when I've crossed some imaginary line of Diana's domain." Nellie's shoulders rose and fell, then she straightened. "I'm not trying to diminish what Diana did. Or make her seem like she wasn't a good wife and mother. But I feel like I'm constantly walking a tightrope because of the fear that I might be."

She gestured to the rope on the ground. "Is my asking for a clothesline a negative commentary on her housekeeping? I don't know. But half the time, I feel as though my asking for something different from how Diana did it is taken as a criticism of her."

Luke took a deep breath. She was right; they'd had several discussions about things Nellie did differently from Diana. Ruby complained especially loudly about those changes.

Bringing in a new wife to take over where his late wife had left off wasn't as simple as he'd thought it would be. He'd done Nellie a grave disservice, thinking her transition would be easy. You couldn't just drop a person into shoes she'd never been meant to fill.

"I'm sorry," he said finally. "I guess things are more complicated than I'd thought they would be."

He looked down at his hands, realizing that he had probably not done as much as he should have to make Nellie's transition any easier for her. After all, she had asked to discuss several topics, like the family finances, church and family traditions, with him, but he'd put it off. And instead of being cooped up in the tiny house with her today to help with the children and see what things were like for her, he'd chosen to be out here, building an extra room that he thought would make her life easier, when he hadn't even asked her if that was what she wanted.

"I know you do things differently from Diana," he said slowly. "Truth be told, I don't know how she did things. I didn't care as long as everyone was happy and healthy. I left a lot of things for you to figure out, because I..." Luke took a deep breath as he finally turned his attention back on Nellie. "I was struggling so much, trying to do all the things my family needed, and I don't know what I was doing. It's been a relief, having you here to do those things for me. I suppose it's been so nice having some order to my house that I tuned out the children complaining."

Nellie seemed so small, leaning against the back of the house. Luke patted the spot next to him. "So come, sit by me, and let's talk about the things you need to talk about. I haven't done a good job of listening or trying to see things from your point of view."

As he spoke, Luke could see how Nellie would feel so isolated in her new home. He treated the men he supervised with more respect, and had Nellie been an employee, he would have been clearer in his expectations of her and her duties. She wasn't an employee, but a wife, so she deserved more respect from him, not less.

"Thank you," Nellie said as she took the spot he indicated. "I do feel as though you haven't been willing to discuss important matters with me. When we met, you said we would talk about things, but it seems like we've spoken very little since I arrived."

"I'm sorry," Luke said. "I'll do better in the future, starting now."

Nellie rewarded him with a smile. Until now, he'd forgotten how pretty she was. Luke shook his head. He wasn't supposed to be noticing her beauty. Theirs was not a love match, but one of practicality and necessity. Had he had any other options, he wouldn't have married her at all.

Swallowing, he tried to banish that thought from his mind. It wasn't fair of him to think such things, not when Nellie was clearly doing everything she could to hold up her end of the bargain. And had his heart not already been taken by Diana, he might have considered Nellie in a different light.

"I understand your reluctance to talk about money," Nellie said slowly. "It's clear you don't have much, and as I told you when we married, that's fine by me. I grew up poor, and I know how to stretch a dollar. What you've given me so far is more than adequate for my current needs. But the children need new shoes, and I'd like to buy some material to make them new clothes. What they have is threadbare and too small. Plus, Christmas is coming, and while I don't believe in extravagances, I do think it nice to have a few little extras, as well as some gifts."

Christmas.

As Nellie continued speaking about the things she'd like to do for the children, that one word continued to repeat itself over and over in Luke's head. Christmas had been Diana's favorite holiday. She would get together with the ladies from church to bake special treats. There would be laughing and conspiring, and excitement would fill the air. The church had all sorts of activities, and there were teas, dances and charity functions filling their social schedule.

Which meant reentering Leadville society and pretending that everything was fine after the loss of his wife. Yes, he wanted his children to live normal lives and to be able to move past the tragedy. But what about for Luke? His wife had died. The woman he'd thought would be his companion for all of his days was gone, and he couldn't find a way to make merry without her.

He stole a glance at Nellie, who'd just finished telling him about all the things she'd like to do for the family for Christmas. It was the time of year to reflect on Christ's birth, but all Luke could think about was his wife's death.

"Whatever you'd like to do is fine," he said, letting the words flow out as quickly as possible so he didn't have to commit to anything else. Nellie and the children could participate in the various activities. He would just stay home.

"But what are the children expecting?" Nellie asked, her voice as firm as it would be were she chastising one of the children. "What are your family's traditions and customs?"

Luke took a deep breath. Christmas was Diana's holiday. She'd taken care of all those details. And he'd delighted in watching her. All the things he remembered… Luke shook his head. He didn't want to do those things anymore.

"There's nothing specific to our family," he said finally. "In truth, I don't much feel like celebrating Christmas. But I know that the children will be expecting something."

Nellie placed her hands over his. "You're still grieving Diana."

He nodded. "She loved Christmas."

Having the warmth of Nellie's hands over his made Luke feel comforted. Her gentle smile and warm touch made him think that perhaps his grief might be bearable after all.

She'd made a mess of things, bringing up Christmas like that. Nellie should have known there was a reason Luke hadn't mentioned the upcoming holiday when it was on everyone else's lips. And now she'd torn open the wounds he was desperately trying to hold together for the sake of his children.

Still, when she went inside after their talk, he followed her in and immediately jumped into the work of setting the house to rights. On today's agenda: cleaning the sleeping loft.

Only, the children hadn't continued with their jobs when Nellie had left to find out about getting a clothesline to air out the blankets. A good washing would have to wait until spring, but at least she could hang them and beat out some of the dust and debris to freshen them for now.

"Why didn't you bring the blankets down from the loft?" Nellie asked when she'd taken off her coat.

"We've never done this before, so I don't see why we have to do it now." Ruby stared at her defiantly.

"Because it stinks up there, and the only way to have things smelling good is to give everything a thorough cleaning." Nellie met the girl's gaze with one of her own. "So you and your brother need to get up there and throw down all the blankets so I can get them hung to air out."

Nellie turned to Luke. "Which is why I'd like a clothesline. I'd prefer to wash them, but in this cold, they won't dry in time for bed."

"I'm happy to help," Luke said, then looked over at Ruby. "Why are you standing there? Nellie asked you to do something."

Amos immediately climbed up the ladder to do as Nellie asked. But Ruby continued to stand there, her hands on her hips and eyes blazing.

"Our mother never made us do anything like this."

"Perhaps not," Luke said. "But I agree with Nellie

that we need to do more to keep our house clean. If she thinks we need to air out our blankets, then I support her fully. We may not have done as much when your mother was around, but it's time we all work together and do our part."

"I thought the whole reason you brought her here was because I was doing too much work," Ruby said, crossing her arms in front of her. "If she's here to do the work, then maybe she should get up there and get the blankets down."

The trouble with marrying for convenience and being honest about it was that even the children knew that Nellie was basically a glorified housekeeper. Which she mostly didn't mind, except that the children had no business treating her like a servant.

Luke marched up to his daughter. "That was one of the most disrespectful things I've heard you say. Not only do you need to apologize to Nellie, but you will spend the rest of the day doing extra chores to help her. She's performing a great service to our family, and it's time you start appreciating her."

"She does nothing for the family," Ruby said, turning her gaze back to Nellie. "I know that Mrs. Fitzgerald fixes all of our meals, including packing our lunches. I wouldn't be surprised if she's the one who comes in and cleans during the day while we're at school."

Luke looked at Nellie. "That's not true, is it?"

Nellie let out a long sigh. The trouble with keeping her secret was that it also meant letting out Diana's secrets, as well. "It is," Nellie said calmly. "Apparently, Myrna and Diana had an arrangement in which Myrna did the cooking for your family, and Diana did all the sewing and mending for Myrna's family."

She pointed at the stove. "Surely you can see that there's no way a person can cook such fine meals on this. That's what Myrna and I were discussing that first night when you came home. Neither of us wanted to dishonor Diana's memory, so we felt it best to keep the arrangement between us."

Then she smiled at Ruby. "Although…I have cooked some of the meals using Myrna's stove. That chicken and biscuit meal you liked so much? I made it."

Watching the horror spread over Ruby's face at actually liking something that came from Nellie's hands gave her a small degree of satisfaction. The girl had virtually licked her plate clean that night.

Nellie let out a long sigh as she returned her attention to Luke. "I apologize for not telling you, but it seemed easier to continue on with things as they've always been done because I know how much Diana's little stove means to you. It's just impractical for running a household. I did what I could to make do. I'm sure Myrna would be more than happy to verify what I've said."

"I told you, I don't like imposing." Luke shook his head. "I can't imagine what Seamus must think of me, taking advantage of his wife's good nature like this."

"The same thing he must have thought when Diana and Myrna had a similar arrangement. I understand he was quite pleased at how well I repaired the holes in his socks."

Something must have triggered a memory in Luke's mind because he started to shake his head slowly. "But Diana's meals were often terrible. Yours are good. If Myrna cooked both, I don't understand."

Nellie went to his side and put her hand on his arm. "I think Diana added a few of her own touches so you wouldn't know. She was probably afraid that if you knew just how poor of a job she did with all the home-making, you'd think less of her."

The sorrow in Luke's eyes as he looked down at her made Nellie's heart ache.

"How is it that you know my late wife better than me?"

"She doesn't," Ruby said, stamping her foot. "She doesn't know my mother at all. She's making it up so you won't be cross with her. But I know better. Mother did cook all those things, and she wasn't afraid of anything."

Ruby's defense of her mother made Nellie's heart ache even more. This was why she'd agreed to continue the arrangement with Myrna.

"Your mother had many fine qualities," Nellie said, modulating her voice so she sounded calm and at ease. "Clearly she loved you very much, and I've not heard a word spoken against her. Please don't misunderstand my comments to mean otherwise. I think it was her deep love for your father, and her desire to please him, that made her mislead him about her talents in the kitchen."

Luke's nod made Nellie feel better about the situation. She gave his arm a squeeze, and she could see by the rise and fall of his shoulders that he'd taken a deep breath and was finding the calm within.

"I should have seen through it," he said. "But you're right—we all loved her so much that we overlooked a lot of things. I didn't question anything because…"

A smile filled his face. "I wish you could have met her. She was so wonderful. No matter where Diana went, she lit up the room because she was filled with so much love and joy."

Nellie returned his smile. "I've heard that about her." She turned her gaze back to Ruby. "And I would never want to dishonor your mother in any way. I can't help but think that this anger and defiance isn't what she would have wanted. She wanted everyone to be happy, all the time, and I know she would have wanted you to find a way to be happy without her."

"You didn't even know her!" Ruby turned and scrambled up the ladder.

Closing her eyes, Nellie took a deep breath. Luke covered her arm where she'd been holding it with his free hand.

"It's all right, Nellie. You meant well."

She looked up at him. "What's all right? At the moment, I feel as though I've made a mess of things."

"What you just said to Ruby. You're right. All Diana ever wanted was for people to be happy."

Nellie had heard the same thing from Myrna, along with similar sentiments from the women she'd met at church. But perhaps she shouldn't have repeated it.

"As for your deal with Myrna," Luke continued, "I don't know what to say about that. It seems I didn't know a lot about the goings-on in my household, and that isn't right. It sounds as though you're just continuing a previous arrangement that's satisfactory to all, but if you don't mind, I'd like to discuss it with Seamus to be sure."

Nellie nodded, enjoying the warmth of his hand on hers. Even though the situation was tense, she felt like she had an ally in this fight. "Of course. I didn't mean to deceive you. It just seemed easier this way."

He studied her face, like he was trying to uncover a puzzle. "Are there any other secrets you're keeping from me? I'd prefer to get them all out now."

Secrets. Nellie had plenty of those. Especially when it came to her past. But those were not things she'd be telling anyone. She'd done her very best to ensure that nothing from her past would come back to haunt her. The men couldn't possibly know that she had the means to go to Denver. And because they'd married in Denver, there was no way anyone would track her to Leadville.

Which meant no one ever needed to know anything.

Nellie smiled up at him. "No. Honestly, it's been hard enough keeping my arrangement with Myrna from you."

And that was the truth. When it came to the present and future, there would be no secrets she kept from her husband. As if to remind her of one more secret, Nellie could feel the coins burning a figurative hole at her waist and in her toes. But since that money was from her past, and was to be her escape route should Luke be keeping some dark secrets of his own, that one didn't matter.

Chapter Six

Since the admission about the cooking, Luke felt as though his relationship with Nellie had taken a more positive turn. True, Ruby seemed more resentful than ever of her stepmother, but Amos and Maeve seemed to be responding favorably to Nellie's care.

"Hello, neighbor," Seamus called from across the alley. "I see you've finally gotten the new room done."

Luke put down his hammer and strode over to where his friend stood. "Yes, I think it'll be a nice addition to our home. I hadn't realized how cramped our quarters were."

Seamus took off his hat and scratched his head. "You know, there are a number of houses for rent in the neighborhood. James Sinclair just moved into the one on the corner of Second Street, and I was surprised at how reasonable the rent was."

Looking around at the tiny lot upon which his equally small house sat, Luke sighed. He and Diana had talked about finding a different house shortly before her death, but it seemed wrong to leave the home they'd built together. When they'd moved to Leadville only a few short years ago, this place was the only thing they could find, and Luke had been proud to purchase it outright, even though it had taken all their savings. Did it make sense to pay rent on a house when this one was paid for? He couldn't bear to sell it, not when he and Diana had put so much of themselves into this place.

"I know you mean well, but this is our home," Luke finally said.

"You just got a raise. You can afford it." The trouble with his friend being his boss was that Seamus knew a little too much about Luke's finances for his own good.

Luke shook his head at his friend. "The price of coal just went up, and even though I'm supplementing with wood, heating this place is getting harder and harder. I can't imagine what it would take to heat something larger."

Stroking his beard, Seamus entered Luke's yard. "That stove you've got is more ornamental than efficient. And while you've done a good job building this cabin, it's not as well insulated as it could be. Last winter, Myrna gave Diana some papers to put up on the walls to keep in the heat, but Diana never did anything with them."

Seamus and Luke had already talked about the stove situation. Seamus confirmed the deal Diana and Myrna had made and that it was continuing with Nellie. Actually, Nellie had done so much mending for the Fitzgeralds that Seamus wanted to pay her, but with everything the Fitzgeralds had done for Luke after Diana's death, it didn't seem right to accept his money. Luke had looked into getting a new stove, but it was just beyond his means, so he'd need to start saving to make it work.

As for the additional paper on the walls, Luke shook his head. "Diana loved that wallpaper. She saved her pin money for quite some time to be able to buy it. I'm sure it would break her heart to cover it up."

"Diana is dead," Seamus said quietly. "I can't imagine she'd want her family to freeze to death to preserve some wallpaper that she isn't around to enjoy anymore."

Luke closed his eyes. "I know she's dead. I can't seem to forget that fact, and it sure makes life harder to live without her."

A warm hand touched Luke's shoulder, and he opened his eyes to see Seamus's gentle face near his.

"I know you miss her. I can't imagine what I'd do without Myrna. But you can't keep living with one foot in the grave when you have three children who need you. Besides that, you have another wife. A woman who deserves to be seen for the wonderful woman she is, and not a fill-in for a dead woman."

His friend's words were like a punch to the gut. Except Seamus didn't know what he was talking about.

"Nellie understood the situation when she married me. Ours was not a love match."

"But she would be a good woman for you to love. She spends a lot of time with Myrna, and I know the affection my wife has for her. Nellie might have been a convenient choice for you, but if you let her, if you let yourself, you could find happiness again."

Find happiness again. Luke looked down at the man's hand resting on his shoulder, then brushed it away.

"I appreciate your words, but as you said, you don't know what you'd do if you lost Myrna."

Seamus's brow furrowed. "You're right, I don't know. But I do know that if I had a woman like Nellie step into Myrna's shoes, I'd be a blessed man indeed, and I wouldn't squander that blessing trying to preserve the past."

Nellie emerged from the Fitzgeralds' house, laughing at something Ellen, Seamus's daughter, said. Ellen handed Nellie a large crock, then followed, carrying a basket.

"Hello, gentlemen," Nellie said as she approached them, seemingly oblivious to the tension between the men. "You are in for a treat for supper tonight. Myrna and I spent all afternoon making noodles with Ellen, who learned this new recipe from one of her church friends."

"Don't forget the bread," Ellen added, nudging Nellie. "Pa, you aren't going to believe how light and fluffy Nellie's bread is. It's like eating a cloud."

"I don't know that I want to eat any clouds," Seamus said, grinning. "I can't imagine it would fill a man up."

"Oh, but it will," Nellie assured him, a smile spreading across her face. "I'm told my bread sticks to a man's ribs."

As Luke watched the banter between Nellie, Ellen and Seamus, part of him wished he could be part of that same easy routine. But another part of him felt like he was somehow betraying Diana. Ellen had been Diana's best friend, and yet, from the way she laughed with Nellie, it seemed as though Ellen had completely forgotten Diana.

"Luke, can you get the door?" Nellie asked, giving him the kind of smile meant to turn a man's heart. Or at least, that was what it would have been to him were his heart not completely unable to be turned.

He did as he was bade, ignoring Seamus's eyes on him. Once the door was closed behind Nellie and Ellen, Seamus said, "You know, it's not a crime to let yourself have feelings for someone else once your wife dies. It doesn't diminish the love you have in your heart for Diana. In fact, it's a tribute to her love, that it taught you how to love even deeper. To be able to love someone else. It's a gift, loving someone, and you shouldn't be ashamed of it."

"I'm not ashamed of anything," Luke said, stepping away from the other man. "Everyone knows I loved Diana."

"So then why are you afraid to love someone else?"

"I'm not." His wife hadn't been gone six months— why was it so wrong to grieve her still?

"Every time you look at Nellie, there's a longing in your eyes, like you want her. But you turn away quickly, like acknowledging those feelings are somehow going to burn you. None of us are promised tomorrow. It would be a shame if you wasted your today ignoring what's in front of you."

Luke's stomach twisted as he stared at his friend. "You don't know what you're talking about. And I'll thank you to not bring this up again. You don't know what I'm going through, so you can't possibly understand."

He didn't wait for a response as he turned and went back into his house. Though he had a few more boards he'd have liked to secure better on Nellie's room, it would do for now.

"Running's not going to help," Seamus called after him.

What did Seamus know? At least Nellie understood that the grieving process was personal, and he couldn't be expected to give up his heart simply because everyone else thought it was a good idea.

Ellen sat at the table, laughing at something Nellie had said. Nellie held up a teapot.

"I was just making some tea. Would you care to join us?"

"No, thanks," Luke said, staring at the teapot Nellie held. "I don't recognize that. Where did you get it?"

"It was in the back shed." Nellie smiled at him as she rubbed the cracked pot. "I couldn't find anything else to use, so I've been rummaging through the old shed. Myrna said it was mostly junk, but I've found a few useful items."

"We have a teapot. I bought Diana a very nice one for her birthday last year."

"That's Mother's!" Ruby said, jumping up from where she'd been reading a book to Maeve. "I'll not have her using Mother's things. When she first came, I took everything nice of Mother's and locked it in her trunk."

Ruby held up a key that was hanging from a string around her neck. "And she can't get into it while I'm at school, either."

Luke wasn't sure what caused him the most physical pain: the anger and selfishness in his daughter's face, or the look of devastation on Nellie's.

As much as Luke hated to admit it, Seamus might have been right about a few things.

"Your mother can't use those things anymore. It's silly to keep them locked away so no one can use them when they might be useful to our family. Give me the key."

Luke held out his hand, but Ruby stood there, shaking her head.

"No. Those are my mother's things. Not hers."

Wind whistled through one of the cracks in the wall, a place where he hadn't dabbed enough mud to keep the wind out, where the thin wallpaper Diana had put up had torn. Luke sighed. Was he being just as selfish as Ruby, clinging to something as silly as having the nice wallpaper Diana had wanted instead of doing more to take care of his family's needs?

"They're also mine," Luke said quietly, looking at his daughter and holding out his hand. "And I bought all those pretty things so they could be used, not locked away in a trunk where no one could enjoy them."

"I won't have her wearing Mother's dresses." Ruby turned her glare on Nellie.

Nellie wiped her hands on her apron and stepped forward. "I would never do such a thing," she said softly, a gentle smile filling her face. "From what I hear, your mother was much smaller than me, so I doubt any of her things would fit me."

Luke watched as Nellie came closer to his daughter. "But I have been thinking," Nellie continued. "You are in need of some new dresses. I can't help but notice how short your skirts have become, and how your wrists stick out at the ends of your sleeves. I was going to ask your father for money to buy material to make you something new, but if you'd like, I could remake a few of your mother's dresses to fit you. That way, you could have a piece of her with you every day."

A lump filled Luke's throat as he saw how Nellie was trying to reach out to Ruby. Only a few weeks before Nellie came, Ruby had asked him if she could wear her mother's dresses. But they were too big on her and wouldn't have been appropriate. Nellie's idea would give Ruby what she wanted.

But was Ruby willing to accept Nellie's olive branch?

Ruby bit her lower lip. "How do I know you won't ruin them?"

Ellen turned around in her seat. "Oh, I can vouch for Nellie's sewing. You should see what she did to help me remake my gown for the Christmas ball. Pa said I couldn't have the new material I wanted, but what Nellie did—oh, I will have the prettiest dress there!" With a smile, Ellen added, "But if you want to do an experiment first, I have an old dress I was going to donate to the church ministry. I'd be happy to let you have it so Nellie can remake it and show you what she can do. You are so blessed to have someone so talented with a needle in your household. Why, you are going to be the best-dressed family in all of Leadville."

Ruby's scowl didn't leave her face, but it didn't deepen. "My mother was talented with a needle."

"Oh, she was!" Ellen agreed. "I will treasure her embroidery forever. But Nellie has an eye for dressmaking that I've never seen the likes of. Where did you learn such things?"

"My mother was a seamstress," Nellie said, smiling. "She taught me everything I know. I was helping her with dressmaking when I was Ruby's age."

For a moment, Nellie appeared lost in the memory, a soft expression drifting across her face. In all the time Luke had known her, he'd never heard Nellie refer to any of her family, other than to say she had a sister who wouldn't be able to come to the wedding.

Then Nellie turned her attention back to Ruby. "I do know what it's like to miss your mother. Mine died far too soon, and there isn't a day that goes by that I don't wish for her back so I could talk to her. But I have my memories, and the things she taught me, so even though I have no mementos like you do, my mother is always in my heart, and always a part of my life."

A little more of the hostility left Ruby's face as she took a step toward Nellie. "Why don't you have mementos from your mother?"

Nellie shrugged, but Luke could see pain written across her face. "A lot of reasons. But it doesn't matter. I've learned that things are just things, and as easily as we come by them, they can be lost. The Bible tells us not to store up our treasures here on earth, and

I believe it's because God knows how impermanent they are. The dresses and whatever else you're hoarding in the chest can be eaten by moths or burned by fire, or some other tragedy can befall them. I have no need of them for myself, but I hope you'll enjoy them while you have them, because you never know how long they'll last."

Ruby slipped the key off her neck and handed it to Luke. Even Luke felt ashamed of the way he clung to the past after Nellie's speech about the impermanence of things.

"I'll take that old dress of yours," Ruby said, turning to Ellen. "And if she does a good job with it, I'll think about letting her do the same to some of my mother's."

Something twisted in Luke's stomach as he realized that Ruby was still acting as though Nellie were nothing more than a servant. But they'd made so much progress today that it didn't seem right to take her to task over this, as well.

"I would be delighted," Nellie said, acting like Ruby hadn't just slighted her. "But I will require help, and since it's going to be your dress, you'll have to help me. Being able to make your own dresses, or remake someone else's into your own, is an important skill, so you'll have to learn just as I did."

Anger flashed across Ruby's face. "But—"

"I think Nellie is being more than fair," Luke said, closing his fingers around the key and wondering how he could help not only himself, but also his daughter, move past the grief that engulfed them. While he could list all his reasons for hanging on to the pain of his loss, as he saw Ruby struggle with the same things, he realized he wanted more for his daughter.

But how could he expect her to break free from the pain if he wasn't willing to do so himself?

Nellie finished arranging her things in her new room. Myrna had given her a blanket she'd made, and once the blanket Nellie was knitting was finished, it would be a lovely room. It was sweet of Luke to build it for her, but she hated the way the new room seemed to intensify the way Ruby glared at her. Every time Nellie went in or out, Ruby hovered nearby, scowling.

Still, as Nellie looked around the small room Luke had tacked on to their tiny cabin, she couldn't help but feel a small level of satisfaction. Amos sat at the kitchen table, reading, and little Maeve was sitting on the floor in Nellie's room, playing with a rag doll. It almost felt like home.

Well, it was home. But despite his promises of friendship, Luke continued to keep Nellie at a distance, and Ruby's hostility made the place uncomfortable most of the time. Somehow, though, Nellie would have to find a way to make it more of a home for everyone.

Though Luke showed no signs of his anger and pain turning outward, he chose to keep his distance from everyone. While he occasionally extended warmth to his children, his coldness made Nellie wonder if they would ever be friends. She had no illusions that he would ever fall in love with her, but shouldn't they at least be working on making their relationship friendly? Mostly Nellie felt like hired help, only unpaid, and from the few interactions she'd seen between Luke and his coworkers, she wasn't sure she was treated as well as them. Not that Luke was ever cruel to her—and building this room for her showed compassion—but was this enough?

Had Nellie married too hastily? She sighed. Of course she had. But at the time, it seemed like the best option for staying hidden from Ernest's creditors.

"Ruby," Nellie said, walking over to the chest of drawers the Fitzgeralds had given her. "Why don't I get my sewing things, and we can work on your new dress? I found some ribbon at the mercantile this morning, and I think it will look very nice on the edges of the dress Ellen gave us."

Luke hadn't been pleased at the Fitzgeralds' gift, considering they'd given her all the furniture in her room—the bed, the chest of drawers, a nightstand and even a pretty lamp to go on it. Myrna had told Nellie that she wanted to buy new furniture for their guest room. Some friends were selling theirs, and Myrna wanted it, but Seamus wouldn't let her, since they already had furniture in that room. Nellie accepting the gift of furniture allowed Myrna to purchase what she wanted. Since Luke wouldn't allow Nellie to accept payment for the dresses Nellie had helped Myrna and Ellen make, Myrna felt that giving Nellie the furniture was a fair trade.

Even though Ruby hadn't responded, Nellie pulled open the drawer where she kept her sewing things. Most of Nellie's belongings had gone to satisfy the creditors, who weren't even close to satisfied with her meager offering, but it was nice to have a place to put what few things she had.

As she grabbed her sewing kit, Nellie noticed that her journal was missing. The slim, leather-bound book had been a gift from Mabel. It contained the only picture Nellie had of her family—Nellie, Mabel and their parents, shortly before their mother had passed away. For whatever reason, the creditors had allowed Nellie this one keepsake. From time to time, Nellie liked to write in it, pretending she was writing to Mabel, sharing things from her life that she would have liked to have shared with her sister if only she could.

Nellie turned to Ruby. "Have you seen my journal? It seems to be missing."

Ruby's face remained the solid wall of bitterness and hate. "Why would I know anything about your things? Do you have anything of your own, or did you steal it all from my mother?"

The girl's words were a knife to Nellie's heart. She shouldn't let the anger get to her—after all, this wasn't about Nellie personally, but about the grief Ruby still felt over her mother's loss.

But at some point, Nellie just wanted the hostility to end.

"The journal was mine. And since you are so intent on preserving your mother's things, perhaps it will help you to know that the only thing I have from my mother, other than my memories, is in that journal. It's a picture of her. Much like the one of your mother that you keep hidden in your pillowcase."

"That is my private property. You have no right taking it!"

Nellie would feel bad for Ruby, except that she was fairly certain that Ruby had done the same to her.

"I didn't take it," Nellie said calmly. "I happened to notice it when I was cleaning. And I see you looking at it every night when I pop my head upstairs to make sure everyone is settled in."

Ruby's glare intensified.

Nellie merely smiled. "I used to talk to my mother's picture. I knew it would never answer back, but sometimes just feeling like I was talking to her gave me the strength to deal with whatever I was struggling with. During my toughest moments, it always helped to have that reminder of her love for me."

The expression on Ruby's face softened. It still wasn't friendly, but hopefully it indicated that she was considering Nellie's words. Realizing that Nellie wasn't trying to diminish Ruby's love for her mother in any way.

"Did your father remarry soon after her death?"

Nellie sighed. Her experience was not at all like Ruby's in this regard, and nothing she said would help her case with the young girl.

"He did not," Nellie finally said. "My father made a number of choices that I can't see your father making. I wish he had chosen to marry instead."

Her father had turned his back on the Lord, much like Luke, only where Luke kept it a private matter between himself and the Lord, Nellie's father had embraced a sinful life. It was one of the reasons why both

Nellie and Mabel had turned to the church, and both had married the first seemingly decent man they could find. Mabel's husband turned out to be just fine, but Nellie's life had become a living nightmare.

Funny how both of Nellie's marriages had been about escaping bad situations. But she had to hope that at least this one could be redeemed.

"You're only saying that because you want me to accept you. Well, I won't. You can pretend to be my friend and make me dresses all you want, but I will never let you be my mother."

Ruby turned and ran out of the room, then went up the stairs to the loft.

So much for trying to relate to the girl.

With a sigh, Nellie looked through her drawers again in the hope that she might have missed the journal. But it was gone. It wasn't just the picture, or even the fact that Mabel had given her the journal. Nellie had written a number of very personal things in there, and while she never went into specifics about some of the terrible things she'd undergone, a child didn't need to read the contents. Plus, Mabel had written a very encouraging note to Nellie in the front of the journal, and just as Nellie found comfort in looking at her mother's picture, she'd also found comfort in Mabel's words.

Why had Ruby been so cruel as to take it?

Nellie shook her head. She didn't have proof that Ruby had taken it, and it was unfair to blame the girl just because she was hostile toward Nellie.

"Nellie!" Amos called from the other room. "Look what I made!" The little boy held up a drawing. He was supposed to have been reading, but Nellie found she couldn't fault him, not with the smile lighting up his face.

Especially since Amos and Maeve seemed to be the only ones in the household with ready smiles for Nellie. It was said that the way to a man's heart was through his stomach, and that certainly had proved to be true with Amos. Once Nellie had made good on her promise of chocolate cake, the boy had become an ally. While she wouldn't say that he loved her, he did treat her with respect, and in the weeks since coming to Leadville, he'd begun to open up in small ways, like he was doing now by showing her his drawing.

Amos held up a picture of a Christmas tree with gifts underneath. "My friends are all talking about Christmas, and I drew a picture of what I love about it."

The pain in her heart at the child's simple love of the season nearly undid Nellie. Since Luke's brief admission that Christmas had been Diana's favorite holiday, the topic had hung between them like a thundercloud that hadn't yet burst. It seemed a disaster was in the making, and Nellie didn't know how to avoid it without breaking a little boy's heart, or making a little girl feel like Nellie was doing one more thing to usurp her mother's power. And that didn't even include what the holiday would do to Luke's grief.

"You like the Christmas trees and presents?" Nellie smiled at him, wondering how much of the boy's real joy was in the presents.

"Oh, yes!" Amos pointed to a spot on the paper. "And that's mistletoe. I love mistletoe."

Mistletoe? As in the plant everyone kissed under? "Why mistletoe?"

Amos smiled. "Because it makes everyone happy, and people hug and kiss, and all the bad feelings go away. If we had mistletoe, then maybe everyone in our house wouldn't be so sad."

A sound behind her made Nellie turn. Luke had come in, and by the stricken look on his face, she could tell he'd heard Amos's pronouncement about mistletoe.

"I don't know if it's that simple," Nellie said, turning her attention back to Amos. "But it is a nice idea."

"Oh, Nellie…" A serious look, almost too mature for the little boy, crossed his face. "Don't you know that Christmas is the time when wonderful things happen? Mama used to say that Christmas is a time of hope because God gave us a very special present. You just have to believe."

Tears filled Nellie's eyes as she realized that she'd forgotten the true beauty of the Christmas message. She'd been so caught up in how she was going to get Luke to go along with her plans for the family that she'd forgotten the true spirit of the season.

"You're right, Amos," Nellie said, smiling at the boy and blinking back her tears. "God gave us a wonderful gift and we should be celebrating that. Why don't you help me plan the family Christmas celebration?"

Though she'd already made up her mind in this matter, Nellie turned to Luke. "Unless you have any objections?"

He shook his head, but Nellie could see the pain in his eyes. Was he thinking of his loss? Or had he, like Nellie, realized just how far he'd fallen short in his assessment of what Christmas meant? Could Luke find healing in the Christmas story and reconcile his relationship with God?

While they were things Nellie had promised Luke she wouldn't interfere with, she couldn't help but send a quick prayer heavenward that God would use this season to touch Luke's heart and bring this lost man back into God's fold. Nellie couldn't do anything for Luke's heart, but God could.

Chapter Seven

Luke hated the disapproving way Amos looked at him because he wasn't joining in their excitement, especially with Nellie seeming to agree with the boy. He knew Nellie wanted to discuss Christmas. But wasn't it enough for him to tell her that this holiday, with its memories of Diana, was almost too much for him to bear?

And mistletoe?

Why did Amos have to bring that up, of all things? If there was mistletoe in the house, then Luke would be obligated to kiss Nellie at some point. And if there was kissing…

Luke shook his head. Absolutely not. He would not kiss Nellie, no matter what Amos thought. The family's problems were not going to be solved by hugs and kisses. Amos was just a child; he didn't understand the deeper meaning of hugs and kisses.

Diana had taken the mistletoe tradition and expanded it, making it a rule that everyone in the family would hug and kiss under the mistletoe, no matter how many berries remained. Because that was who Diana was. Hugs, kisses and affection flowed from every cell in her body. He couldn't, wouldn't, do that with Nellie.

Seamus's words about being able to love another came back to Luke, but he shook them off. Some forms of love might work that way, but the deep love between a man and a wife was different. Seamus had never lost a wife, so how would he know? Even Pastor Lassiter, whose beloved wife had died, had not remarried. Not that Luke wanted to hear anything the pastor had to say. After all, it was the pastor's fault Diana had died.

Luke climbed up the stairs to the loft and saw that Ruby was sitting on her pallet, staring at a picture of Diana.

"Are you missing your mother?" he asked.

A tear-streaked face looked up at him. Of course she missed her mother. They all did.

Luke went and sat beside his daughter, then put his arms around her. "I'm sorry. I miss her, too."

"Then why did you marry Nellie?"

Luke let out a long sigh. "I've told you. Several times. I can't raise this family alone. Nellie's been good to all of us. Our house is cleaner than it's ever been, she makes delicious meals, she's helping you with new dresses, and she takes care of your brother and sister. She's not your mother, but she's a good woman, and we have to…"

Luke's throat clogged as he started to say that they had to give her a chance. He felt like a hypocrite giving that advice, when deep down, he knew he wasn't giving Nellie a chance, not really. He refused to open up to her, refused to see the possibility of a future with her. Though he'd promised friendship, he hadn't even tried at that.

"I know." Ruby made a grumpy sound. "But why doesn't she go where she's wanted? Like to her sister's. If she and her sister love each other so much, why isn't Nellie there?"

"I want her," Luke said quietly. "And for whatever reason, Nellie is choosing to be with us instead of with her sister. We should be honored that such a fine woman would choose our family."

As he spoke, Luke let Ruby's questions roll around in the back of his head. Why did Nellie choose to marry him rather than find refuge with her sister? Yes, it was difficult to be a widow with no protection, but surely with her sister, Nellie wouldn't be in such a difficult situation.

Was it possible that there was more to Nellie's story than she'd told him? Nellie had been so afraid when they'd first met, and even now, at times, she shied away from him. Luke hadn't questioned it because he didn't want to make her share her heart with him when he was unwilling to do the same.

He took a deep breath. If there was more to Nellie's story, it was none of his business. As he'd told Ruby, Nellie was a fine woman, and his family was fortunate to have her.

Nellie poked her head up into the loft. "I'm sorry to bother you, but I promised Myrna I'd go with her to the church to plan their Christmas celebration. Amos and Maeve are coming, so I thought I'd see if Ruby would like to join us."

Ruby stilled beside him. She knew what Christmas meant to the family. And her mother.

"I'll give you a few minutes to decide. I need to get Amos and Maeve bundled up. It's chilly out there."

Luke couldn't help but smile as Nellie went back down to get the children ready. The temperature had been below freezing for days, and though it was slightly warmer today, it still wasn't anything approaching chilly, which would feel like a heat wave right now.

"Do you want to go?" Ruby looked at him, an eager expression on her face. Though he'd gotten Nellie to agree not to try to get him to come to church, he hadn't made the children make the same promise. And Ruby always asked.

"I have some things I need to do around here," he said, giving her the excuse he always did.

"Everyone misses you at church." Her innocent words hurt more than he could have imagined.

Maybe they missed him. Or maybe they felt guilty about what had happened to Diana. It seemed like every time he ran into one of his old church friends, they all tried convincing him to go back to church. And had no helpful things to say about dealing with his loss.

"Some other time," Luke said, starting for the ladder. "But you should go. I know your friends there will be happy to see you."

"So would your friends." Ruby followed, a deeper sadness seeming to surround her now than when she'd first come up to the loft. It pained him to know that his actions were hurting his daughter, but she didn't understand how much it hurt to face all those people again.

Luke didn't answer as they made their way down the stairs. Nellie already had the other children bundled up, and she was slipping on her coat.

"Are you coming, Ruby?"

Ruby shrugged. "Papa says there's a lot to be done around here. It isn't right to leave him to do all the work."

"I'll be fine," Luke said. "I just need to finish a few things for Nellie's room. Nothing you can help with."

At the mention of Nellie's room, Ruby's resolve to stay seemed to diminish. She gave him a resigned look. "I suppose I could go, but it won't be as much fun without you."

He bent and kissed her on top of her head. "Well, try. Your friends will all be there, and I'm sure they have some fun things planned. After all, it's Christmas."

Just because he wasn't excited about Christmas didn't mean he had to spoil it for his children. Luke glanced down at Ruby, whose face held an expression of both hope and uncertainty. Because she was just a child, she probably had the same eager anticipation as her brother. But she was old enough to remember how special Diana had made the holiday.

"All right, let's go," Amos said, a wide grin filling his face, making the dimples in his cheeks pop. "I'm going to ask Mrs. Fitzgerald about finding mistletoe."

"Mistletoe?" Ruby's voice was strained as she looked over at Luke. "We can't have mistletoe. That's…"

"Tradition!" Amos crossed his arms over his chest. "It's not Christmas without mistletoe."

Clearly Ruby remembered how they all kissed and hugged underneath the mistletoe. How could they continue that tradition?

"I'll ask Mrs. Fitzgerald," Nellie said. "But I won't get any until we've all agreed."

Nellie gave Amos a smile, then turned her gaze to Ruby. "I know it's going to be hard for you, since it will remind you of your mother. We'll make it as comfortable as we can for everyone."

Compromise. Luke felt ashamed at how he'd been treating her. She was working so hard to find solutions that worked for all of them, and he'd been hiding in his grief. Only thinking about his own comfort. Deep inside, he knew he owed her more.

"I like that idea," Luke said. "And maybe Nellie can share some of her Christmas traditions with us."

The smile that lit up Nellie's eyes encouraged Luke. Hopefully it meant that she understood his desire to start working together more. And maybe, this would be the beginning of their friendship.

The women were gathered in the church, talking among themselves, and Nellie couldn't help but smile at the sight. Though she'd been to a few gatherings since coming to Leadville, it still felt almost unreal that she was part of such an incredible community.

"Nellie!" Myrna waved her over with a smile. "I want you to meet some of the ladies."

Every time Nellie walked through the doors, Myrna

had someone else for her to meet. So far, it seemed almost impossible to get to know anyone besides Myrna because there were so many people. She didn't know where to start.

"Can we go play?" Amos tugged at Nellie's skirt.

The other children were on one side of the room, gathered around a table where a brave woman had set up a table with crafts for the children.

"Of course. Have fun."

She set Maeve down to follow her brother and sister as they ran off to join their friends. The children's laughter was invigorating, and Nellie's joy grew as she turned back to Myrna.

"This is such a wonderful idea. What are the children working on?"

Myrna gestured at one of the women standing nearby. "Patricia Steele has spent all year organizing a knitting project. All the women have been knitting blankets, hats, gloves, socks and scarves for the people we minister to. The children are decorating some papers to wrap them in. We'll take them to the houses of ill repute on State Street and give them to the women residing there."

Nellie had heard that the church had a ministry to those women, but she'd mostly tuned it out, not wanting to give away her own sordid past. Still, it was a lovely thing for the church to do. Would her circumstances have been different had she had some contact with a group like that?

"I'm sure they'll enjoy that," Nellie said, looking

over at her children as they helped the others with the project. Even Maeve seemed to be participating.

Wait. *Her children?* Nellie shook her head. As much as she loved them and thought of them as her own, they would never be anything other than Diana's. Luke might say one thing, but the way he treated her made it clear that she would always be in Diana's shadow.

Fortunately, Myrna didn't know the direction of her thoughts as she led Nellie over to the woman she'd pointed out. Patricia Steele stood with a woman who looked to be around Nellie's age, perhaps a bit older, and another, more garishly dressed woman.

"Ladies, I want to introduce you to my dear friend Nellie. She married my neighbor Luke Jeffries, and I'm sure you will all come to love her as I have."

The women all exchanged glances as if they knew exactly who Nellie was. Luke's new wife. The one meant to replace Diana—and the one who never could.

"I'm Patricia Steele." The woman Myrna indicated earlier stepped forward. "And this is my good friend Laura Booth, and, um…"

Patricia hesitated for a moment, and the garish woman shook her head. "I'm sure she knows who I am. Miss Betty, at your service. I suppose the likes of you ain't never met a woman like me, but I promise, I ain't got nothing you can catch."

Nellie grinned. Though Miss Betty had covered her revealing dress with a shawl that had been pinned for modesty's sake, her clothing alone would indicate that she was not your average churchgoing woman. And the brightly painted face and bold stance made it clear that Miss Betty was not part of their society.

"It's a pleasure to meet you, Miss Betty. I'm delighted you could join us. I imagine you don't get out much."

At least she could make this woman feel welcome. Nellie had learned that the best way to ease her own nervousness in a new situation was to find someone equally nervous. Miss Betty seemed to be confident, but Nellie could see the fear in her eyes.

"Do you see?" Myrna said. "I told you she'd fit right in."

The other woman, Laura Booth, smiled at her. "Indeed you did. Nellie, I hope you know how welcome you are. Myrna and Ellen have told us so many wonderful things about you."

Laura's gentle manner of speech immediately made Nellie feel at ease. "Thank you. I'm very pleased to meet you all. What will we be doing today?"

Patricia frowned. "I'd hoped to put together some gift baskets for the ladies at Miss Betty's, but Miss Betty says that won't do."

Nellie couldn't imagine anything not being acceptable to the ladies. When she'd been held by the men Ernest sold her to, the ladies lacked so many basic comforts that she would have been grateful for the gifts the children were wrapping.

"What do the ladies in your place need?" Nellie asked, turning her attention to Miss Betty.

Miss Betty frowned. "It's not that." She looked over at the children, then at the other women who appeared to be putting together baskets of various food items they'd brought.

"I can't imagine why you all keep bothering with the likes of us. I suppose some of the girls have left my employ and gone to live respectable lives, but most people know what they were, and they aren't going to welcome them into their parlors. So why all this work?"

Exactly the reason Nellie hadn't told Luke everything about her past. Even though her stay in a house of ill repute had been against her will, unlike Miss Betty and her girls, she couldn't imagine him, or any of the women in church, welcoming her. Even though Miss Betty was here as a guest, Patricia had stumbled over her name, as though it was difficult to associate with her.

Laura smiled at Miss Betty. "I've welcomed you into my parlor many times. Your girls come to my home for Bible study, whether they've left your employ or not. If anyone has ever felt unwelcome, I apologize most sincerely."

"Not you, Laura." Miss Betty made a noise. "But so many of these other women. If I pass them on the street, they cross over to the other side so as to not be forced to associate with me. What's the point of all their charity at Christmas when they treat us with contempt the rest of the year?"

Another good point that solidified Nellie's decision not to tell Luke everything about her past.

Myrna nodded. "I wish I could give you a good answer. Maybe not all the women here would welcome you, but I know those of us standing here would. Isn't that right, Nellie and Patricia?"

The faith the older woman had in her was something remarkable. Not because Myrna was wrong, but because she clearly understood Nellie in a way that she'd thought only her sister could.

"Absolutely," Nellie said as Patricia echoed her agreement.

Their answers appeared to satisfy Miss Betty, who said, "All right, then. I suppose I should take a look at this year's baskets."

As Patricia and Myrna led Miss Betty away, Laura turned to Nellie. "Thank you for your kindness toward Miss Betty. It's so difficult for a woman in our world, especially without a husband or a father to care for her. She's done the best she can with what she has, and I just pray that God will continue to show her His love, to know that…" She shook her head. "Listen to me, giving a sermon. I'm sorry, I don't mean to go on."

"It's all right." Nellie gave her a smile. "You seem to be passionate about helping others."

At Laura's nod, Nellie had to wonder if they had more in common than she thought.

"I hope you don't mind, but did you…" Nellie glanced in Miss Betty's direction, not sure how to ask if Laura had ever been in her employ.

"Oh!" Laura shook her head, but the mirth in her eyes told Nellie that it was all right. "No. I was not in that situation." Her shoulders rose and fell as she took a deep breath. "But since you are at a disadvantage because we know so much about you, I'll tell you about me. Because to some people, my past is scandalous."

Though Laura's words indicated a bad situation, she wore a peaceful expression. "I'm divorced," Laura said with a firmness that surprised Nellie. "My husband was a horrible man, but because of how our society works, I stayed with him for much longer than I should have. He murdered a woman and is now in jail. Because of those circumstances, I found the courage to divorce him. The people in this church have loved and supported me, which is why I'm here, loving and supporting people who need our help."

Nellie took a deep breath. She couldn't trust Laura with the whole story, but it would be nice to tell someone a little bit about her own past. "My late husband was a bad man, too. That's why I married Luke. Because a woman needs…"

She couldn't finish. It sounded so wrong, admitting that she'd married for something other than the usual reasons for marriage.

"The protection of a husband," Laura finished for her. "I know. That's why I married. Luke Jeffries is a good man, unlike my ex-husband."

Annabelle Stone, the pastor's daughter, appeared to be walking toward them. Though Nellie would have liked to have continued the conversation, this wasn't the time.

"Thank you," Nellie said to Laura. "It's nice to know I'm not alone."

Laura gave another smile that Nellie had come to think of as comforting. "I think you'll find that many women are in similar situations." Then she looked at Annabelle, who was almost upon them. "But there are also those who find love. I'm not willing to put forth the energy for such things. I don't want or need another husband. But I pray that in time, you and Luke will find love together."

A fine sentiment, and if Laura wanted to pray such a thing, Nellie wouldn't argue. But at this point, she'd be grateful for the original deal she and Luke had made: to be friends.

"Please don't listen to her nonsense about not finding love for herself. I believe that everyone can find happiness. Laura just needs time, that's all." Annabelle gave them both a dazzling smile.

"Don't waste your breath," Laura said with a small laugh. Clearly these two had had this discussion many times over, and their affection for one another was obvious.

"It's my breath, I'll do what I want." Annabelle grinned, then a solemn look crossed her face. "I hate to bother you, but Luke has been standing across the street for some time now, staring at the building like he needs something but is afraid to ask."

Was he taking the first step in returning to church? Or was something wrong?

"Thank you for letting me know," Nellie said. "If you'll both excuse me."

She dashed outside, not bothering with a coat. As she started across the street, Luke looked like he wanted to come toward her, but the effort of moving his foot was too great.

"Is everything all right?" Nellie took his hands in hers when she reached him.

Luke nodded. "I was trying…" He shook his head. "It's no use. I can't even set foot on the property without feeling sick. I can see everyone through the windows, having a good time. I can hear their laughter. And then I see Diana lying there, in her coffin, and I can't." His voice was tight, like he wanted to cry.

"You don't have to," Nellie said, squeezing his hands.

Luke looked down at her, his face twisted in anguish. "But the children… Ruby wants me here."

Nellie closed her eyes and said a quick, silent prayer that she'd have the right words for him.

"Give it time. We're giving her time to accept me, and you can give yourself time to work out whatever you need to work out with God."

Before Luke could respond, Ruby came running out. "Papa! You came!"

The terror in Luke's eyes made Nellie's heart ache. He didn't want to disappoint his daughter, but he wasn't ready to go in.

"He did," Nellie said gently. "But I'm suddenly very tired, so I'm hoping he won't mind escorting us home."

The relief on his face made the anger on Ruby's easier to bear. Better for Ruby to have one more thing to hold against Nellie than for Luke to have to struggle so.

"That's a good idea," Luke said. "I'm not sure I'm ready for such a crowd."

Fire flashed in Ruby's eyes.

"Why don't you keep your father company while

I get the others?" A gust of wind came through, and Nellie shivered.

"What were you thinking, coming out without a coat?" Luke asked. "Even Ruby stopped to bundle up before joining us."

"I suppose I wasn't," Nellie said, then she went back inside to gather the other children. They'd be disappointed to have their fun spoiled, but Nellie wasn't sure what else to do.

As she reentered the building, Laura took her by the elbow. "Is everything all right?"

"Yes. Luke thought he was ready to join us, but his grief is too great. We're all going home."

Laura nodded slowly. "If you need anything, I'm here."

"Thank you." Nellie gave her a squeeze, then went to round up the children.

The walk home was quick and silent. Ruby was sulking because she thought Nellie was responsible for keeping their father from joining them. Amos was upset because he hadn't wanted to leave his friends. And Maeve was tired from all the excitement, having missed her nap.

When they arrived at the house, Nellie went to lay Maeve on her bed. She'd taken to using her bed for Maeve's naps so she didn't have to worry about the little girl alone in the loft.

As Nellie passed her dresser, she noticed that one of the drawers hung at an odd angle.

Once Maeve was in bed with a blanket tucked around her, she opened the drawer to set it to rights and noticed that the fabric she'd placed there earlier that day had been disturbed.

The corner sticking out from the edge told Nellie everything she needed to know. Her journal. At least some of what Nellie had told Ruby was sinking in.

Her heart felt a little lighter as she picked up the book and looked through it. Everything appeared to be exactly as Nellie had left it. Even the picture Nellie treasured was still there. So why had Ruby taken it? Had she intended to do some harm, then had second thoughts when she realized just how much it meant to Nellie? She supposed Ruby's motivation didn't matter, but it was frustrating to have to keep pretending everything was all right when it clearly wasn't.

Nellie picked up the dress she was working on for Ruby and went back into the main room. "You'll never guess what I found," she said, pasting a smile onto her face. "My journal."

Ruby still didn't turn her attention to her. Luke gave Nellie a puzzled look.

"Oh, that's right, you missed it." Nellie carefully kept her tone pleasant. "I couldn't find my journal earlier today, and as the children will tell you, I was beside myself. It contains the only picture I have of my family, and I was devastated to think I might have lost it. I don't know how I missed it, but when I laid Maeve down, I noticed one of my dresser drawers at an odd angle, and when I went to fix it, there it was. I'm so grateful I have it. I must have been more preoccupied than I thought."

Luke pressed his lips together, like he knew exactly

what had happened, but his shoulders rose and fell like he was taking a breath instead of responding the way he would have liked.

"I didn't realize you kept a journal."

Nellie shrugged. "Just random observations, particularly as I was traveling. Since I was alone, it felt like I had someone to share things with."

He looked like he wanted to say more, but as the minutes passed in silence, Nellie thought perhaps she'd misread his expression. However, he finally spoke.

"If you ever feel comfortable, I'd like to hear about your travels. And see your picture. You haven't spoken much of your family, and I should like to know more." He cleared his throat. "That is, when you feel ready."

The awkward way Luke spoke made Nellie feel slightly better about the situation. Maybe he was just uncertain about how to connect with her, how to bridge the ever-widening gap between them.

Could the real problem between them be their mutual fear of pushing too hard or saying too much? They'd both said they wanted to become friends, but perhaps neither of them knew exactly how to go about it. Nellie took a deep breath. One of them had to be the first to let their guard down. Tonight, when the children went to bed, Nellie would do her part in taking that step.

Hopefully, between now and then, she'd figure out exactly what to say to him.

Chapter Eight

As Nellie cleaned up the supper dishes, Luke turned to Ruby. "Come help me bring in some firewood."

Ruby stared at him. "Me? But I…" Anger flashed across her face. He knew what she was thinking. And he was tired of it.

"Now."

Luke stood and then pulled out Ruby's chair. "Get your coat."

He didn't wait for an answer, but grabbed his coat, and was pleasantly surprised to see that Ruby had followed his instructions. Before Nellie came, Ruby had always been so obedient, but now he never knew what to expect.

Once they got to the woodpile, Luke turned to look at her. "We need wood, but I also wanted to speak with you."

Ruby didn't say anything but looked at him with the same disdainful expression that never seemed to leave her face these days.

"I know Nellie didn't accuse you, and she's too good of a person to do so without proof. But I know you did something with her journal."

"And?" The challenge in Ruby's voice was unmistakable.

"It needs to stop. You keep agreeing to give Nellie a chance, but you don't. You've barely looked at her, refused to answer her questions, and are being difficult with her. She's been nothing but kind to you in response."

"I returned the journal, didn't I? I was going to slip it in one of the neighbor's trash barrels when they were burning, so that should count for something."

Where had this devious child come from?

"Why would you do that?"

"Because it's not fair! You heard her talk about how happy she is. We're all miserable, but she's happy. So maybe if she had a reason to be unhappy, she'd stop being so cheerful and nice all the time."

Luke's heart constricted at his daughter's words. Nellie might act happy most of the time, but he could also tell that a lot of it was just her way of making the most of a difficult situation. Amos had told him that he'd heard Nellie crying in her bedroom last night when he went to get a drink.

It was one more revelation that had made Luke question his own behavior toward Nellie.

"Have you ever thought that maybe Nellie acts happy, when deep inside she's just as sad as we are?"

"So she's only pretending to like us?" Ruby snorted.

"That makes a lot of sense. Why should I be nice to her if she doesn't even like us?"

"That's not what I said. I think she does like us. But she also misses her family. And her husband recently died as well, under what had to be difficult circumstances for her."

Luke tried to be as vague as he could about Nellie's situation, since he didn't have her permission to share. Even if she wasn't sad about her husband's death, losing him still had to be hard. Based on how quickly she'd adapted to the community here, and how eager she was to be part of all the church activities, Luke imagined it had been the same for her in her old home. The scandal she must have faced would have been devastating.

Luke sighed. All this time, he'd been wondering about the secrets she kept from him. But as he tried finding the right words for Ruby, he started to see the shame she must feel about her past—or, at least, her late husband's.

"I guess I didn't think of it that way," Ruby said slowly. "She did tell us about her mother dying, and how hard that was. When she talked about her sister, it seemed like she really loved her."

Though Ruby sounded sincere in her realization, they'd had this conversation before. At what point was it going to change his daughter's behavior?

"We're going to bring some wood in, and then you're going to ask Nellie what you can do to help with your new dress. You will be kind to her, and you will converse with her. There will be no more of your outbursts." Luke took a deep breath. He hated to think that it had come to this, but nothing else had worked. "You keep saying you will do better, and then you don't. I've tried to be patient, but enough is enough."

Luke closed his eyes and tried to think of how Diana would have handled the situation. She probably would have laughed it off and said that Ruby would do things in her own time. But Luke couldn't live with the tension in his house—of Nellie valiantly pretending that everything was fine, and Ruby being so defiant. There would be no more discussion on the matter. Luke had done his best to reason with Ruby, to get her to understand why things were the way they were. But nothing seemed to work.

He opened his eyes and gave her a hard look. "Now let's get some wood for the fire."

They gathered the wood in silence, and when they brought it in the house, Nellie was waiting with her ever-present smile.

"You were gone so long, I was just about to see if you needed any help."

"We're fine," Luke said. He turned to Ruby. "Did you have something you wanted to say to Nellie?"

Ruby said nothing.

Luke put the wood away, and once Ruby had done the same, he looked at his daughter to see if she would do as he'd asked. Still, she said nothing.

"Ruby and I had a talk," Luke said, looking at Nellie. "I'm ashamed of how she treats you, and I should have told you that sooner. You are my wife, and you sacrifice a great deal for my children. I haven't expressed my appreciation, and I haven't stood up for you the way I should. That changes tonight."

The tears in Nellie's eyes told him that he should have done this sooner. But he hadn't been ready to face his own pain, his own uncertainty. Now he wished he'd been a stronger man.

"Every time Ruby is rude or unkind, refuses to speak to you, or is otherwise uncooperative, she will be punished." Luke turned and looked at Ruby. "Nellie has my full permission to punish you as she sees fit, but my hope is that she gives you the most unpleasant task she can think of, such as cleaning out the chamber pots."

"What?" Ruby's eyes widened as she looked from Luke to Nellie, then back at Luke. "You said—"

"I know what I said." Luke took a deep breath. "But you've used up all your chances to do the right thing. Now, did you have something you wanted to say to Nellie?"

Ruby glared at him. "I believe I'm too tired for sewing tonight. I'm going to bed."

She was so much like her mother, it made Luke's heart ache. So strong-willed that it seemed almost impossible to make her do something she didn't want to do. But there was no other choice in this matter.

"And I believe I asked you to do something first. You can either do as I asked, or I will ask Nellie to select a punishment for you."

Nellie shifted uneasily next to him. "Luke, I don't know what you asked Ruby to do, but surely we can..." She let out a long sigh.

"That's another thing that's going to change," Luke said. "You have to stop making excuses for her, and stop accepting her behavior. If Ruby isn't being re-spectful, or if she disobeys you, you need to give her consequences."

Though Luke's heart thundered against his chest, he continued. "Also, I would like to ask you to only work on Ruby's dress when Ruby is helping you. If she is not going to help you, then she does not need a new dress. I know she wanted it done in time for the church Christmas celebration, but that's going to depend on her. If she's not willing to do the work, then she can show up in her oldest, most ragged dress."

"You wouldn't!" Ruby's face reddened.

"I will," Luke said. "Nellie asked you to help her as a condition of making the dress, and so far, Nellie has done all the work. Nellie is no longer allowed to do anything for you unless you are helping her."

"Anything? What about supper?" The haughty tone in his daughter's voice made Luke's stomach churn. He hadn't raised her to act like this.

"Actually, I would love help with supper," Nel-lie said, the doubt finally leaving her face. "Though Myrna, Ellen and I take turns with various jobs, an-other set of hands would be welcome. And it's the only way you'll learn how to cook something besides eggs."

"My mother taught me how to make eggs!" Tears streamed down Ruby's face.

"And they are delicious. But a young lady must know how to cook more things. Which you will learn."

"I hate you!" Ruby screamed, then she ran to the stairs and clambered up to the loft.

Luke started to go after her, but Nellie put a hand on his arm. "Let her go. I know you're trying to enforce consequences with her, but we've given her a lot to process right now. There will be time enough for her to reap what she's sown in the morning."

And suddenly, Luke felt the same sense of partnership as he had when they were in Denver, when he'd first met Nellie and seen her as the solution to his problems. It hadn't been as easy as he'd hoped it would be, but for the first time, he was starting to think it might be possible.

Something had just changed, and Nellie wasn't quite sure she could describe it. But as Luke patted the hand she'd rested on his arm, she felt that the man she'd married had returned to her.

Amos came up to her, holding Maeve's hand. "Nellie, we don't hate you."

She let go of Luke and knelt in front of the children. "I know. But your sister misses your mother, and it's hard for her."

"We miss her, too," Amos said. "She smelled like flowers, and spring." He crinkled his nose. "Not in the beginning of spring, when it smells yucky like all the bad stuff that shows when the snow melts, but when it's all gone, and the flowers come."

Nellie smiled. "That's a nice smell. I can see why you like it. I would miss it, too."

Amos nodded sagely, like he held all the wisdom of

the ages, and then some. "You smell like cimanonin... no, cimanon...er..." He looked up at her for an answer.

"Cinnamon." Nellie couldn't help but look on the boy with affection. "I like cinnamon."

"I do, too," Amos said. "Especially on the oatmeal you make us for breakfast. I miss our mama, but I like you, too."

He hugged her, and for the second time that evening, Nellie felt her eyes fill with tears. Especially as Maeve, who probably didn't understand any of what was going on, wrapped her arms around Nellie, as well.

Amos gave her a kiss on the cheek. "I know it's not time for mistletoe yet, and we don't have any, but this feels like when we all would kiss and hug under the mistletoe."

She kissed him back, then planted a kiss on top of Maeve's head. "We don't need mistletoe to hug and kiss. We can do it whenever we want."

Then Amos turned his gaze to Luke. "Papa, we don't have to get mistletoe this year if it makes you and Ruby sad. We have Nellie, and she's enough for me."

Even if things never changed with Luke and Ruby, Nellie could never leave this sweet child and his equally sweet sister. Amos and Maeve, while not her children in the usual sense, filled her heart with so much love, she couldn't imagine feeling anything deeper.

Nellie held the children close to her, then gave them a final squeeze. "I think it must be getting close to bedtime. Why don't you go get ready for bed and help your sister do the same, then we'll have one final hug and kiss?"

"All right." Amos grinned and turned to scamper off, but then he stopped. "Will you tuck us in tonight?"

Everyone knew how terrified Nellie was of climbing that ladder. Well, the climbing wasn't so bad, it was the going down. But if that was what Amos wanted…

"Not tonight," Luke answered for her. "Nellie and I are going to sit by the fire, have a cup of tea and talk about Christmas."

The light shining in Amos's eyes made Nellie's heart even more full. But beyond that was the way Luke looked at her. With hope, promise and the same kind of recognition she'd seen in him when they'd first met. All night, she'd seen signs of this slight change in him, and now she was beginning to believe it was actually happening. They just might be able to talk and get to a place where things weren't so awkward and strange between them.

Nellie watched as Amos gently helped Maeve wash her hands and face. When Nellie had first come, the children had been horrified at how often Nellie asked them to wash up. But she believed that keeping clean was the best way to stay healthy, and now even Amos, who would be happy if he never washed, took to the task without complaint.

"You've taught them well," Luke said, coming to stand beside her. "Ruby might be a challenge, but it seems like Amos and Maeve have taken to you."

Turning to look at him, Nellie smiled. "They have, and I'm so grateful for that. I can't begin to thank you for the joy they've brought to my life."

"And I can't thank you enough for what you've done

for my home and family. I find…" Luke paused, then he turned his gaze out the window.

Snow had begun falling, and Nellie could barely make it out in the dark, highlighted by the lights in the street. The streetlights were a luxury most towns didn't have, and Nellie could see why Luke was so quick to point out that while Leadville was full of wealth, tiny cabins like their own peeked out from behind the mansions. Maybe that sounded wrong to some, but to Nellie, when the two children were running up to her to give her a final hug and kiss good-night, she couldn't imagine living in a more perfect place.

"Tiss, Newwie!" Maeve tugged at her skirts, and Nellie picked up the little girl, then gave her a kiss. Maeve responded with a slobbery baby kiss Nellie was tempted to wipe off but found she didn't have the heart to.

Maeve reached for Luke. "Tiss, Papa!"

Luke took Maeve out of her arms and rewarded his daughter with a hug and a kiss. Nellie didn't get much of a chance to enjoy the moment between father and daughter because Amos had wrapped his arms around her legs.

Nellie bent to give the little boy a hug and a kiss, and she breathed in the warm scent of the freshly washed child. With a pang, she wished Ruby could be a part of this, but she knew it had to come in Ruby's time. They could force her to behave, but Nellie wasn't going to force affection. Perhaps it would be best not to have mistletoe this year.

"Good night, Nellie," Amos said, giving her a final squeeze.

"Good night, Amos."

Luke set Maeve down, then kissed and hugged his son. The children giggled as they made their way across the room, up the ladder and into the loft.

"I'd like some tea, if it's not too much trouble," Luke said once the children had disappeared from view.

"Of course. I have a nice blend of herbs that I came up with to help with sleep, if you'd like to try it."

"That sounds fine."

It was a polite answer, but there was something more intimate in Luke's tone than Nellie had heard from him before. As she made the tea, she could see that he'd moved the chairs closer to the fire.

"It's already getting chilly in here," he said, sounding thoughtful. "The storm has barely begun, but by the looks of things, we're in for quite a lot of snow."

Nellie looked out the window. "Looks like there's already at least an inch or so. But we'll be fine. We have plenty of wood, plenty of food and good company."

She didn't know why she added the part about good company, except that when she turned to look at Luke, she was pleased to see he had a smile on his face.

"I found a deal on a new stove. Some people are renting the Carmichael place, but they wanted a bigger stove. Ed offered to sell me the one already in there at a fair price. I have enough saved to cover it." Then he let out a long sigh. "I just hate to use our savings."

Nellie took the kettle that she kept on the stove and

filled the teapot. "That would be nice, but don't feel obligated on my account."

"Honestly, I feel more obligated continuing to use the Fitzgeralds' stove all the time. They give us so much, and I hate that we're taking advantage of their hospitality."

Luke moved the small end table from the other room so Nellie could set the tea things on it. She also set out a few cookies she'd saved from the baking she'd done with Myrna.

"I wish you wouldn't feel like we were taking advantage. Yes, it is inconvenient to go across the alley to cook, but their friendship means so much to me. Myrna has often commented on how she loves having me and Maeve over. She quite despairs of Ellen ever getting married, since Ellen has now decided to become a schoolteacher. For Myrna, it's like having the extended family she's always wanted."

Luke gave her a smile as he sat in his chair. "Seamus says the same thing, but I was afraid he was just being polite."

"Seamus doesn't strike me as the sort to mince words. I can't see him telling you that just to be polite." Nellie poured him a cup of tea. "Besides, this has been the arrangement since long before I got here."

He took a tentative sip of the tea, then gave Nellie a satisfied look. "This is very good."

"Thanks. Myrna had some dried herbs that a friend had given her, and she didn't know what to do with them, so I showed her how to blend them into a tea. She liked it so much that she's been having other ladies at church try it, and they've been having me make some blends for them, as well. It made me think about doing some for us, and well, here we are."

"You have a real gift in the kitchen." Luke reached for one of the cookies Nellie had brought over. "I assume these have cinnamon in them?"

"Thank you. And yes, they do. I will admit to being rather liberal in my use of cinnamon. I hope you don't mind."

Luke leaned over and reached for Nellie's hand. "I hope we get to the point in our relationship that you stop saying that. If I minded, I would say so."

The look he gave her brought a strange sensation to Nellie's stomach. So warm, tender and… She shook her head. Those were dangerous thoughts. He might be her husband, but she couldn't allow herself to be attracted to him. It was all this flattery. She wasn't used to such things. Not from a man. Not from her husband.

"I'll try," Nellie said, looking away.

Luke made a noise, as if he had something to say but thought better of it. That sort of thing had been bothering Nellie about their relationship, but right now it felt like a safer choice. How could she admit to him that sometimes, when he looked at her a certain way, she felt like a schoolgirl in the throes of an infatuation?

It would pass, just like those schoolgirl dreams and silly flights of fancy. Luke wouldn't have that effect on her—someday.

Unfortunately, when Nellie looked away, she hadn't taken her hand from his. She felt the pull of his grasp, asking her to come back to him.

"I'm sorry I haven't made more of an effort to spend time with you and work on our relationship," Luke said when she finally brought her gaze back to him.

"It's all right." Nellie took a sip of tea to mask the fact that she didn't really know what else to say. Especially when those blue eyes seemed so full of sincerity...and something else.

But what? Luke reminded her often enough that he'd buried his heart with Diana. So what could he feel for Nellie when he couldn't love her as a man loved a wife?

Luke looked nervous, like he, too, didn't quite know what to say. Only in Luke's case, he seemed to have something on his mind.

"I've kept you at a distance," Luke continued, his gaze still firmly on her. "And that hasn't been fair to you. When I was talking with Ruby earlier, asking her to give you a chance, I realized that in some ways, I'm not giving you a chance, either. Can you forgive me?"

Nellie took a deep breath. She hadn't expected this from him. One of the reasons she'd accepted Luke's marriage offer was his seeming honesty, even when it would have been better to be less forthright. Until this admission, she hadn't realized how much she'd missed that in him.

"Yes," Nellie said, giving his hand a squeeze. "I know it's hard for you, missing Diana, and I've tried to give you your space."

A strange expression crossed Luke's face. "I appreciate that. I suppose I don't know where to draw the line. Ruby's behavior, even with how much she misses her mother, is not acceptable. And there are times I know I am not as…open…to you also, but I find I don't know how to handle this as well as I thought I did."

His brow had furrowed, and Nellie realized that he had, indeed, been struggling with the balance between honoring his dead wife and moving on with his life.

"You've never been rude or unkind to me, if that helps." Nellie gave him what she hoped was an encouraging look.

"It does." A sort of half smile twisted his lips. "But I feel like I owe you so much more."

He leaned into her, and for a moment, Nellie thought Luke might be trying to kiss her. But a clatter behind them made them both jump, and when Nellie turned to see the source of the noise, she saw Ruby standing there, a murderous expression on her face.

"Maeve is fussing, and I can't sleep." She glared at Nellie like it was all her fault. In Ruby's mind, it probably was.

"I'll come up," Luke said. "See if I can get her settled. Thanks for letting us know."

"Why don't you bring her down to me?" Nellie turned her gaze back on Luke. "You've got work in the morning, and you need your sleep."

"Thanks. That sounds good."

It wasn't until Luke started up the stairs that Nellie felt the weight of Ruby's stare leave her back. What had Nellie done this time to upset Ruby? Surely Maeve's fussing wasn't enough of a crime to warrant such anger.

But as Luke gave Nellie a tender glance before starting up the ladder, she understood. Ruby had caught part of the exchange between her and Luke, and she, too, had probably thought Luke was going to kiss Nellie.

The flutter in her stomach that she'd been trying to ignore returned and grew to her heart.

What if Luke had kissed her?

Before Nellie could even begin to address that thought, she heard Ruby stomp across the floor and up the stairs. Luke quickly came down after Ruby had gone up, Maeve in his arms.

"She's quite warm," he said. "No wonder she's fussing."

Nellie took the little girl out of his arms. "I've got some herbs that will help. You get some sleep. I'll take care of her."

Worry creased his brow as he looked down at her. "Are you sure? Should I call the doctor instead?"

The wind howled as if to answer his question.

Nellie pressed a kiss to the top of Maeve's head. "It's going to be all right, Maevey."

"Newwie." Tears rolled down Maeve's cheeks.

"It's not safe for you, or the doctor, to be out in this weather. But she's got tears, which is actually a good sign. I've treated many a sick person, and I'm not worried. Get some rest."

Luke looked at her doubtfully. "We've always called the doctor when the children are sick. Or Myrna."

She put her hand on Luke's arm. "I know what I'm doing. But if she gets any worse, I'll wake you and you can get Myrna. Maeve is going to be fine."

Luke looked like he was going to argue, but Nellie gave him another squeeze. "Get some sleep. If Maeve is truly ill, then I will need you to be well rested to help take care of her. The best thing you can do for your daughter is go to bed."

Finally, he nodded. Then he bent and kissed Maeve on her forehead. "Feel better, Maevey. Papa loves you."

Maeve lifted her head slightly. "I wuv you, too."

As Luke went up the ladder, Nellie carried Maeve over to where she'd just been sitting by the fire. The tea had cooled enough that Maeve would be able to drink it, and Nellie was pleased to see that the little girl drank quite a bit. The herbs would also help fight whatever was making Maeve sick.

But then Maeve emptied the contents of her stomach all over Nellie, and Nellie knew they were in for a long night.

Chapter Nine

"Where is my breakfast?"

The angry tone jolted Nellie from what had been a sound sleep. She'd barely drifted off, or so it felt, when she looked up to see Ruby standing above her.

Nellie started to stretch, then felt Maeve beside her. She touched the back of her hand to Maeve's forehead. Thankfully, it was cool.

"I was up all night with your sister. You might recall coming down to let us know she was sick."

Ruby continued to glare at her.

"There are some leftover biscuits on the shelf, and some preserves. That will do for your breakfast."

Maeve whimpered in her sleep, and Nellie smoothed her hand over the little girl's hair to comfort her. Maeve snuggled closer to Nellie.

"She's not going to remember our mother, thanks to you."

Nellie closed her eyes and said a quick silent prayer

for patience. Maeve was ill, but all Ruby could think of was how it somehow violated their mother's memory.

A few deep breaths settled her nerves, then Nellie looked up at Ruby. "And that is where you come in. You will share things about your mother with your sister, and you'll help me by making sure we preserve the traditions that your mother started. But you have to stop seeing me as the enemy, and start seeing me as an ally in keeping your mother's memory alive."

Hard footfalls sounded, and Nellie saw Luke standing behind Ruby.

"Shouldn't you be at work?"

Luke nodded. "I saw you were both sleeping peacefully when I woke, but I couldn't stay focused without knowing Maeve was all right. I took the rest of the day off to help with her."

"I think she's better," Nellie said. "At least, her fever is gone and she's sleeping peacefully."

The lines on Luke's brow eased slightly as he turned to Ruby. "I heard what you said to Nellie. That wasn't very nice. Now, I need you to do as Nellie suggested, and get some biscuits for you and your brother. You have to leave for school soon."

Then Luke looked around the room. "Where is Amos?"

Amos staggered into the room, still in his nightclothes, his face flushed. "I don't feel so good."

Nellie sighed as she struggled to get out of bed. "Get him a basin. He's probably going to be sick to his stomach soon. If you wouldn't mind getting him some blankets, we can put him on a pallet in the main room. It'll be easier than going up and down the ladder."

Luke gave her a funny look as she swung her legs out of the covers. "What are you wearing?"

She looked down at her clothes. "Oh. Maeve was sick all over me, so I had to change dresses, but she was fussy and wouldn't let me go. I ended up putting on a blouse that was easier than the one that matched this skirt."

"Are you sure we don't need a doctor?" The lines returned to Luke's brow.

"If it would make you feel better. But I'm fairly certain it's just a run-of-the-mill bug that will work itself out in time."

Amos's face suddenly looked pale. Nellie gestured at Luke. "Your son needs to get to a basin now."

Fortunately, Luke didn't argue and did as she'd asked, and by the sounds coming from the other room, he'd been just in time. Though Nellie had never had children of her own, she'd seen illness run through families in her church and had helped nurse enough sick people that she felt confident in what she was doing. But what if the children were truly ill and in need of a doctor?

Nellie shook her head as she glanced back at Maeve, whose peaceful slumber was that of a child in recovery. She'd probably be running around by the afternoon like nothing had happened.

As Nellie shifted her weight off the bed, Maeve whimpered again, reaching for her.

"Ruby, for the third time, please go get yourself

some biscuits so you aren't late for school. Maeve seems to want me, so I think I should stay with her so she can rest."

Nellie sank back into the comfort of the blankets and put her arm around the little girl, who snuggled back into her, a contented look filling her face.

"Maeve really got sick on you?"

"She did. Wash day is not going to be fun, that's for sure."

"You're not upset?"

"Why would I be? She's a child, and I'm sure she didn't know she was going to be sick until it was too late. It wasn't as though she did it on purpose."

Ruby looked at Nellie warily. "What if she did do it on purpose?"

The question wasn't really about whether or not Maeve had gotten sick on Nellie on purpose, that much Nellie could tell. Instead, Ruby was more likely asking about her own bad behavior, and how Nellie felt about that. Could there be a way to bridge the gap between them?

"I suppose," Nellie said slowly, "it depends on why Maeve did it. I think sometimes we do bad things, not because we are bad people, but because we're hurting, and it seems like the only way to make that hurt stop is if someone else is hurting more. At least then we aren't alone in our pain."

Ruby nodded like she understood. "So if Maeve got sick all over you on purpose, it was because she wanted someone to be sick with her so she wasn't so lonely?"

"Exactly." Nellie looked down at the sleeping child.

"But I don't think Maeve would do that, because I think she knows that she is loved, and even if she is sick and makes a big mess all over my favorite dress, I'm not going to love her any less."

"But she's still sick," Ruby said. "So she still must feel pretty awful."

This was definitely about Ruby's grief. And yet, this child seemed to understand a need to sort through those feelings with Nellie. Even if it meant all three children getting sick all over Nellie, if she could make Ruby understand her own emotions surrounding her mother's death and Nellie's arrival, she'd do it in a heartbeat.

"I imagine she does feel awful. But making me feel awful isn't going to get her well any sooner. In fact, it might delay her recovery because then I will be too sick to take care of her, and with no one to take care of her, she'll just stay sick."

Ruby let out a long sigh, like she hadn't considered the idea that perhaps making someone hurt just because you were hurting didn't solve anything, and only created more pain.

"Now, you're really going to be late if you don't hurry."

"Do you think I could stay home today?"

Nellie couldn't read the expression on Ruby's face, but she seemed lost, somehow. Maybe it was the conversation, or maybe Ruby was beginning to come down with the same bug the other two children had.

"I could help you," Ruby said. "Papa said I was supposed to help you, and with both Maeve and Amos sick, you could probably use it."

Not only was that the most Ruby had ever said to Nellie, it was also the kindest and most genuinely helpful.

"Thank you, Ruby. That's very thoughtful. I know your father doesn't approve of you missing school to help with your siblings, but I think with the illness in the family, it might be best for you to stay home today, as well."

Ruby gave Nellie the first genuine smile Nellie had seen from the girl—at least, one directed at her.

"I'm hungry. I should get a biscuit. Would you like one?"

Nellie had always been told not to look a gift horse in the mouth, but she'd never understood it until now.

"That would be lovely, thank you."

As Ruby left, Luke walked in, a smile on his face. "Wow. That was…"

Nellie nodded. "Apparently the fact that her sister ruined my best dress and I'm not mad had some effect on her."

"Good." Luke came in and sat on the edge of the bed. "Amos is resting, and I think it's a wise decision to have Ruby stay home."

Then he looked at her, the weariness in his eyes somewhat lightened. "I think you're right that they don't need a doctor. I'm sorry if I sounded like I doubted you. This is the first time they've been sick without Diana here, and I panicked."

"It's all right." Nellie leaned forward and squeezed Luke's hand. "You've already lost so much, I can't imagine how it must feel to be worried about losing someone else."

Ruby returned, carrying a plate that held two biscuits. "I also put some tea on," she said. "It shouldn't take long for the water to boil."

Nellie accepted the plate and gave the girl a smile. "Thank you. I appreciate your help."

A shy expression darted across Ruby's face. "I can get tea and biscuits."

Luke leaned forward and gave his daughter a squeeze. "You can do a number of good things, and I appreciate your effort in helping Nellie today."

Then he started to let out a long sigh but stopped midbreath. His face paled as he jumped up. "I think I'm ill, as well."

As Luke dashed out of the room, Nellie looked over at Ruby. "Well, I guess it's even better that you're staying home today. Hopefully you and I don't end up with the bug, but in the meantime, we'll take care of the others. Why don't you go upstairs and get all the remaining blankets? We'll make up beds for everyone down here."

For the first time since Nellie had come to their home, Ruby didn't give her a nasty look or make a rude comment in response. She merely nodded, then went to do as Nellie asked.

Progress.

Two days later, Luke was finally feeling more like himself. Nellie had been correct in that it was just a bug. Both Maeve and Amos were also feeling better.

However, Luke had just tucked a rather pale-looking Nellie into bed, where she promptly fell asleep.

"Is Nellie going to be all right?" Ruby asked as he exited the room.

"I think so." Luke ruffled her hair. "The rest of us got through it well enough."

A knock sounded at the back door, and Luke opened it to find Seamus and Myrna standing there. "How is everyone feeling?"

"Better, but I think Nellie might have come down with it," Luke said, moving aside to let them pass.

Myrna held up a large pot. "Just as I suspected. She looked a little peaked when she came by to ask if I would mind fixing breakfast this morning. I started working on this soup as soon as she left. It'll keep you all fed, and it'll also help everyone regain their strength. Lots of folks are coming down with this bug, but it seems to be passing quickly enough."

"Several of our men are out sick," Seamus said, nodding gravely. "I hate to ask, but we've got so much work backed up, I'm hoping you feel up to coming in for a while today."

Luke looked over at the door to Nellie's room, then at Ruby. He'd agreed to let her stay home one more day, but he hated having her miss school again to take care of everyone.

"It's all right, Papa. I've been helping Nellie care for you and the others. I can do the same for Nellie."

"And I will help," Myrna said, setting the pot on the stove. The large pot dwarfed the tiny stove, and once again, Luke thought about the stove he'd mentioned to

Nellie before illness struck their family. Though she'd been noncommittal about the purchase, he hoped it hadn't already been sold. After all the sacrifices she'd made, she deserved to have something to make her life easier. Even if she continued her arrangement with the Fitzgeralds, it would make him feel better to provide an extra measure of comfort for her.

Myrna hadn't waited for his response before busying herself in their tiny kitchen. She looked over at Ruby. "Go get all the soiled laundry, then bring it over to Ellen. Then you and I are going to give this place a good scrubbing." The older woman paused as she saw a stack of dishes sitting on the table. "It looks like Nellie was already getting organized to do that very thing. I tell you, that girl has so much sense in her. You couldn't have found a finer wife for yourself."

As Myrna jabbered on and on about what a treasure Nellie was, Luke gathered his work things. "I guess that means I'll be working today, Seamus. Give me a few minutes to get ready, and I'll be in."

He passed Ruby on the way to the loft. Her arms were full of dirty laundry. The change in her over the past couple of days was almost hard to believe.

"Papa?" Ruby stopped in front of him. "Is there any way you could stop by the post office to pick up a letter I asked them to mail? I changed my mind. I don't want to mail it anymore."

He stared at her. They didn't know anyone far enough away to correspond with. Or at least Ruby didn't.

"Who did you write to?"

Ruby shook her head. "It doesn't matter. I shouldn't have, and I want to take it back. Could you please go ask them to get it for me?"

Her brow was creased with worry. But what could a child have possibly mailed that would be so terrible?

"I'm afraid it doesn't work that way. Once you mail a letter, it's gone."

"Please, Papa." She looked almost frantic. "It wasn't so long ago, just before everyone took ill. Surely there's still time."

"Mail goes out the same day you send it. There's nothing that can be done."

Ruby let out a long sigh as she shifted the laundry in her arms.

"What did you mail? Surely it can't be that bad."

Tears fell down Ruby's cheeks as she shook her head. "I found Nellie's sister's address when I took Nellie's journal, and I wrote to her, asking her to take Nellie away."

Though he wanted to chastise Ruby for trying to cause trouble, they'd already talked about how wrong it was for her to take Nellie's journal. And clearly, she'd learned her lesson about interfering. So what was a father to do?

Luke wrapped his arms around Ruby, causing her to drop her bundle. "There now, I'm sure it's going to be fine. Nellie's sister will probably have a good chuckle over your letter and write to Nellie in response, and it will all be sorted out."

The big blue eyes Luke loved so much looked up at him. "Do you think so? You were right about us needing her. I couldn't have taken care of everyone the way she did. I'd have been mad if Maeve got sick all over my favorite dress."

He couldn't help but smile at his daughter's admission. Who would have thought that it would take a nasty illness to get his daughter to finally accept Nellie?

"I do. Nellie has spoken very fondly of her sister, and I'm sure it won't be an issue. Perhaps it will encourage her sister to come for a visit, and I know that would please Nellie greatly."

Though the words sounded positive as they came out, Luke had the niggling of a doubt in the back of his mind. Nellie had been hesitant about involving her sister in their wedding, and though he'd suggested visits at a later date, she'd brushed him off in a way that made him wonder if there wasn't more to the story.

"I hope so," Ruby said. "I've always wanted an aunt."

Diana had been an only child, and Luke had lost touch with his brothers years ago, too many wars and conflicts separating them. His brothers had been soldiers, going wherever the fight was, and they'd never been good at writing. Hopefully they were well, wherever they were.

A clatter in the kitchen brought Luke back to the task at hand. "I'll speak with Nellie about it later. You gather those things and go help Myrna. I need to get ready for work."

Luke changed into his work clothes quickly, and when he came down, he noticed that Myrna had given each of the children a job. Maeve looked more like she was making a mess than helping, playing in the bubbles of the washbasin, but at least she was occupied, and Myrna obviously knew what she was doing.

"Before you leave," Myrna said, "I've prepared a tray for Nellie. I heard her stir in the bedroom, and while I'm sure she doesn't feel like much, it would be good for her to at least attempt to get something in her."

"Of course." Luke took the tray. "Thanks for taking such good care of my family. I'd hate for yours to take ill, as well."

Myrna sighed. "Truth be told, I think our family gave it to yours. A couple of days before your family took ill, I was feeling poorly myself, and Nellie spent the entire day while you and Seamus were at work taking care of me, and then Ellen, who came home from a ladies' meeting at the church feeling quite ill herself. If it hadn't been for Nellie, I don't know what we'd have done. I know you tell Nellie all the time that you don't like imposing, but you have to realize that neighbors and friends watch out for one another. It's no imposition because we're all each other has."

Something in Myrna's expression made Luke's heart soften. He'd like to think, wherever his brothers were, that if they were in need, someone would be there to help them. Diana used to say that if they had each other, that was all they needed, but even she had a large group of friends she spent time with. Maybe Luke had been too hasty in refusing help.

"Thank you for being there for us," he said, then turned to go into Nellie's room.

Nellie was standing beside her bed, struggling to put an apron on over her dress.

"Get back in bed," Luke said, setting the tray on the dresser.

"I hear all kinds of commotion out there." Her voice was weak, and Luke remembered feeling exactly the same way. Wanting to be useful to his family, but lacking the strength to do much more than sit up in bed.

"Myrna is here, and she's got the children helping her set things in the house to rights. You need to stay in bed and get some rest."

"But there's so much to do," Nellie said, her voice sounding even more pitiful than it had a few moments ago.

Luke pulled back the covers and patted the bed. "You wouldn't let any of us get out of bed before we were better, and I insist that you follow your own advice. You're not well enough to be up, and you know it."

"But they need me." Tears filled Nellie's eyes. "Ruby will use this as an excuse to hate me again."

She looked defeated as she lay down. When she swung her feet onto the bed, Luke saw that she'd attempted to put her shoes on but had faltered with the fastenings.

"Let me help you," he said. Without waiting for an answer, he reached over and took off her shoes. Nellie let out an exhausted sigh, like that brief exertion had been too much.

When he pulled off the boots she always wore, he noticed that her feet were much smaller than the shoes. He set them on the ground, but not before feeling the inside and realizing that she'd stuffed some material in the toes to make them fit.

He glanced over at the now-sleeping woman. She'd insisted on his children getting new shoes, all the while wearing improper footwear herself. She'd promised to love them like her own, and clearly Nellie had done more than that. How many sacrifices had this woman made for him, for his children, for his neighbors?

The depth of compassion in her shamed him. True, he'd tried reaching out to her the night they all came down sick. But all this time, in her own way, Nellie had been loving his family, expecting—and receiving— nothing in return.

Luke looked harder at Nellie and realized that he'd spent so much time avoiding this very thing because he knew what he found would be remarkable. Even now, pale with illness, she had a beauty to her that he couldn't describe.

Though she'd tried putting her long black hair up, most of it was already falling down around her face and shoulders. Diana had been as blonde as he and the children, so there was no comparison here. Both women were equally beautiful in their own right. Admiring Nellie took nothing from Diana. But it meant admitting in his heart that perhaps Seamus had been right. Was Luke being foolish for not letting their marriage be everything it could be?

More foolish thinking. He had no idea what Nellie wanted, or even if Nellie would be comfortable with more than what they had. After all, she'd been just as eager for their arrangement as he'd been.

Still, as he tucked the blankets around her, Luke couldn't help but press a kiss to the top of her head. It was not a grand romantic declaration. But it was a start. Of what, he didn't know, but when he looked upon her sleeping face, Luke knew he owed it to her, to himself and to the children to figure it out.

Chapter Ten

When the family, including Nellie, was finally well again, Nellie became painfully aware that Christmas was approaching more quickly than she would have liked. She still had too many unanswered questions. Amos was more than happy to give her a list of how the family must celebrate, but Luke and Ruby hadn't given her enough of a sense of what was appropriate to come up with a plan.

As Nellie walked down the street to pick up Amos and Ruby from school, she couldn't help but notice all the bright displays in the storefront windows.

She'd already made some new dresses for Maeve's dolls out of fabric scraps, and both Amos and Ruby would be getting new clothes they weren't expecting, so she felt she'd done a good job of preparing gifts for the children. But as she looked in each cheerful shop window, Nellie couldn't help but think they were ill-prepared for the coming holiday.

Each evening, Nellie and Luke sat by the fire, drinking tea and talking about their days, but the intimacy that Nellie had seen a hint of the night the illness hit the family seemed to be lacking. There was a distance in Luke, and Nellie couldn't quite figure out what it was. Was he angry at having to accept help from the Fitzgeralds?

Nellie shook her head. The two families seemed closer than ever, and she knew that Seamus had been trying to convince Luke to return to church for Christmas. She would be singing with the choir, and the children were going to be doing something special for the congregation, as well. Luke had resisted when Nellie had invited him, but Seamus continued to persist.

"Tandy?" Maeve pointed to Taylor's Mercantile, where the family did most of their shopping. Mrs. Taylor was a generous woman who spoiled each of the children who came in with a small piece of candy.

"Not today. I think you are sweet enough, and we must hurry to get to the school in time. The children have a recitation for the families, and we don't want to miss it."

Maeve's brow furrowed, but she didn't fuss.

As they crossed Harrison Avenue, a group of women from church waved at her.

"Nellie! Are you going to the school? Walk with us," Annabelle greeted her warmly.

As Nellie approached, she saw that Flora Bellingham was in the party. Nellie sighed. Though Flora had nothing to do with Diana's death, Nellie knew that Luke still blamed her because her husband had owned the mine where Diana had been killed. Luke hadn't told

Nellie all the details, but a dark look crossed his face whenever the Bellingham name was mentioned. Nellie had done her best to be polite at church, but she'd very carefully avoided talking to the other woman out of respect for her husband.

But it would be rude to ignore Annabelle's offer. And even ruder not to smile back at Flora when she chimed in with a cheerful "Yes, please do join us."

"I'd be delighted," Nellie said, stepping in with the group, grateful there were several other ladies present, including her new friend Laura, with whom she could easily converse.

Only, Nellie found herself next to Flora, who smiled shyly at her. "I'm so glad I get to spend time with you, even if it's just for a moment. I've been eager to make your acquaintance."

And Nellie had been avoiding it. "Thank you. That's kind of you to say."

She hoped her answer was enough to be polite but not draw Flora into conversation. Luke was going to try to leave work to watch the children's program, but they were still backed up from everyone being out due to illness, and he didn't know if Seamus would let him go.

If Luke saw Nellie with Flora, it might disturb the already fragile peace they'd found in their relationship.

"I do hope you don't think me impertinent, but I would dearly love to get to know you better. After everything that's happened, I want to know, that is, I need to know, how Mr. Jeffries and the children are doing."

Nellie tried not to sigh. This was exactly the sort of

discussion she was not prepared to have, particularly without discussing it with Luke first, and in the middle of town to boot.

"I appreciate your concern. However, I mean no disrespect when I say that I know what you're asking, and it's not something I'm comfortable discussing here. In fact, it might be best if you had your husband address the matter with mine."

Flora looked put out at her answer. "But that's the trouble. Your husband refuses to speak to him, or anyone else for that matter, about what happened. The Jeffries family has been an important part of our community, and Mr. Jeffries has cut everyone off. It was such a blessing when you came, bringing the children to church and becoming involved in our community. But there's still a piece missing, and we want to find a way to reconciliation."

Nellie almost didn't hear Flora's last words, because she saw Luke striding toward them. He'd obviously seen Nellie speaking with Flora.

"Papa!" Maeve tugged at Nellie's hand to pull her toward Luke.

"I'm sorry," Nellie said to Flora, hoping her words were loud enough for Luke to hear. "Any reconciliation you desire will have to be with my husband directly."

Turning, Nellie ran smack into Luke's steely chest.

"Just what do you think you're doing?" he asked, his voice full of anger as he stepped away from Nellie.

"Luke, I—"

"Not you." He barely glanced at Nellie as he turned his gaze on Flora. "You. Tell your father, your husband

and your pastor to stop. Money cannot replace what was taken from me, and none of your pretty words can ease the pain in my heart."

Then he looked over at Nellie briefly before he faced Flora again. "And leave my wife out of this. I've allowed, no, encouraged, her to become involved in the church, and to bring the children along. But they will not be part of your pathetic attempts to make right that which can never be made right. Am I clear?"

Nellie put her hand on Luke's arm. "Of course. I did nothing to encourage this."

For a moment, she was tempted to ask him to at least consider letting her hear Flora out, but the anger flashing in his eyes told her it would be a lost cause. Hadn't she learned not to go against a man in a foul temper? True, Luke had never harmed her in any way, but that didn't mean that given proper provocation, he wouldn't.

"I know," he said. "You're much too kind and generous to refuse anyone, but in this, I must ask you to avoid associating with this woman. It's clear her motives aren't about befriending you, but trying to make up for what was done to Diana."

Something in Flora's eyes said that Luke was wrong, but clearly Flora didn't understand the depth of Luke's grief.

"I am so tired of this!" Ellen pushed past Flora to stand in front of Luke. "You keep blaming the church. You keep blaming the Bellinghams. But you know who you should blame? Me. Diana didn't want to spend the day at a dirty, stinky mine. However, I'd signed up for the trip, and I was missing her dreadfully, so I begged her to come for a day. The pastor assigned us to wash dishes at the creek. But I knew Diana hated washing dishes, so I asked Flora to trade jobs with us. I was the one who decided we would be serving water. Not Flora. Not the pastor. Not George Bellingham. Me."

Fire flashed in Ellen's eyes, and Nellie could see the pain her friend had been silently suffering. She'd known that Ellen had been in the accident with Diana, but the depth of what she'd experienced hadn't occurred to Nellie until now.

Luke tensed under Nellie's hand, and Nellie gave him a gentle squeeze. Oh, she knew she wasn't the woman he wanted, but at least she could give him some comfort.

"And because you need someone to blame so badly, let me tell you what I haven't told anyone other than God and the pastor, because it hurts so much when I think about it. I lived, and Diana died, because Diana pushed me out of the way. Had she not pushed me, I would be dead, and Diana would still be here. So stop hating them, and hate me instead."

Luke didn't say a word. Nellie looked up at him to see that he was staring at Ellen with an expression she didn't recognize. When she turned her gaze to Ellen, she saw tears running down her friend's face. Nellie's heart ached as she longed to reach out and comfort her friend, but she knew that she had to be there for her husband.

Some of the ladies whispered among themselves, and Flora took Ellen by the arm, wrapping her arm around the other woman and leaning to speak in her ear. At least someone could comfort Ellen. From Nellie's conversations with her, she knew that Ellen counted Flora as a very good friend. So, whatever the full details of the accident, clearly the two women had been able to forge a friendship despite what had happened. Maybe there was hope for Luke finding healing after all.

Annabelle stepped forward. "I don't mean to interfere, but Luke looks like he could use a private moment. We're having a bunch of children over at the parsonage after school, so why don't I take Maeve with us to the school, and she, Ruby and Amos can spend the rest of the afternoon with us?"

It was a kind offer, and Nellie knew that since the children were friends with Annabelle's nieces and nephews, it wouldn't be too much of an imposition.

"Thank you. I hate to miss their recitations, but I do believe my husband needs me."

She looked up at Luke for confirmation, but his expression was blank. Clearly Ellen's words had come as a shock to him, and he was probably reliving the tragedy of Diana's death.

Nellie bent to Maeve. "Will you go with Mrs. Annabelle and be a good girl? You can go to her house and play with the children."

Maeve's eyes lit up. "I pway wif da chiwwen?"

"Yes, darling."

Maeve ran over to Annabelle. "I come pway!"

Nellie couldn't help but smile. The best part of her involvement with the church was the number of children running around, and the families that delighted in them. Though she didn't want to criticize Luke, since he had his grief to deal with, it had been hard on the children to be isolated from the time of their mother's death until Nellie had come into their lives.

"Please tell the children I'll come for them as soon as I can. I'm so sorry to put you in this position."

"Not at all," Annabelle said. "We've all been worried about Luke, and we're grateful he and the children have you. Take all the time you need. I'm sure they will have too much fun to miss you."

Nellie tugged at Luke's arm. He still stared off into the distance, not speaking, and seemingly unaware of the conversation around him.

"Let's go, Luke."

Fortunately, he didn't seem to notice that she'd just handed their daughter over to the pastor's daughter. Nellie had spent a great deal of time with Annabelle, and she knew that Maeve would be fine. But she didn't want to have that argument with Luke right now. Actually, she didn't want to have any argument with him, especially when he was clearly so upset.

He allowed her to guide him home. Once there, Nellie coaxed Luke into a chair by the fire, where they'd had so many pleasant chats. Hopefully it would provide him with comfort now.

As Nellie prepared some tea, Luke finally spoke.

"All this time. It was Ellen. She killed Diana."

Nellie set the kettle on the stove with a thud. "I know you're hurting. I can't imagine the pain of hearing more about Diana's death. But you need to stop with the blame. Ellen didn't kill Diana. She asked

Diana to come, yes, but Diana chose to go up on the mountain that day. And Diana made the choice to push Ellen out of the way."

Luke let out a disgusted sigh. "No wonder the Fitzgeralds have been so helpful. They felt guilty that their daughter killed my wife."

"Stop!" Nellie knelt in front of him. "Ellen said that the only person she told was the pastor. And I'm sure he didn't tell them, because he's very good at keeping confidences. They didn't know. Ellen didn't kill anyone. Can you imagine how horrible she feels, knowing the pain you're in, and knowing that Diana's choice saved her life?"

Finally, Luke looked at her like he actually saw her. "Just whose side are you on?"

"Yours," Nellie said. "And I'm trying to help you so you can move on with your life."

"I don't know how," Luke said, brushing past Nellie as he got up and strode across the room. "Diana's gone, and it feels like nothing will ever be good again without her."

"Then you're a fool." Nellie fought tears as she thought about every good thing that had happened in their home over the past few weeks. She'd thought that the biggest risk she was taking was that Luke would lash out and hurt her physically. But as he stormed out, she realized that even if he'd reached out and struck her with a hot poker, it wouldn't hurt as much as the ache in her heart.

Luke had told her that his heart wasn't available, and Nellie had thought she could live with that. But the more time she spent with him and his family, the more she realized that she wanted more. At this point, though, even friendship seemed to be a hopeless cause.

So what now? She smoothed her skirts and felt the press of the coins at her waist. She could leave Luke, but that would mean leaving the children. They weren't afraid to love her, especially now that Nellie and Ruby had come to a level of understanding. And Nellie loved them far too much to ever leave. Especially knowing how Luke's grief had isolated them so much.

No, whatever Luke's burdens were, he'd have to find a way to deal with them. And Nellie would have to carry on somehow. He'd made his feelings quite plain. Nellie's heart would heal. She could be the housekeeper who was also a wife, but in name only. Just as she'd agreed to be.

And to think she'd done all this in the hopes of attaining safety. Because right now, this felt like the least safe place to be.

Luke got halfway to the smelter before he was able to process Nellie's words. He'd been intent on confronting Seamus, quitting his job, and then…well, he didn't know what.

But the one thing that stopped him was finally realizing what Nellie had said. Seamus hadn't known.

His daughter was a murderer, and Seamus didn't know.

Luke shook his head. No. More of Nellie's words came to him. Ellen hadn't killed Diana. Diana had caused her own death, pushing Ellen out of the way.

Was he supposed to be mad at Diana, then? For being so reckless as to not think of the cost? The family she'd leave behind? The husband who'd miss her desperately?

He saw Pastor Lassiter walking toward him, Seamus at his side. By the expressions on the men's faces, they clearly knew about the conversation Luke had had with Ellen on the street. His heart ached so much. The last thing he wanted was to talk to them, to hear how he had to let it go and forgive. Right now, Luke wasn't even sure who he was supposed to forgive.

"Luke!" Pastor Lassiter called out to him, and Luke looked around for an easy way to avoid the man. While he spied an alleyway he could have turned down, the determination on Seamus's face told him that the men would just follow him.

Luke stopped. "I don't want to hear it," he said.

Seamus looked at him like Luke was a child. "But you're going to. I know you're angry. Everyone in town knows you're angry, and have been since Diana died. But what good does holding on to that anger do? How does it help you? How does it help your children?"

The memory of Nellie gently explaining to Ruby that getting someone else sick just because you felt sick and didn't want to be alone came back to him. They'd been talking about Ruby's grief without saying that was what it was, and now Seamus was challenging Luke in a similar way.

But they didn't understand how much it hurt. True, it became easier every day, but it didn't mean the pain was gone.

"I don't know," Luke finally said. "But everyone trying to make me feel better only makes it worse."

He turned his gaze on the pastor. "You're going to give me more of your turn-to-God nonsense. But I ask you, where was God when the explosion hit? When my wife, the mother of my children, died?"

Seamus stepped into Luke's line of view. "I don't know. But I do know that in the midst of that situation, where unspeakable evil was taking place, your wife chose to sacrifice herself for my daughter. Which is the most beautiful example of the sacrificial love the Lord teaches us to have for one another. Though you ask where God was, I will spend every day for the rest of my life thanking God for your wife and the love she had for my daughter."

"How is that fair?" Luke shook his head. His friend had been spared unspeakable loss, but Luke would have to live with his own loss for the rest of his life.

Tears filled Seamus's eyes. "It's not. But the Bible doesn't promise us fair. Should I sacrifice my daughter, have her die so that we both are faced with crippling grief for the rest of our lives? Would that make you feel better, for us both to lose?"

Nellie's illness argument again. "No. I don't want you to lose your daughter. I don't want anyone to experience the kind of loss I have."

Pastor Lassiter stepped forward. "Everyone dies. The question isn't if your loved ones are going to die, but when. So then, the challenge for all of us is how do we love in the limited and unknown time we have? How do we make the most of every moment?"

The question seemed almost too simplistic for the pain in Luke's heart.

A wagon rolled by, loaded with cut trees to serve as Christmas trees for some of the local families. Luke knew Nellie was waiting for him to tell her what he wanted to do for the family celebration, but every time he thought about Christmas, he thought about the wonderful things Diana would do and how the best part of those traditions, Diana's laughter, would be missing.

How could he choose a tree when he remembered how Diana would always insist on finding the largest tree, so big it nearly didn't fit in the house, and would make everyone squeeze around it because it made her happy?

Luke hated those trees. But he loved how happy they made everyone else. That was the magic of Christmas for him.

He turned his attention back to Pastor Lassiter. "And what do you do when you loved those moments because of who was in them?"

The pastor nodded slowly. "It isn't the same, but there are others to fill those moments, if you let them."

"Nellie." Luke's voice was flat as he spoke her name. How many times had Seamus encouraged him to love his wife instead of keeping their arrangement as it was?

"In part. The Bible does teach us to love our wives, and Nellie is an exceptional woman. But there are also your friends, and your children. Surely you have had happy moments with them since Diana's passing."

The other man's words shamed him. Not because

they were meant to, but because Luke realized what a disservice he was doing to his family and friends by not acknowledging the good moments he'd had with them. His happiness hadn't been all about Diana, even though with her gone, it sometimes felt that way.

"I suppose I'm not being fair in saying that nothing is good without Diana."

A twinge of guilt hit him as he realized the words he'd spoken to Nellie. What a terrible man she must think him, given that he'd basically discounted every wonderful thing she'd done for him.

He'd been trying so hard to at least build a friendship with her, to see if there could be something more, and yet, every time Nellie let down some of her defenses, he'd been the one to throw up insurmountable walls. The problem in his marriage wasn't Nellie—it was him.

Pastor Lassiter came around and clapped him on the back. "You're human. And the truth is, I had my own bitter moments after losing Catherine. Some days, I would pray that God would find it in His heart to take me so I could be with her. I hid my grief because I thought I had to be strong for Annabelle, whose bitterness was apparent to all. But the Lord knew, and over time, he brought new family into my life that I never imagined."

A softness came upon the pastor as he smiled. "Some days, I still wake up and feel the empty place in the bed next to me, and I miss Catherine terribly. There are times when I still wish I could turn to her and ask her advice. But I live in the hope of Christ that I will see her again."

Luke could relate to the pain of missing his wife in those same moments. And in many more. As for seeing her again, Luke shook his head. He'd turned his back on God so many times, he no longer had that same hope.

"And for those of us who are not as good as you?"

"It's not about being good," Pastor Lassiter said softly. "None of us would qualify if that were the case. Instead, the Lord asks us to look to Him and do our best to follow Him. He knows we stumble, and that's why He is there to pick us up."

As Luke nodded slowly, he noticed Nellie and Myrna coming toward him. Myrna had her arm around his wife, and Luke was struck by the deep bond between the two women. Though he'd often tried highlighting the differences between Nellie and Diana, watching Nellie now, he realized that he'd chosen two very similar women as brides. Diana had also deeply loved those around her and had been loved in return. Nellie was the same.

But could he let Nellie love him? Could he bear to love Nellie? No, *bear* wasn't the right word. Loving someone wasn't a chore. Yet something inside him fought the notion harder than he'd fought anything else.

"Nellie told me what happened," Myrna said when the women reached him. She looked at Luke with so much love and sympathy, Luke didn't know what to do. "I cannot imagine how you must be feeling. I know how angry you are at Diana's death. But if I may, I would like to say that is who Diana was. She was the kind of person who would lay down her life for her friends, and she would not be the woman we loved if she stood by and watched someone she cared about suffer. I know it doesn't take away the pain of your loss. But I can't imagine the heartache Diana would be feeling if the situation had been reversed."

Luke wanted to be angry at Myrna's words, at trying to justify the fact that Diana had died while Ellen had lived. Only... Myrna was right. If Diana had lived and Ellen had died, Diana would be filled with unspeakable guilt. Because she tried so hard to make everyone else happy, Diana would have seen Ellen's death as a failure on her part.

"Thank you," Luke said quietly. "I know you are all trying to help, and I appreciate that. But you all want me to let go of my grief as though it were as simple as putting down a package. It isn't."

Pastor Lassiter returned to Luke's side and put his arm around him. "I know it's not. But you also can't bury yourself and use the loss of your wife as an excuse to avoid living."

Had Luke been avoiding living? It didn't seem like it. He went to work, made sure his children had what they needed and took care of things around the house. But as he looked around at the concerned expressions of his friends, he had to wonder if he wasn't seeing his actions clearly.

Sympathy shone in Nellie's eyes, and once again, Luke felt ashamed at how he'd been treating her. Despite his promises of friendship, even his own personal commitment to giving her a chance, he hadn't. The distance between them was greater than ever, and as much as he hated to admit it, he'd been using his grief as an excuse.

"What am I supposed to do now?" Luke asked. "I can't forget about Diana. I can't pretend that I don't feel what I feel."

The pastor gave Luke a squeeze. "You have every right to your feelings. But ask yourself—what would Diana have wanted for her family in her absence? Would she have wanted you to stop going to church? To ignore her favorite holiday? Your family is participating in our Christmas program, and Seamus tells me you aren't even going. How would Diana feel about those decisions?"

Though Luke expected there to be judgment in the pastor's eyes, there was only kindness and love. "Before you tell me I have no right to ask those questions, I want you to know that answering those questions is the only thing that got me through the first few months of being without Catherine. The days I could hardly get out of bed, I was always roused by imagining the disapproving way my wife would have looked at me for my foolishness. Catherine died, and I lived, and the only way I know how to honor her is to continue living in the manner she'd want me to. To carry on her legacy of love."

Diana wouldn't have wanted Luke to miss out on Christmas. She wouldn't have wanted him to be so stubborn in ignoring Amos's pleas for decorations, including mistletoe. And though she wouldn't have been excited at the idea of Luke with another woman, she wouldn't have been happy about how he was treating Nellie. Had Diana lived and Nellie come to Leadville some other way, they probably would have been friends.

Luke stepped out of the pastor's embrace and turned to Nellie. "I suppose we should get the children and take them to find a Christmas tree."

Chapter Eleven

Nellie couldn't stop smiling as the children pelted each other with snowballs. The pastor had offered to take the family in his wagon to a place nearby where a resourceful rancher had turned his frozen pond into an ice-skating rink, and people could take advantage of the plentiful trees on his property to find their own Christmas tree.

Since it was so cold in Leadville in winter, especially today, where the icy wind promised to bring snow in the coming days, they'd decided to go in search of their tree first. That way, when the children were tired and cold from ice-skating, they could go home rather than trudge through the snow to get their tree.

With Christmas just over a week away, and the weather so unpredictable, it was best to get their tree now, rather than wait and potentially not have one.

"What do you think of this one?" Luke pointed to a nearby tree. The children dropped their snowballs and ran toward him. Nellie cuddled Maeve closer to her, grateful for the additional warmth of her little body.

"Down!" Maeve tugged at Nellie. Unfortunately, the little girl didn't stay cooped up for long, always wanting to be running around with the others. But she'd soon grow tired again and want Nellie to pick her back up.

Nellie set the little girl down, and Maeve tried running through the snow, but she quickly slipped and fell into a snowbank. When Nellie went to pick the little girl up, Maeve was laughing, which made Nellie's smile widen.

They reached the tree Luke indicated, and Nellie shook her head. "It's much too big. It will scarcely leave room for all of us in the house."

"We like them big," Luke said, a catch in his voice.

Nellie looked to the children. "I think we should go smaller. What do you all think?"

Amos grinned. "The bigger, the better! I want that one!"

He pointed to a tree so tall it wouldn't fit in a grand mansion, let alone their house.

"That's definitely too big," Nellie said, laughing.

Ruby pointed to a small tree, scraggly and unkempt, so odd looking that it could almost be considered a shrub. "What about that one? It looks like it could use a good home."

In their stove, maybe. Nellie couldn't see anything festive about this particular tree. But something shining in Ruby's eyes made Nellie hesitate.

"What do you like about that tree?" she asked instead.

"I don't like big trees," Ruby said. "The big trees our mother picked out made such a mess. This one would fit nicely in the sitting room."

Though her words weren't a grand proclamation of anything, they were a sign that Ruby was starting to let go of the crippling grief she'd clung to.

Luke turned to them. "You didn't like the big trees?"

"No. They took up too much room, and we couldn't play. Mama would get mad at us for being in the way, but we didn't have anywhere to go. Nellie said we get to remember our mother in the traditions that we love, but we also get to make our own traditions. And I think we should make the tradition of getting the tree we like the best, rather than finding the biggest one."

Something in Luke's expression changed, though he still didn't look like he was entirely happy. Amos also joined them, nodding thoughtfully.

"I like that idea," Amos said. "But can we still have mistletoe? It's what I love best about Christmas."

Ruby smiled at her little brother. "I like mistletoe, too."

Amos ran to his sister and wrapped his arms around her, nearly knocking her over. "Nellie said we could only get mistletoe if you and Papa agree, so now we just have to convince Papa!"

There was something especially charming in the affection Amos so freely gave Ruby, particularly because when Nellie had first come into their home, the siblings weren't as warmly disposed toward one another. Amos had resented Ruby's bossiness, and now, just as Luke had hoped, the siblings were getting along much better.

Nellie stole a glance at Luke. Did he realize the significance of this interaction? He'd been staring at the tree so intently, Nellie wasn't sure what he'd seen or heard, or even if he was paying attention at all.

Amos let go of his sister and ran to his father. "Can we have mistletoe, Papa? Please?"

The action seemed to jolt Luke out of his thoughts. He looked down at his son. "Mistletoe? Why are you so insistent on mistletoe?"

"Because!" A wide grin split Amos's face. "Everyone kisses and hugs, and they're all happy. We need more happiness in our house. And maybe if Nellie kisses you, then you would be happy, too."

"Nellie can't kiss Papa!" Ruby declared, shaking her head furiously. "It's not right."

A lump formed in Nellie's throat. Apparently, there were limits to the changes Ruby would approve of. Even Luke looked stricken at the thought.

But they had almost kissed. Or so Nellie thought. And Ruby had seen it, as well. Would Nellie and Luke ever kiss? Sometimes Nellie hoped so. But then she thought about how it would just be a physical gesture to Luke, whereas if Nellie kissed him, she'd be doing it with all her heart. It was a difference that would absolutely destroy her.

Still, they couldn't let the fear of what a kiss meant prevent the family from keeping a cherished tradition.

Nellie walked over to Luke. "There's nothing wrong with people who care about one another showing it with a kiss." To prove her point, she stood on her tiptoes and kissed Luke on the cheek. Then she turned toward the children. "You see? There's nothing terrible about my kissing your father. Now each of you come here so I can give you one."

Amos ran to her, arms outstretched. Nellie bent and picked him up, despite the fact that he was almost too big to be carried, and she held him tight and gave him a big kiss. "I love you, Amos," she said.

"I love you, too." He rested his head on her shoulder, and though Nellie would have liked to enjoy the moment a bit longer, Maeve had wrapped her arms around Nellie's legs and was shouting, "Me!"

As Nellie put Amos down and took Maeve into her arms, she stole a glance at Luke. He looked bewildered, but not upset. She probably shouldn't have surprised him with the kiss, but she was tired of everyone making such a big deal over physical affection when it was Nellie's heart that was breaking, not theirs.

Ruby looked at Nellie, uncertainty filling her face. She'd never hugged or kissed Nellie, nor had she ever told her anything remotely close to "I love you." Nellie didn't want to push the girl any harder than she'd already pushed. They'd gained too much ground already for it to be lost on something that would come in time.

Nellie smiled at Ruby. "Would you like one?"

She hesitated, and Nellie knew that Ruby still fought the battle consuming Luke. Part of her missed the deep affection the family had once shared. But she was afraid that it would be a betrayal to her mother's memory.

"I think your father could use a bigger hug and kiss than I can give. Would you give him one for me?"

Ruby nodded slowly, as though she realized that Nellie was trying to give them all the space they needed. Or maybe it was relief that she wouldn't be forced to accept or reject Nellie, but would still get the love she needed.

Once again, Nellie's words seemed to shake Luke out of whatever place he'd gone to. He put his arms around his daughter, then bent to give her a kiss on the forehead. "I love you, Ruby," he said.

Ruby didn't say anything back, at least as far as Nellie could tell. But when Luke released her, he pointed to the tree Ruby had selected. "And I think we will get the tree you want."

When Luke turned to Amos, Nellie was encouraged by his expression. Whatever darkness had overcome him just a few moments ago was gone.

"And we should definitely get mistletoe."

Amos ran to his father and wrapped his arms around him. "Thank you!"

Luke bent and kissed his son. The family finally seemed whole, or at least as whole as they could be while in mourning.

Once they'd loaded their tree into Pastor Lassiter's wagon, Luke watched as Nellie helped the children get into ice skates. Though the pastor had asked Luke to call him by his given name, Frank, it seemed too personal, and Luke wasn't sure yet if the man was friend or foe.

Keep living as Diana would have wanted.

Easy enough to say, harder to do. Luke had tried following Diana's tradition with the Christmas tree, but he'd been relieved when Ruby had chosen to change things up.

He still wasn't sure how to feel about the mistletoe, but he'd told his son yes, and he'd bought a bunch from the rancher before he lost his resolve. Nellie's demonstration kiss was meant to make him feel better, but it only made him more confused.

He'd liked the touch of her lips against his skin. All warmth, love and kindness. But just as quickly as it had happened, the feeling was gone, and Luke found himself touching his gloved hand to the spot her lips had been, wishing for more.

"She's wonderful with the children, isn't she?" Pastor Lassiter asked, stepping beside him.

"Some days, I can't believe how well things have worked out."

Luke turned to him. "When I met Nellie, I thought it was something only the Lord could have arranged so perfectly. But then I thought about how He'd taken Diana from me, and I can't understand how He would be so cruel, then do something so kind. Was it the Lord, or was it coincidence?"

"The Lord works in mysterious ways," Pastor Lassiter said, shrugging. "It's not our place to question the motivation or what God is thinking, but to choose to love and follow Him, no matter where it takes us."

"So even though He took the most wonderful thing in my life, I should be happy about it?"

Pastor Lassiter shook his head. "Not necessarily. Your question makes a lot of assumptions about the Lord, which may or may not be true. I've searched for answers about Catherine's death for a long time, and I don't believe I will ever get them, not in a way that satisfies me. I've learned that I must still trust in the Lord's goodness, even in those dark moments, because there is so much I am not capable of understanding."

More words Luke didn't find comforting. How could he trust in the Lord's goodness when something so tragic had happened to him?

But as the children's laughter rang out across the pond, Luke knew that once again, he wasn't being fair. Could he judge the Lord's goodness based on one action? Or did he have to look at the sum total of his life? And even if Luke looked at just his life, was that fair, when there were so many people in this world? Could he, a mere man, accurately view a God so much bigger than anything Luke could understand?

"Don't lose faith, son." Pastor Lassiter clapped him on the shoulder. "Though things seem dark, you must always look to the light."

"Papa!" Amos skated across the pond to him. "Join us!"

Though they'd been in Leadville for several years, Luke and Diana had never taken the children skating. Diana hated the cold and preferred indoor activities. This was one more new memory he was making with the children.

"I haven't been skating since I was a boy," Luke told his son, smiling. "I'm not sure I remember how."

Pastor Lassiter gave him another pat. "You'll remember. Come on, let's get some skates."

After only a few small mishaps, Luke found that not only did he remember how to skate, but how much he'd enjoyed it. What a delightful way to bring back good memories and pass them on to his children. He took turns skating with Amos, Ruby and even little Maeve, but Luke noticed that even while Nellie helped the children on the ice, she still wore those ill-fitting boots of hers.

Until now, he'd forgotten about the boots. It made him realize again just how much he'd taken Nellie for granted. True, she'd only been well for a couple of days, but getting her boots that fit, particularly in this weather, should have been a priority.

Luke skated over to her. "Why don't you have skates?"

"I don't know how." Nellie shook her head. "It's easier for me to help the children in normal shoes, because otherwise, we'd all be falling over each other."

Amos skated past them, looking happier than Luke had seen him in a long time. Ruby followed, laughing like she didn't have a care in the world.

How had he gotten so wrapped up in his grief that he'd forgotten what joys his children could be?

"Get some skates," Luke said. "I'll help you."

Pink tinged Nellie's cheeks, partially from the cold, but he suspected also partially because she wasn't used to him paying her personal attention. Their conversations were always about the children, the house and their plans.

"You deserve to have fun, too."

"I am having fun," she said, smiling. "I'm having the most wonderful time I've had since coming here."

"You'll have even more fun on skates."

Nellie went to the small hut where they had the skates. He hovered close enough to hear them talk about Nellie's shoe size. Luke hadn't thought about a Christmas gift for Nellie, and he wasn't sure he'd wait until Christmas to give them to her, but first thing tomorrow, he'd buy her a pair of boots that fit.

Once they got Nellie a pair of skates, Luke helped her onto the ice. She wobbled as he held her upright.

"You can do it. Just like you were telling the children."

Amos skated up to them. "Let me show you!"

He demonstrated the motion, which Nellie copied as Luke held her steady. After a few turns around the ice, Luke didn't need to hold her as tightly, but he found, with Nellie's infectious smile and laughter, he didn't want to let her go.

"This is more fun with skates," Nellie said. The smile filling her face lit her eyes, and Luke couldn't say he'd ever seen her looking prettier.

Ruby skated up to them, holding Maeve's hand. For someone so small, the little girl was doing remarkably well. Then again, she didn't have so far to fall, nor did she have the same fear of falling as everyone else. Maeve would fall, laugh and get right back up.

It seemed like no matter what the little girl did, she was filled with joy.

"Want Newwie!"

Maeve let go of Ruby's hand and skated to them. Or rather, right into Nellie's legs, nearly knocking her off balance. Luke tried steadying her, but his footing slipped and he came crashing down to the ice, taking Nellie and Maeve with him.

Somehow, Ruby got caught in the pile as well, and before they could right themselves, Amos came by. "That looks like fun! I want to join you!"

Before Luke could say anything, Amos flung himself on top of them all, laughing.

Luke tried righting himself, but with all the sharp skates and bodies flailing, he couldn't get up. If they weren't on ice, he might not have wanted to. His family hadn't been so close or laughed so much in a very long time. It would be a shame to end this wonderful moment.

A hand reached out to them. "Let me help you," Pastor Lassiter said.

Once they got untangled, Luke realized that the family's red cheeks were starting to get a little too red. It seemed they'd reached their limits of the cold.

"Let's go inside for a hot drink." Luke turned to Pastor Lassiter. "Then we should probably think about heading home."

"Yes," the older man agreed. "It will be getting dark soon, and then the cold will be unbearable."

They entered the warming hut, and while Luke ordered drinks for them all, he watched his family by the fire, smiling and laughing in a way none of them had in months. For the first time, he realized that the entire time they'd been skating, he hadn't thought about missing Diana once. Even now, his thoughts were about how pleased she'd be at how much fun the family had had this afternoon.

This was exactly what the pastor had been talking about. Luke could still live and honor his late wife, and in doing so, he was doing her the greatest honor because his family had the one thing she wanted most for them all—happiness.

Somehow he had to find ways to create more of these moments, not just for his sake, but for the sake of his children, who still had so much left of their lives. Maybe Luke didn't know God's plan, or even what God was thinking in all of this. But as he watched Nellie cuddling Maeve, laughing at something Ruby had said to Amos, he knew his family would be all right.

And their family was the very thing Diana would have been most concerned about. Though Luke's heart still ached, the weight of his loss didn't seem so strong anymore. Diana was gone, yes, but her legacy would live on. He didn't have to cling so tightly to her memory to make it happen. The new memories and traditions they'd made today were proof of that.

Nellie looked in his direction, and though her hair was mussed from the wind, she still looked as exceptionally pretty as when they'd been skating. If there was room for new memories and traditions in his family, could there be room for a new love in his heart? Could Luke learn to love his wife?

As Luke considered the question, he realized that his

answer wasn't the automatic no it had been for so long. It wasn't a yes, either, but he felt a new contentment and openness to accept whatever came his way.

Chapter Twelve

Nellie was pleased with the way their new tree looked in the house. Ruby had been right in thinking that it would work perfectly in the sitting area. The family had brought out the ornaments Diana had cherished, but they'd decided to make some of their own, as well.

Though Luke hadn't spoken much of the Fitzgeralds since their confrontation the day before, he'd agreed that she could invite them over to decorate the tree. It was progress, even though the weight of their disagreement hung over them. No, not their disagreement, but rather, Luke's pain over Ellen's admission that Diana had pushed her out of the way.

A knock sounded at the door, and Amos ran to let in their guests. Myrna carried a pot of what was likely soup, and Seamus held a large box. Ellen followed, looking timid as she entered with her bundles.

"I can't imagine what all you've brought," Nellie said, greeting her guests. She hugged Ellen as she passed, and some of the hesitation left her friend's eyes.

"Ewwen!" Maeve immediately wrapped her arms around Ellen's legs, oblivious to the tension in the room.

"I love your tree," Myrna said, joining them in the sitting area after putting the pot on the stove. "It fits the room perfectly."

Nellie smiled. "I do, too. Ruby picked it out."

"I'm glad Ruby is participating more in the family activities. But where is she?" Myrna asked.

Nellie looked around for Ruby, but the girl was nowhere to be seen. Neither was Luke. Apparently, fences were not going to be so easily mended. But why would Luke take Ruby with him when she'd been looking forward to this gathering all day? She'd even helped Nellie do some extra cleaning to get ready for their guests. True, their house wasn't terribly dirty, and the Fitzgeralds had seen it in far worse condition, but it still felt more hospitable somehow. This was the first time they'd invited their friends over in a more formal way.

Amos came up to them, holding up a sprig of mistletoe. "I need someone to kiss me," he said, grinning.

Myrna bent and kissed him on the forehead, then Nellie did the same.

Maeve ran up to them. "Me!"

Nellie couldn't help but lift Maeve up and swing her around as she gave the little girl a big hug and kiss.

When Nellie started to set Maeve down, she said, "More!"

How could she refuse such a delightful smile?

As Nellie spun Maeve around a second time, she noticed Luke and Ruby coming in the back door. Nellie set the little girl down, and Maeve, still giggling from the excitement, ran to her father.

"Papa! Is you's turn!"

Even Ruby smiled as Luke lifted his daughter and spun her in the air.

"You used to do that to me all the time," Ruby said. "But I suppose I'm too big now."

The dark expression Nellie had seen on Luke's face from time to time momentarily appeared, but then he shook his head and it was gone.

"We can make it work." Luke picked up his daughter under her arms and lifted her slightly off the ground, then swung her around.

Though he hadn't done the exact same thing as he'd done with Maeve, it was enough to bring a broad smile to Ruby's face.

When he set her back down, Ruby said, "I guess I'm still your little girl after all."

Her words made Nellie's heart twist in an unexpected way. All this time, Ruby had been trying to be the woman of the house, taking over for her mother, when deep down, all she really wanted to be was her father's little girl.

"You'll always be my little girl," Luke said, pulling Ruby close and hugging her tight against him.

Myrna moved closer to Nellie and said softly, "You have no idea how much this family needed you."

Watching father and daughter interact so tenderly was helping Nellie get a better idea.

A knock sounded at the back door, and Luke pulled away from Ruby.

"Good, it's here!" He smiled broadly, then opened the door.

Two burly men entered, carrying what looked like part of a rather large cookstove. Another man followed with miscellaneous parts in his arms.

"What is all this?" Nellie looked at him, knowing she must sound stupid, since it was obvious what it was. Luke had mentioned there was a possibility that he could get a new stove, but to have it come so soon, and without discussing it…she'd thought they'd come to the conclusion that they didn't need a new stove right now.

"Merry Christmas," Luke said, looking at her with obvious pride.

"A stove?" Nellie stared at him, then at the stove. It was almost too large for the room, a beast. Bigger and nicer than Myrna's.

The men set the large part of the stove near their current stove, then went outside, presumably to get the rest of it.

She closed her eyes and took a deep breath, gathering her thoughts and sending a quick prayer for love and patience in this moment.

"I don't understand," Nellie said when she finally opened her eyes to look at him. "The money…"

Luke shrugged. "Ed needed to get it out of a house he was fixing up for some wealthy gent to rent. The gent wanted something fancier, and this one has a busted hinge on one of the doors, so Ed sold it to me for a good price. Isn't that right, Ed?"

Luke turned to the man who'd brought in the spare parts. "Sure enough," Ed said, grinning. "These rich folks come in for a spell, want the house done up right, then they're gone, and I have to redo it for the next one. Matter of fact, that place on Chestnut you and the late missus were interested in is available again. You know I'll give you a good price."

The dark look returned to Luke's face as he shook his head. "I appreciate it, but the stove is all we need. We're staying put in this house."

"You mean the yellow house with the porch Mama liked so much?" Ruby asked, looking up at her father. "It had a parlor for her to do her entertaining, and we could have a bedroom instead of the loft."

Then Ruby turned to Nellie. "And, oh, the kitchen. Why, it was as big as this whole house! You've got to convince Papa to get that place. It's all Mama ever wanted."

Luke had never mentioned wanting to move, though it made sense, given that even with the added-on room, their cabin was barely big enough for a couple, but with children, sometimes it seemed like they couldn't breathe in such a small space. Nellie didn't have any complaints, though. After all, it was a comfortable home, and everyone seemed happy enough in it.

"We're not moving," Luke said.

At his words, Ruby's face fell. The tone in his voice was the one Nellie had gotten used to as being borne of the pain he'd suffered. Clearly Ruby knew it, as well.

But at least this wasn't one more way Luke was blindly following the path Diana had set for them. Sometimes Nellie felt like she'd stepped into this other woman's life and wasn't given a chance to make it her own.

One of the stove parts fell to the ground with a clatter as the two men returned, carrying additional pieces of metal. Nellie looked over at where they'd set the stove, and she immediately felt bad for thinking such a thing. True, most of what happened in the house was about Diana and what she wanted, but every once in a while, there was a glimmer that Nellie would have her chance, too.

"It's a mighty fine stove," Myrna said.

When Nellie turned her attention back to her friend, she realized that this wasn't about getting Nellie a nice new stove. No, this was Luke's response to finding out about Ellen. A way to have a more distanced relationship with the family he considered responsible for his pain.

"We'll have to wait until morning to get it hooked up. Let the little stove burn out and cool down so we can change out the pipe to the chimney." Ed and Luke began discussing the logistics, but Nellie wasn't paying attention. All she could see was the sadness on her friends' faces.

They knew what this gift meant, too.

"That doesn't mean we can't still work together," Nellie said, trying to sound more cheerful about the situation than she felt. "Look, Myrna, I believe it has one of those warming sections like you were wishing you had."

Myrna didn't respond, so Nellie continued. "In fact, I think this might be a wonderful way for us to try some of those new recipes Ellen keeps finding in her magazines."

Nellie turned to Ellen, whose expression was even more grief-stricken than her mother's. The poor woman blamed herself. But she'd only been trying to help, to get Luke to stop being so angry with people who didn't deserve it. Not that Ellen deserved it, either. She'd probably suffered enough. Though Nellie hadn't had a chance to speak with her friend privately since Ellen's revelations, she knew that Ellen probably suffered more guilt than anyone could comprehend.

"Please say you'll come over and we'll try out my new stove together," Nellie said to her friends. "You always say that many hands make light work, and I find it so much more pleasant to cook with such fine company."

"Thank you," Myrna said quietly. "You can count on us."

If only Myrna didn't sound like she was about to cry. Nellie looked over at Seamus to see what he thought of his friend's actions, but the older man had busied himself with showing Amos and Maeve something he was carving. Ruby hovered above them, watching, not fully participating in the activity.

Luke looked up from whatever Ed was showing him, then went over to Nellie. "You don't like it? I thought you would appreciate being able to better do your job."

Her job. Nellie swallowed the frustration that rose up at his words. She had to remember that was all this was to him. He might not have employed her, but when one chose to be a wife in name only, for the sake of taking care of a man's house and children, that was really all it was. A job.

"I was doing just fine," she said slowly. "But I appreciate all the thought that went into this gift, and I'm sure it will benefit us all for years to come."

The puzzled look didn't leave Luke's face. He'd clearly thought she was going to be pleased with the gift, and here she was, acting completely ungrateful.

"Thank you. Truly." Nellie gave him a smile, trying to sound more cheerful than she felt. "I never expected something so generous."

Some of the tension left Luke's face, and he appeared to be relieved. He'd thought she'd been worried about the money. In part, she had, but mostly, as she looked at her unhappy friends, she couldn't help but think how a new stove would change their relationship.

Luke tried to enjoy the festive evening with Nellie and the Fitzgeralds. But as he watched everyone laugh and interact, he felt like an outsider. It was strange, since they'd been his friends much longer than they'd known Nellie. Something had changed between them all, and Luke wasn't sure they'd get it back.

The right thing to do was to tell Ellen that there were no hard feelings, that he didn't blame her. But he wasn't sure it was completely honest.

He wasn't sure what he felt anymore. It wasn't fair that Diana had to die, but he wouldn't say that Ellen deserved to die, either. They'd put some men in jail for their part in the explosion at the mine, but knowing those men would never be free to hurt anyone else did nothing to replace what Luke had lost.

Nellie laughed at something the children said.

Luke turned to watch them. They were stringing popcorn to put on the tree, and Nellie was tossing some at the children to catch in their mouths.

Every moment that he dwelled on Diana's death, trying to figure out who was at fault, was a moment he missed out on with his children. They'd had fun yesterday, and he found that the ever-present ache that had become his best companion since Diana's death had been strangely absent.

But did not missing his late wife mean that he no longer loved her?

"Papa! You's turn!" Maeve tossed popcorn at him before he could answer himself, and it ended up going everywhere.

He glanced over at the disappointed looks on the faces of all the adults in the room. Even Ruby seemed to wear an expression of disapproval. This was meant to be a fun family night, and he was the one spoiling it.

"Sorry," he said, giving her a big smile. "Try again."

Maeve needed no further invitation to toss another large handful of popcorn at him. Thankfully her hands were small, but they'd still have a mess to clean up later.

Luke caught some of the popcorn in his mouth.

"Hooray, Papa!" Maeve ran to him and jumped on his lap. At least he was able to give her a sense of happiness and belonging.

Now he had to figure out a way to provide the same for all the other sour faces in the room.

"I could use a glass of that punch you made, Nellie," he said, trying to sound cheerful. "Would anyone else like some?"

Joining in their activity only seemed to shut it down. They all sat there, silent, staring at him.

Luke got up and served himself some punch, then took one of the cookies they'd been enjoying all evening.

"This is a delicious cookie, Ellen. I hope you'll share the recipe with Nellie so she can bake some from time to time." He gave the young woman a smile, hoping she would see it as an attempt to restore their shaky friendship.

Ellen gave a weak smile but didn't respond. Myrna, however, gave him a cutting look as she said, "We've never minded baking them and bringing some over to share. It's the neighborly thing to do, and it provides a good excuse for us to share a cup of tea."

Luke looked down at the cookie he'd just been enjoying. Suddenly it wasn't so tasty. This wasn't about the tension over Ellen's revelation about Diana's death. No, this was about the stove.

He turned to Seamus. "You were the one who suggested I get a new stove. Now that I've gotten it, everyone is acting like I've gone and done something terrible."

There were far more terrible things than getting a woman a new stove, especially one as nice as the one he'd bought for Nellie.

"I suggested a lot of things," Seamus said quietly. "But you were eager to tell me I had no business telling you what to do. I just find it strange that you're finally starting to make some changes now. My family is no longer good enough for yours to spend time with, now that…"

Seamus shook his head. "I'm sorry, I don't mean to spoil the evening for the children." He turned to Ruby. "How about you show me that ornament Myrna helped you make?"

Luke tried to take a deep breath, but his lungs felt nearly paralyzed. Was that what his friend thought of him? That he was so angry about Ellen that he'd cut off the Fitzgeralds?

But as he looked at the downcast faces trying to pretend they were having a good time, he realized that was exactly what they thought. As he tried justifying his behavior to himself, he found he couldn't.

He'd shut out everyone he blamed for Diana's death. He'd caused an ugly scene in the middle of town just the other day.

"I'm sorry," Luke said quietly. "That's not what I meant at all."

None of them appeared to accept his apology. Or believe his words. And how could he blame them? Though he'd been sorting out a lot of things in his mind, even thinking he'd made decisions, he hadn't shown any of them a change in his behavior.

This stove, which had been his first attempt at moving on, meant different things to all of them.

Luke took a deep breath as he looked at his wife, who seemed so forlorn sitting with the Fitzgeralds.

When he'd broached the subject of a new stove with her before they'd all taken ill, she'd been hesitant.

"I'm sorry," Luke said to her. "I honestly thought I was doing something nice for you. I wanted to get you a gift to make your life easier, and to show that I am committed to making our marriage work. I wouldn't get rid of Diana's stove for sentimental reasons, even though I know we could use more heat."

With a sigh, Luke looked over to the new room he'd built. "I see you shivering in the mornings when you're getting the stove going. I hate seeing you dash back and forth in the cold, making sure our supper is taken care of. I guess I thought that if I got you a new stove, you'd be warmer, and you'd see that I pay attention to your needs."

He watched the expression play on Nellie's face, like she almost didn't believe that he cared for her. Her disbelief hurt him more than he thought it would.

As much as Luke hated to admit it, he hadn't been the best husband, father or friend lately. If the life he was living was all about trying to keep Diana's memory alive, he was doing a poor job. She'd be ashamed of the man he'd become after her passing.

"I know it's not yet Christmas, but I got you another gift," Luke said, trying to keep his voice steady and not betray the anguish threatening to spill over. "I wanted you to have your gifts as soon as possible so you could start using them, only now I'm afraid you'll take this one the wrong way, too."

He got up and walked over to the chest where he

kept his things. "I might as well give it to you now, and if you don't like it, I'll return it."

The boots rested on top of his wedding picture. His and Diana's wedding, that is. He and Nellie hadn't had a photographer commemorate their union. At the time, he'd justified it as not being necessary, since theirs was a marriage of convenience, but the longer he and Nellie were married, the more he realized that there was no such thing. Marriages were about working together, planning together, dreaming together.

Luke had done none of those things for Nellie. He'd made all the decisions, expecting Nellie to care for his children and keep house, even though he'd initially told her they were in this together.

"I'm sorry," Luke whispered to the picture of him and Diana as he grabbed the parcel he'd had Mrs. Taylor wrap for Nellie.

Luke handed Nellie the gift. "I noticed your boots are too large and probably aren't keeping your feet warm enough. When we were ice-skating, I made note of your size."

Tears streamed down Nellie's face as she took the boots out of the package.

Did that mean she liked them? Or that she hated them as much as the stove?

"Mrs. Taylor said they're quite fashionable, similar to what many of the ladies in church wear. She thinks they'll fit, but if they don't, she said we could get you a pair that do. I just…"

Nellie started to sob quietly, and Luke's stomach knotted.

"Please don't cry, Nellie. All I wanted was to do something nice for you, since you do so much for my family, but you never ask anything of yourself. You've bought new things for everyone, yet you still wear the old clothes and worn boots you came with. I thought you should have something nice, too."

He shifted his weight, wanting to hug her or pat her hand or something. They'd once been able to comfort one another with ease, but he'd never hurt her before, never had to make up for his callousness.

Nellie stood and wrapped her arms around him, sobbing as she hugged him tight. The children had stopped their game at some point in the exchange, and Maeve had come over to hug Nellie's legs.

"I'm sorry," she said. "I was so ungracious about the stove because I thought you were using it as a reason to separate me from my friends."

"No cwy, Newwie," Maeve said.

Nellie pulled away and wiped at her eyes, then picked up Maeve. "It's all right, Maevey."

Myrna handed Nellie a handkerchief. Luke took a moment to glance at his other children, who wore the same worried expression as Maeve. He'd ruined what was supposed to be a special evening for all of them.

Shifting Maeve on her hip, Nellie turned to Luke.

"You have given me some of the finest gifts I have ever received. No one notices my needs like that, and I'm very grateful for both the stove and the boots. I'll make good use of both."

The constriction in Luke's heart eased as he returned her smile. "I'm glad you like them."

Ruby and Amos seemed to relax and returned to their game, though Maeve still clung to Nellie.

Seamus stood and held out his hand. "I'm sorry, friend. I wrongly accused you, and I apologize."

Luke shook his head. "You were right to do so. I've been shutting everyone out, and it's natural that you would think I was continuing my cantankerous behavior. I've been a terrible friend, and you've all stood by me."

He turned his gaze on Ellen. "I keep thinking about what Diana would have wanted, and she'd be ashamed at how poorly I've been treating everyone in her absence. You were her best friend. If she saved you, then she'd be horrified if I were to shun you as a result. I won't have her actions rendered meaningless because of my selfishness."

Ellen began to cry. Her shoulders shook with sobs as Myrna took her daughter in her arms.

"I feel so guilty," Ellen said. "I didn't have a family who needed me. Why would Diana, who had so much to live for, die, when I…"

The rest of her words were lost in her sobs, and Luke realized the weight of the pain Ellen carried. In all of this, he'd thought only about his own grief, his loss, but never what anyone else was going through. Especially Ellen.

"Just as she would have wanted me and the children to live our best lives, she would have wanted the same for you. To live your dreams, and in doing so, honor her."

Some of the heaviness lifted from Luke's chest as he

spoke. He looked at his children, who'd gotten mixed up in an adult situation they weren't old enough for. "I'm sorry I've been so caught up in my own pain that I haven't paid attention to yours. That's not what your mother would have wanted."

Ruby looked up at him, tears in her eyes. "I didn't do what Mama would have wanted, either."

Then Ruby got up and brought the ornament she'd been working on over to Nellie. "I made this for you. Our family tradition is that we all have ornaments with our names embroidered on them. I know I didn't do as good of a job with the lettering as you would, but I wanted to make it. I'm sorry I was so mean to you when you came. Mama would have punished me for sure."

Nellie took Ruby into her arms and held the crying girl. "I know. You were hurt and scared. I forgive you."

With as much grace as Luke had learned to expect from Nellie, she looked up at him and smiled. "And I forgive you, Luke."

Her words chased away the remaining heaviness in his chest, and Luke finally felt like he could breathe. But there was one more set of amends he needed to make.

"If you all don't have any objections," he said, "I'd like to join you for church in the morning."

The smiles that greeted him were all Luke needed to finally feel like he was back on the right track. However, Amos scowled.

"What's wrong, son?"

Amos let out a long-suffering sigh. "Could you please stop making everyone cry so we can have some fun? There are still some games on my list that we need to play."

"Absolutely. I think it's time we all focused on celebrating this glorious holiday." This time, when Luke smiled, he could feel it all the way down to his toes. As much as he'd been dreading the season, he had no doubt that the family was going to have a merry Christmas indeed.

Chapter Thirteen

Nellie couldn't help but hum one of the songs they were working on for the Christmas performance at church. Yesterday after they'd attended service as a family, including Luke, Seamus and some of the other men from church came over and helped Luke install their new stove. She was wearing her new boots, and though she'd found it odd getting used to having shoes that fit, her feet were more comfortable than they'd been in a long time. Oddly enough, she didn't miss the comfort of the coins in the toe of her shoe, reminding her that she had a way out.

She didn't need a way out. Not anymore. A man like Luke, who'd fought so hard to be a better man and was willing to admit his mistakes, was the kind of honorable man her mother had always told her to pursue. If he'd been so overwrought at hurting someone emotionally, he'd never hurt her physically. More important, Luke had genuine compassion for others, which Nellie had never seen in her late husband or any of the men he'd sold her to. Until coming to Leadville, she'd forgotten that genuine compassion existed in others. She'd been too busy trying to survive.

"Tookie?" Maeve pointed to the stack of cookies Nellie was arranging on a plate for the children. Annabelle had invited the older children over to make Christmas gifts for their families, and they were due home anytime.

A knock sounded at the door. Nellie wiped her hands on her apron, then picked up Maeve. "Not yet, but as soon as your brother and sister come home, we will."

When Nellie opened the door, her smile fell into the pit of her stomach. How had he found her?

"Hello, Nellie." Big Jim, the head of the gang Ernest had sold her to, stood in front of her. "Looks like you've done pretty well for yourself."

He let out a long whistle as he stepped into the room. "It's not more than a shack, but I know what property values in Leadville are. You are sitting on a gold mine." Big Jim chuckled. "Well, I guess the money is in the silver here, but you know what I mean."

Nellie stared at him. "We don't have anything at all. Look at this place. My husband works in a smelter."

Her husband. Nellie took a deep breath. She'd married Luke because without the protection of a husband, Big Jim and his men could do anything they wanted to her. But now she was someone's wife. Part of a community. She didn't have to roll over and do what Big Jim, or any of the rest of them, wanted.

"You need to leave," Nellie said, trying to stay calm, aware of the child in her arms.

"I don't think so." Big Jim looked around the room. "Seems you got yourself set up real nice here."

He picked up a cookie from the plate and took a bite. "A little dry."

Nellie watched as Big Jim ate the rest of the cookie, wondering how she could get rid of him before the children came home. He finished the last bite of cookie, then with one sweep of his arm, he sent the plate of cookies crashing to the floor.

"Tookies!" Maeve's cry made him laugh.

"There will be more than a few cookies getting broken if we don't get our money."

Though he had a pleasant tone to his voice, his face looked so menacing that if Nellie didn't need to be strong for Maeve, she'd probably start crying herself.

"We have no money," Nellie said. "We're barely getting by on what we have. I'm married now. You can't just come in here and demand money, thinking I'm going to pay it. It's not even my debt."

"I own you," he said in a low voice.

"Slavery is against the law." It was harder now to keep her voice calm. It might be illegal to buy and sell people, but Nellie knew she wasn't the only woman handed over in exchange for a man's debts.

Big Jim gave a snicker, same as when Nellie had tried to defy him before. And then he'd backhand her so hard she'd fly across the room. Nellie took a step back. If he hit her, she could go to the sheriff, and this time, the sheriff could do something.

"You think they're going to believe a woman over

me?" The sound Big Jim made didn't even seem human as he flipped over the kitchen table.

Maeve started to cry harder, and Nellie cuddled her tighter against her body, pressing the little girl's head to her chest.

"One of the women I go to church with is married to a deputy. They'll believe me."

She didn't know Mary Lawson and her husband, Will, all that well, but they were connected to Pastor Lassiter, and Annabelle had often told Nellie that the Lawsons would do anything to help anyone in trouble.

Big Jim walked up to her casually, like he had no fear of the law. "You don't think I know how to handle some low-ranking deputy?" He gave a snort. "I've bought and paid for more deputies than boots."

Some of the bravery Nellie felt started to fade. The deputies had laughed at her when she'd gone to them before, and she'd noticed a number of lawmen counted among Big Jim's clients. Could anyone here help her? Or did Big Jim's influence extend all the way to Leadville?

He reached out and tugged on one of the loose curls around her face. "And I'm sure once that husband of yours learns all about the things you did at my place, he'll be grateful to be rid of you." With a chuckle, he added, "He might even pay me to take you away. Keep you from corrupting this sweet child of his."

When Big Jim tried to touch Maeve, Nellie swatted him away. "Leave her alone."

"Who's going to make me?" Big Jim stepped away,

then with a sweep of his arm, he knocked everything off the counter.

"What do you want?" Tears ran down Nellie's cheeks. "I don't have any money. I'm just one woman. What am I to you that you can't just let me go?"

Big Jim walked over to the stove, where Nellie had dinner simmering. He dipped his finger in, tasted it, then picked up the pot and flung it across the room.

"You're an example. To every stupid woman who thinks they can run off and get away with it. And to every idiot man who thinks he can cheat Big Jim."

"Ernest is dead. Isn't that enough?"

"Not when the deed to the house he gave me was faked. Who knows how many of those deeds he made up? Now I've got five other guys fighting me in court with the same exact piece of paper, claiming they own the house. Prime real estate, and I'm not getting a dime. You think I'm just going to let another moneymaker get away? Not without a price."

Nellie swallowed her tears. Tried to calm herself, knowing that Big Jim enjoyed making women cry.

"How much?" Nellie asked.

Big Jim gave her a nasty grin. "You were always a favorite at my place. It'd take you a while to earn what you owe, considering Ernest's debt, and everything I spent trying to get you back. But there's a game in town, and I'm willing to let you go if I can get my stake. One thousand dollars."

Looking around the room, and having had the financial discussion with Luke, Nellie knew that even if they sold everything they owned, it wouldn't come close to that amount. Surely Ernest hadn't lost that much money gambling. Their old house hadn't been worth that much, either. But Nellie remembered watching them beat a man for not paying on time, then telling him it would be double when he brought the money for the next deadline. Interest, they called it.

"You're crazy," she said.

He laughed. "I was definitely crazy to accept Ernest's wagers, that's for sure. But I am perfectly sane in telling you that I will recoup my losses."

Big Jim stuck out a finger and wiped a spot where the stew had landed, then licked it.

"Too salty. I can't keep you as a cook, but I'm sure we'll find another bed for you to use working upstairs. The men liked you."

Nellie closed her eyes. How a man could enjoy hurting a woman and making her cry, she didn't know. But that life—she simply couldn't go back to it.

The front door opened, and Ruby and Amos came running in.

"Nellie! Look what we did!"

Amos held up a package, then stopped. Ruby opened her mouth but didn't say anything.

"Ah," Big Jim said. "The rest of the children."

He walked up to Ruby, a grin filling his face. "You must be Ruby. Such a charming letter you sent to Nellie's sister, begging for her to take Nellie away. If it hadn't been for you, we would have never found her. I'll have to send you a finder's fee once I get what's rightfully mine. Don't you worry, you pretty thing. Nellie will be out of your hair soon enough."

Ruby shrank back, terror in her eyes as she looked from Big Jim to Nellie.

Nellie's stomach ached. Everything she'd done to keep Big Jim and his men from finding her, and all it took was a resentful little girl to ruin it all. Ruby hadn't known what she was doing, but it didn't matter. The damage had been done.

"Please leave," Nellie said, trying to keep her voice firm. "You have no quarrel with these people. You've caused enough harm."

Big Jim turned and looked at her. "You have three days. I'll have my money, or I'll have payment in some other way. Even if it means taking you and the children. I'm not sure you're worth a thousand dollars anymore."

"But that's Christmas," Nellie said. "Can't it wait until after the holiday? For the children?"

He gave her a look of the same deep disgust he'd given her while she was with him and his men. "Do I look like I care about someone else's brats? Unless they can make me money, that is."

As if to prove his point, Big Jim walked over to their Christmas tree, picked it up and tossed it across the room.

"I'm sure it will be a merrier Christmas for them without you. Get me my money or else."

Big Jim strode out of the house, looking more confident than a lowlife like him deserved to be.

The children were all crying, and as Nellie looked around the room, she couldn't help but do the same. Their supper was ruined, and when Big Jim had thrown it, bits of stew had landed on all their decorations, effectively destroying them. Everything the family had worked so hard for was now worthless.

"Who was that man?" Ruby asked, coming alongside Nellie and wrapping her arms around her.

Amos joined in, and though the weight of his arms on her body was meant to comfort her, it only made the growing desperation eating at her insides worse.

What if Big Jim had hurt the children?

What would he do when he came back?

"He's a very bad man," Nellie said, taking a deep breath to steady herself.

The front door opened, and Luke stepped in.

"What happened?"

The children ran to him, and Nellie set Maeve down so she could join her siblings.

"A very bad man was here," Amos said.

"And it's all my fault," Ruby added.

Nellie meant to say something, but as she opened her mouth, the only thing that came out was a very large sob. Everything she'd worked for, everything she wanted in life, had been so close to her grasp and was now being taken away.

They didn't have the money. And Nellie wouldn't ask that of Luke even if they did, not when he had the children to provide for.

"No," Nellie said, finding her voice as a strange sense of calm overcame her. "It's my fault. I shouldn't have come here and put you all in danger."

Luke stared at the mess in his home. He'd sent Amos to the Fitzgeralds' for help. Myrna had taken Nellie into

Nellie's room, and the two women were holed up there. Seamus had taken one look at the inside of the house and gone for the sheriff. The children couldn't tell him anything about what happened, other than the fact that a very bad man had been there and he wanted a thousand dollars by Christmas or he'd take Nellie away.

He'd tried asking Nellie for more details, but she only shook her head slowly, tears running down her cheeks.

A thousand dollars.

What had this man been thinking, demanding that much money? True, the house and land were worth quite a bit, given that land prices in Leadville were climbing with every ounce of silver coming out of the mines. But that sum was too dear for their tiny place.

The front door opened, and Will Lawson, one of the town deputies, entered with Seamus. The last time Will was in this house was to tell Luke that his wife had been killed. Luke took a deep breath as he tried to push away the memory.

Will shook his head as he looked around the room. "Whoever this man was, he meant business. Where's your wife?"

"In the other room. She won't talk to me. Just keeps crying."

"Probably in shock." Will gestured toward the bedroom door. "May I?"

"Of course."

Will knocked on the bedroom door. "Mrs. Jeffries? Nellie? May I call you Nellie?"

Luke couldn't hear her response, but she must have answered in the affirmative.

"Nellie, I need you to come out and talk to us. Give us information about the man who was here so we can catch him before he hurts anyone else."

The gentle way Will spoke to Nellie made Luke wish he had the same skill. It seemed like everything Luke said to Nellie came out wrong. No wonder Will had a reputation for being such a great lawman.

Nellie finally emerged from the room, her face red and splotchy from crying. "The man was Big Jim Jones," she said quietly. "My late husband sold me to him as payment on a gambling debt he owed. I ran away. Big Jim came here to bring me back."

She spoke so simply, so matter-of-fact, that Luke had a hard time understanding the words. "What do you mean he sold you? You can't sell a human being."

The sadness in Nellie's eyes as she looked up at him nearly broke his heart. "Of course you can. Maybe people don't talk about it, or pretend they don't see it, but it happens every day."

She pointed out the window. "You think all those women in houses of ill repute on State Street are there by choice? Maybe some, but most of them don't go into that life willingly."

Luke stared at her for a moment. "You mean to say that you were one of those women?"

Surely not. He must have misunderstood her meaning. But as the silence grew, the truth kicked him in the stomach.

"So you would…"

He couldn't even say the words. Luke took a deep breath. Nellie didn't seem anything like those women.

"You told me you were a widow."

"I was." Fire flashed in Nellie's eyes, the first sign of life he'd seen in her since he'd come home. "A couple weeks before my husband died, he turned me over to Big Jim as payment on his debt. I didn't go willingly."

Myrna put her arm around Nellie and whispered something in her ear. Luke should have been doing that. But as he looked around the room, all he could think about was how his family could have been harmed.

How had he allowed himself to be taken in by a woman with such dangerous connections?

"I'm so sorry," Will said to Nellie, guiding her to one of the chairs that Seamus had righted. "My wife works in the church's ministry to those women, and we've met several who'd been forced into that profession by a father, a husband or sometimes a man who'd kidnapped her. I'm glad you found a way to get free. I can assure you that we will do everything we can to keep you safe."

Luke stared at Will. "I don't understand."

He knew the church had ministries to down-and-out people, including those women, but Luke never knew that some of those women lived that lifestyle against their will. Nor could he imagine Nellie doing anything she didn't want to do. None of this made sense.

"Nellie's plight isn't uncommon. It's not talked about much in polite society, which is why I appreciate all the work Pastor Lassiter does. So many of the less fortunate in our society are in that position not by choice, but by circumstance."

The Fitzgeralds murmured their agreement. They, too, often helped in the church's ministries and probably were aware of what Will was saying. But it didn't make it easier for Luke, knowing the danger his family had been in.

Tears streamed down Nellie's cheeks. "I tried to go to the authorities, but they didn't believe me. Said I should return to my husband or father, and then one of Big Jim's men showed up claiming to be my father, and they made me go with him. The next time I ran away, I went to my sister's. But they burned her barn down and said her house would be next if she didn't hand me over. Mabel didn't want me to go, but I couldn't let her family lose their home."

Luke had to admit it was a heartbreaking story. Part of him felt sympathy for Nellie, but as he looked around the room that had been destroyed by Big Jim, he mostly felt rage.

"So you would endanger my family instead? My children?"

The children were upstairs in the loft, and Luke wished the walls weren't so thin. They could probably hear every word. Amos and Maeve wouldn't understand. But Ruby, who'd already lost so much, would.

It was one more reason for her to be angry with Nellie.

His children shouldn't have to know that such evil existed in this world. He and Diana had done everything they could to protect them from the darker side of Leadville. Which was part of why they'd remained in this cabin, tucked away in one of the few decent neighborhoods in town.

Yet trouble had still come to their door, thanks to Nellie.

"I did everything to protect them," Nellie said, standing. "Before I ran away the last time, I made it seem like I hated my sister. I lied and said that she threw me out, so they wouldn't have any reason to cause her more trouble. And when I finally got away, I laid so many false trails that I thought for sure they'd never find me."

More tears started to stream down her face as her body shook. "I did everything I knew to do."

"But it wasn't enough!" Luke shouted. "I've already lost a wife, and now you put my children at risk?"

"Stop!" Ruby's voice echoed from the loft entrance, then she scrambled down the ladder.

"I did it," Ruby said. "It's my fault the men came. That letter, the one I asked you to get back? I found Nellie's sister's address in her journal and I wrote her a letter, begging her to take Nellie back because she was so awful and we hated her so much."

Watching his daughter cry tore at Luke's heart. No child should have to endure so much pain. Especially when Ruby had nothing to do with any of this.

Ruby shook her head. "I didn't mean it. I was mad, and when I realized how terrible it was, I tried to take the letter back, but you said it wasn't possible."

Then Ruby looked at him with accusation. "If you'd gotten the letter back like I asked, the man would have never found Nellie. He said so. Even told me I would get a reward for helping him find Nellie." Her words came out in breathless catches, the sobs stealing the air from her lungs.

Ruby turned to Nellie. "I'm sorry. I'm so sorry. I didn't mean it. I didn't know it would bring bad people here. You said nice things about your sister, so I thought that even though I was sending you away, it was to a good place."

As much as Ruby wanted to take the blame, this was not her fault. The blame lay squarely on Nellie's shoulders, for her sins of omission.

Nellie held a hand out to Ruby, but Luke held his daughter back. This was not the time for Nellie to be making amends with his daughter, but to be answering to him for endangering Ruby.

"Ruby, you go back upstairs and stay with your brother and sister. They need you."

The little girl still shuddered from her tears. "But everything's going to be fine, right? The bad man isn't going to take Nellie away, right?"

Luke didn't have the answers to her questions, mostly because he had no idea if anything was ever going to be fine again. How could the rug continually be pulled out from underneath him like this?

"Please go upstairs," Luke said again, and he noticed that Nellie nodded at Ruby in encouragement.

The Fitzgeralds looked at one another like they were nervous he was going to ask them to leave, too, but it was better for them to hear what was happening first-hand, rather than speculation later.

Once Ruby had gone upstairs, Luke brought his attention back to Nellie. "You should have told me. If you hadn't been so secretive about your past, we could have—"

"What would you have done?" Nellie wiped at the tears in her eyes. "I saw the disgust in your eyes when you realized the things I must have done with other men. And yes, I did them. At first I cried the entire time. But then I learned that if I cooperated, I didn't get so many beatings. It's what we all did to survive. Only people like you don't understand that, so you sit in judgment because somehow you're better than me for not being so stupid as to marry the wrong sort of man."

Nellie shook her head slowly. "I guess I'm pretty dumb, because I did it twice."

The look she gave him nearly broke his heart in two. Which was crazy, because she was the one who'd deceived him. So why did it bother him so much that she was upset for suffering the consequences of her actions? Actions that could destroy them all?

"I honestly thought you were the sort of man who judged a person by their character, and I'd hoped that over the past few weeks, I've shown you who I am. But now that you know about my past, you treat me with the same disdain as the society ladies who snicker behind their fans about women of that profession."

How was it that she'd been the one to do wrong, and yet the accusations were being leveled at him?

"That's not fair," Luke said. "You deceived me. You put my family in danger. Those aren't the actions of a woman of good character."

Nellie nodded slowly. "Perhaps you're right. I should have been more forthcoming about my past. I apologize for the inconvenience to your family."

Then she turned to Will, who'd been scribbling in his notebook. "I know you mean well, but these men are dangerous, and you can't stop them. I won't put Luke and his family in harm's way. If you can give me a safe place to sleep tonight, tomorrow I'll see about finding Big Jim and going with him. If I leave willingly, no harm will come to anyone."

"No," Will said flatly. "We have experience in these matters. You go with Big Jim and you'll be dead within a couple of years, if he lets you live that long. And he'll go on doing the same thing to countless other women. He needs to go to jail, where he can't hurt anyone else."

"I agree," Myrna said as she put her arm around Nellie. "You've done nothing wrong, and you don't deserve to spend the rest of your life suffering for someone else's mistakes."

Seamus went to the other side of Nellie and copied his wife's gesture. "Anyone can see that those things you had to do were to survive, they aren't who you are. We will stand by you, give you a home if you need it and do whatever else it takes to keep you safe. You will not return to that life."

The sadness on Nellie's face made Luke want to cry, as well. "No. I've done enough damage, thinking I could outsmart these men. My sister lost her barn, and probably her livelihood. I can't cause Luke or the children any more pain."

She gave Myrna what Luke recognized as being

the smile she used when she was trying to make the best of an impossible situation, like when Ruby had been difficult for her. "I love you all too much to put any of you in danger, as well. It's best I go with Will, and in the morning, I'll do what I need to do to keep my family safe."

Nellie sat back down in the chair, then lifted her foot and started unlacing her boots. "I'll need a few moments to pack my things."

Looking up at Luke, she said, "I won't take anything bought with your money. I'm sure these boots will fetch a decent price because folks buy used boots all the time. That's how I got mine. I am truly sorry for any pain I've caused you, and I know I can never make up for it, but I hope someday you'll find it in your heart to forgive me."

The memory of discovering her old, worn, too-big boots shamed him. She'd taken nothing from him, sacrificed herself for his children, and here she was, doing it again.

"Keep the boots," Luke said. "You deserve to have warm and dry feet."

She deserved a lot more than a pair of boots, and she hadn't deserved his harsh treatment. He'd spoken rashly in a moment of anger at seeing what could have happened to his family. Nellie would have never intentionally endangered his children. How could he have forgotten the way she so lovingly cared for his family?

"No. You've made it clear what I am to you."

Except it wasn't clear. Not at all. Not when the prospect of her leaving, of her returning to that life, filled him with more dread than he'd ever known. He'd thought that Will coming to his home to tell him Diana was dead was the worst moment of his life.

But watching Nellie prepare to leave was nearly as difficult.

Chapter Fourteen

Nellie had always known that theirs was a marriage of convenience. She'd always known that Luke would never stop loving Diana, and that he would always be so blinded by that love that he'd never be able to love anyone else.

But she'd never imagined he'd treat her with such contempt.

As she went to her room to pack her bag, she tried to think of what she could tell the children, how she could express her love so they'd understand she was leaving to keep them safe.

"Nellie…"

Luke called to her, but she found she couldn't turn to face him again. Couldn't bear to see the accusations in his eyes and the hatred for a woman who'd deceived him. She hadn't thought of it as deceit at the time, but she'd also been deceiving herself.

"Please, Nellie. I need to apologize. I was too harsh."

He followed her into her bedroom, leaving the door open, but the space still felt too confining.

"You were honest," she said quietly, looking at the knitted blanket on her bed, the one she'd worked on in the evenings while the children did their lessons. Did this blanket belong to her, or should she leave it for Luke and the children?

"I was angry. My home had been turned upside down, quite literally, and I found out that the woman I married was not the woman I thought her to be."

Nellie turned and looked at him, not bothering to hide the tears that had started falling again. "But that's just it. I am the same woman I've always been."

"You can't leave us," he said. "What about the children? What will we do without you?"

She hadn't thought about that, how much Luke needed her help with the children. And the housekeeping. And all the other tasks a wife who was not a true wife did.

"You have an extra room now. You can hire a housekeeper."

Nellie dug at the place in her waistband where she kept her coins and pulled them out. "Here. This should help. I have a few more in my old shoes. It's not much, but it can go toward fixing what I've made a mess of."

Luke didn't take the money she offered. His hands remained at his sides, and he stared at her. "I don't want your money. I want you to stay. Please. I will spend the rest of my life making up for my thoughtless words. Just stay."

A few hours ago, that request might have been

enough. But as she'd listened to Luke berate her for endangering his family, she'd realized that all of the feelings she'd been having for him were not returned. Luke would never love her. He just had a use for her.

Which made him no different from the men who paid Big Jim for her services. At least those men never pretended to care about her. Never made her feel like she could be something more than what she was.

"I meant what I said about wanting to protect your family. Will means well, but Big Jim and his men have a lot of power. I don't think Will understands how dangerous they are. I do. I'm not going to put the people I love at risk."

Three faces peered into the doorway, and the pain written on them brought a new level of despair to Nellie. She didn't want to go back to that life. Nor did she want to leave them. But what else was she supposed to do?

"Please, Nellie, you have to stay," Ruby said, entering the room.

The pain in the little girl's eyes was almost too much for Nellie to bear. Maeve squeezed through the people crowded at Nellie's bedroom door and ran to Nellie.

"Newwie. Pwease don't go 'way."

Nellie couldn't help but lift Maeve into her arms. What had she been told about her mother's death? Did Maeve just think that her mother had gone away and never come back? Nellie would be doing the same thing, in a sense.

"I have to," Nellie said. "You don't understand how bad these men are. They won't hurt you if I leave."

Obviously, they'd been determined enough to continue watching Mabel's house and to find out that Nellie—Ruby—had written. Or perhaps they'd threatened Mabel somehow, told her that if she had any contact with Nellie, she had to tell them or risk something terrible. She'd heard them threaten Mabel that the next time she helped Nellie, it wouldn't just be the barn they burned down.

A sick feeling filled Nellie's stomach. Were Mabel and her family all right?

Nellie looked past the children to Will, standing behind Luke. "If you want to help someone, please, help my sister. They got my information from Mabel. I don't know if they hurt her, or threatened her, or what they did to her. I know it's terribly expensive, but can you send a telegram?"

Will nodded. "I will. But I want you to do something for me in return."

"Anything." Nellie held Maeve closer to her. Protecting these children, protecting her sister, was the only thing that mattered to her.

"Stay. Let us capture Big Jim and his men. I know you're worried about the safety of your sister, but if you don't let the law deal with Big Jim, he's going to hurt other women, other people's sisters. Other people's children. Let's think about them, too. He might have sway with the law where you're from, but me and my men, we're always on the side of justice."

Nellie took a deep breath. She hadn't thought of it that way. Will had tried to tell her something similar earlier, but she'd been too focused on Big Jim's power.

None of the lawmen she'd gone to before had even tried to get her to stand up to Big Jim. They'd told her she was in the wrong and sent her back. Will wanted to help her. That had to count for something in a world where no one else had been willing before.

"All right," she said, exhaling a long breath. "We can try it your way. But if you fail, I'm going back with him, and that's that."

Will gave a nod. "Fair enough."

"Not fair enough." Luke spun to face Will. "This is my wife we're talking about. I can't just let her go."

"You have to," Nellie said. "I'm not giving you a say in this matter. Even if Big Jim goes to jail, I can't be your wife anymore."

Luke turned his gaze back to Nellie. "What do you mean?"

She'd thought she'd been certain of her decision to marry Luke, that it would solve all of her problems. But now she knew that it only delayed facing them. And created more. They'd thought they could build a friendship where there was no love, but as the scenes of their marriage replayed in Nellie's head, she couldn't do it anymore. Talking with Laura, even though Laura didn't know all the details, had made Nellie realize that she'd settled for far too little.

"I believe we have plenty of grounds for an annulment. It won't hamper your ability to marry again, if you choose," Nellie said. "But I hope that if you do, you marry for love. I thought that since my first marriage was not one of love, I could be married again without love so long as the man treated me well. But I can't. A marriage without love is nothing more than a business arrangement, and I'm tired of being used for someone else's convenience. If what I've given you is all you want from a woman, then you should follow Mrs. Heatherington's instructions and find a housekeeper."

Nellie looked at the children, whose faces were full of sadness and confusion. "If I get to stay in Leadville, I'll always be here for you as your friend. You can come to me for anything, anytime. But once all this is settled, I have to find a job and a new place to live."

Luke took a step toward her. "You can't be serious."

"I am," Nellie said. "I've been told I have skill as a seamstress, and I'm sure I can find employment."

"But you have a home here."

Confusion was written all over Luke's face, and Nellie didn't entirely blame him. She'd agreed to this arrangement, and now she was backing out without warning. Luke had been right that everything in his life was turned upside down suddenly.

"I'll stay until you can find a housekeeper."

"I don't want a housekeeper," Luke said. "I want you."

Nellie shook her head as she looked down at the little girl in her arms. Even being a mother to this dear child wasn't enough.

"That's not possible. If I'm to be married, I want a real marriage." Tears filled her eyes as Nellie shook her head. "And you don't. You're still holding on to someone I can never be."

Luke opened his mouth like he wanted to argue, but then he closed it. As much as it hurt to realize that he didn't return her feelings, there was something freeing in stating what she wanted. To finally chart the course of her own life, not out of desperation, but out of confidence in who she was.

Maybe she'd never find a man to love her. And that was all right. But if she found her freedom in this fight, she wasn't going to squander it by remaining in a situation where the man she married didn't love her.

That, at least, was a lesson she'd learned by being here. She'd seen the love Seamus had for Myrna. The love between Annabelle and her husband, as well as the deep affection shared among other couples at their church. Didn't Nellie deserve that for herself?

Nellie took a breath as she looked at Will. "If you think it safe enough, I'll remain here for the time being. But I would like to visit the pastor to speak with him about the women's ministry. While I am not in the same dire straits as the women it serves, I do wish to know my options as a woman alone. I'm not so naive as to think that it will be easy without a man's protection. But if they can do it, so can I."

Speaking those words made Nellie feel stronger than she had in a long time. She hadn't wanted to mention Laura by name, but knowing how Laura had overcome her bad situation gave Nellie the courage that she could do the same, as well. Though she was still willing to go with Big Jim if that was what it took to protect the children, the hopeless desperation that had filled her when he'd shown up had disappeared.

"I have no doubt that you'll be fine," Will said, giving her a smile. "And for now, I'd prefer you stay here, inside, until I know more about the situation. I'm going to go back to the office to see what I can find out about Big Jim, as well as any known associates he might have in the area. I'll ask Frank to pay you a visit."

Will's speech was addressed to her, and to her alone. Something about the respect in that bolstered Nellie's confidence, making her believe that it just might be possible to escape Big Jim once and for all, without having to look over her shoulder in fear.

"Thank you," Nellie said. "I'd appreciate that."

Will glanced at the children briefly, then back at Nellie. "I know your main concern is for the children. Rest assured that they will be safe. I will have one of my most trusted men outside at all times."

He made a motion with his hand at the window, and within moments, the door opened, and a man entered. "Did you need something?"

"This is Owen Hamilton. There is no one I would trust more with my own family." Will turned his attention to Owen. "I'm going to do some investigating and make some arrangements. I need you to remain here and keep watch. We don't know if Big Jim is here alone or if he's got men, so I would feel better if someone stayed here."

Owen tipped his hat at her. "Ma'am." He turned and gave a slight nod to Luke, then brought his gaze back to Will. "Would you mind letting Lena know that I might be a while? I know my sister was hoping to slip out to do some last-minute shopping for the girls, so I want her to have the chance to make other arrangements."

"Will do. I'll see if Mary can give her a hand. I

know how much your girls enjoy playing with our little Rosabelle."

Owen grinned. "Babies are hard to resist."

As Nellie watched the interaction between the men and how dearly they valued their families, she felt even safer. These men didn't pay lip service to caring about women and children. Being family men themselves, they understood what was at stake and wouldn't take unnecessary risks to capture Big Jim.

Now, more than ever, Nellie could believe that she might finally be safe. And as she looked around at the children, she knew they would be, too.

Luke wasn't used to feeling invisible. But as he watched the interaction between Nellie and the lawmen, he wondered if they even remembered he existed. But as the men turned to leave, Will gestured at him to follow.

They stepped outside, and Will addressed him. "Right now, we need to do everything to keep Nellie from running. She needs to feel like she's in a safe place. If she thinks the children are in any danger, she will leave, and those men will take her—and I think you know what happens then."

Luke swallowed. He was starting to get a pretty good idea, and he didn't like it, not one bit. Especially because he was now remembering all the times Nellie had acted afraid of him. Those men had done that to her.

"So we use her as bait?" He shook his head. "Even

if the children weren't here, this is Nellie we're talking about. What if they hurt her?"

Will shrugged. "What's it to you? From where I stand, Nellie is nothing more to you than a nanny and housekeeper. You'll find another."

"She is my wife!" Luke was tired of listening to everyone act like he had no feelings at all for Nellie.

"You sure don't treat her like one," Will said, looking over at Owen. "His sister is taking care of his family, but even he acts with more compassion toward Lena than you do to Nellie."

Seamus's lectures about how Luke treated Nellie were nothing compared to this. Those hadn't made Luke feel so hollow inside.

"What are you saying?"

Will shrugged. "If you have any desire to keep your wife, then you'd best start thinking about how to win her heart. It's the only reason you'll get her to stay. If you're not interested in her heart, then let her go."

The thought of not having Nellie in his life made Luke's heart ache in a most painful way. But he wasn't sure he was ready to love another woman besides Diana.

"You don't understand what I've been through," Luke finally said.

Owen stepped forward. "I understand more than you think. I helped put the men who killed your wife in jail. I will do everything I can to make sure you don't bury a second wife. Not only am I committed to protecting her now, but if she chooses to go it alone after, she will not be without assistance."

Then Owen looked him up and down, a measuring

look. "I know what it's like to have to raise children on your own. It's not easy. I will always be grateful to my sister for being willing to help with my girls. But to take a wife means you owe her more than a comfortable place to live. If you can't give her your heart…" Owen shook his head. "I suppose that's why I haven't remarried. I never want my daughters to think they should ever settle for anything less than a man who loves them with all their heart. If that's what you want for your children, don't you think you should set that example?"

Luke had given them that example. Only, Diana had died. But Owen's intense gaze told him that the other man wasn't going to accept that excuse.

"I suppose I should be getting back to my family," Luke said instead.

Will nodded. "We've got work to do."

Wishing he'd had better answers for the men, Luke went back inside. Nellie had left her room and was in the kitchen, setting it to rights.

"What can I do?" Luke asked.

"Nothing," Nellie said flatly. "This is my job."

She hadn't meant to hurt him, Luke realized, mostly because she didn't think she had the power to. Despite all the small gestures he'd thought showed her he cared, it hadn't been enough.

"Do you really think that's all you are to me?"

She stared at him, the blank look telling him everything he needed to know.

More important, though, as he looked at the tiredness lining her face, he finally saw the brokenness he'd been looking past all this time. When he'd first met her, he knew she carried deep wounds, and he'd hoped that one day she'd share those with him. She had, in a most painful way, and he'd reacted badly.

"I'm sorry, Nellie. Sorry for a good many things, and I can't even begin to express them. Because the more I'm here with you, the more I realize how much I've wronged you. I do care about you, and I've done the worst job of showing it. Please give me the chance to make it right."

Her face softened, but doubt remained in her eyes. "There's no room in your heart for me. Not when every other thought you have is about Diana."

She turned, then picked up the bowl she'd been using to store the broken pieces of dishes Big Jim had destroyed on his rampage. "Ruby, can you keep Maeve and Amos out of here for a while? I'm finding a lot more broken glass than I first thought, and I don't want anyone stepping in it. I'd appreciate it if you all stayed upstairs until we get things cleaned up."

Luke hated how Nellie had grown so cold so quickly. Wasn't it just a couple nights ago that they'd finally come to a place of warmth? Where they'd thought they could finally build a real life together? Or had it been just him?

Though someone had already righted their poor Christmas tree, many of the ornaments still lay on the floor, strewn about in one big mess. One of Diana's precious glass ornaments that she'd saved from her parents looked like it had been crushed by a man's boot. There would be no salvaging it.

Luke tried to pick it up, but the pieces were so small, it seemed almost useless.

"I'm sorry about the ornament," Nellie said, coming behind him. "Ruby said it was Diana's favorite."

He turned, noting that her face bore signs of deep regret. After what she'd said a few moments ago, she probably thought it had devastated him. And perhaps it would have, a few weeks ago. But the pained expression on Nellie's face reminded Luke that there were far more important things he faced losing.

"It doesn't matter," he told her, looking her in the eye. "It's just glass. As long as you and the children are all right, I don't care about the things."

He reached out and put his hand on her arm, but she shied away. Did his touch no longer comfort her? Or did the reminder of her past make her fear all men?

Luke brought his hands back in front of him. "I'm sorry. I suppose after everything that's happened, I don't have the right. But I want to comfort you like I used to. Like you've done for me."

She stared at him for a moment, then shook her head sadly. "I don't think we can go back to that. I saw how you reacted to my past. I am a fallen woman, Luke. That's not a fact that's going to change."

As he examined her face, he wondered just how bad it had been, being owned by Big Jim. Until today, he hadn't known that women didn't always go into that profession willingly. And he couldn't imagine Nellie choosing that life. Yet she would. To save his children.

"No, you aren't," he said. "I admit I was shocked when I found out what happened to you, what you had to do to survive. But someone who would choose that life to keep my children safe—that's the most honorable sort of person I know, and I'm proud to have you in my life."

His voice caught as he spoke, but his words didn't change the cold expression on her face.

"I was the one who put them in danger. You said so yourself."

Nellie picked up the broom that lay nearby, then started to sweep up the bits of broken glass. "And look what I've ruined."

The shattered glass was nothing compared to Luke's heart. Maybe Nellie was right in saying that Diana took up too much room in their relationship. But right now, faced with losing Nellie, Luke would be willing to suffer the pain of Diana's death a thousand times over before letting her go.

Somehow, he had to find a way to make it right.

Chapter Fifteen

Though the house had been set to rights thanks to Myrna returning with some ladies from church, Nellie didn't feel safe in their home. No, not their home. Luke's home. Even a day later, the place felt foreign to her. She glanced in his direction, and he smiled at her, giving her an inviting glance. Nellie looked away.

"You can't ignore him forever," Myrna said, handing her a plate. The women had brought different dishes last night, providing supper for the family, since theirs had been ruined. With the amount of food they received, they'd be eating through the new year and still have plenty left over. Especially since so far, Nellie hadn't found the time or energy to eat.

Various people, including Laura, had come to Nellie, pledging their support, offering her a place to stay or offering her work. She could leave at any time if she wanted, but she'd promised Will she'd stay until Big Jim's deadline, giving the lawmen a chance to put him in jail. She stole another glance in Luke's direction. She'd said she'd also give him the chance to find a house-keeper.

A knock sounded at the front door. Luke got up to answer it, and Will entered, followed by Owen.

Myrna gave Nellie a squeeze. "You go see what they need, and I'll watch the children. Be sure to offer Owen some of Mrs. Jackson's apple pie. It's his favorite."

Nellie squeezed her friend back, grateful to have someone like her by her side in such a difficult situation. "Thank you."

Then she greeted the lawmen warmly. "You heard Myrna. Can I tempt you with some pie? I believe Mrs. Jackson's daughter-in-law, Emma Jane, also brought over a nice cherry one. There's coffee on the stove, and it would be no trouble to make some tea."

Owen grinned. "Myrna knows me well. I'd appreciate a cup of coffee and some of that pie, and I'm sure you can twist Will's arm into having a slice, as well."

It felt almost…normal…to be offering these men hospitality. True, she and Luke had only ever entertained the Fitzgeralds, but she'd hoped, that with Luke going back to church and the friendships Nellie had been building, that they'd start having friends over.

Nellie served the two men and refilled Luke's coffee. She tried treating Luke like one of her guests, but their hands touched when she poured the coffee, and she felt a small spark. Pretending like she hadn't felt a thing was one of the hardest things Nellie had done in a while, but things between them felt too unsettled. Though he'd been kind to her since his apology last night, it seemed overly nice, almost smothering.

"I have good news," Will said when Nellie was seated. "Big Jim is wanted on several outstanding warrants. We'll have no problem arresting him and his men and putting them all in jail for a long time." He gave Nellie a smile. "A friend of mine paid your sister a visit. Everyone is safe and well. She never received the letter. Apparently, it was intercepted before it ever got to her. They're investigating the situation as we speak. Your sister was happy to hear that you're well, and if you don't mind my saying so, I think she'd appreciate hearing from you."

"Thank you." Nellie smiled back as she tried to ignore the way Luke leaned in toward her, trying to be comforting, she supposed, but his presence only made her feel more uneasy. What did he want from her? She knew he felt bad about his reaction to Big Jim and wanted her to stay, but a few kind gestures weren't going to change her mind.

Brushing aside thoughts of Luke, Nellie returned her attention to Will. And her sister. Some of the heaviness in Nellie's heart dissipated knowing that Big Jim hadn't bothered her or her family again. "I thought not hearing from me would protect her, but I've missed her dreadfully. I can't imagine the worry it caused her to have someone from the law visit her."

"He's not with the law," Will said. "I remembered what you'd told me about Big Jim's connections, and I thought it best to make discreet inquiries. Fortunately for us, he's burned a lot of bridges in the past few months and he doesn't have as many resources at his disposal."

Nellie could breathe even more easily now. She hadn't wanted to hope too strongly that she could be forever free of Big Jim, but she was starting to believe it possible. A new life, with friends to support her and the freedom to write her sister without worry over anyone's safety.

Owen nudged Will, who gave a slight nod before continuing. "Word is there's a high-stakes game happening on Christmas. Buy-in is a thousand dollars. My guess is that Big Jim is running short on cash, and when he got here and heard about it, he saw it as a way to get ahead."

Nellie nodded. "He mentioned something about a game and being willing to give me my freedom in exchange for his stake."

Luke jumped up. "If money is what this is about, then I'll pay it, gladly. We can go to the bank first thing tomorrow."

"You don't have any money," Nellie said. She shook her head, knowing the exact amount Luke had to his name. It was sweet that he was making all these grand gestures to get her to stay, but he shouldn't be making promises he couldn't keep.

He looked at her, his face as guilty as Amos's when he got into the treats when he wasn't supposed to.

"When Diana died, the owner, George Bellingham, sold the mine. He divided the profit among the victims. The families who lost a loved one got the most, but he also gave consideration to those injured and made sure they were compensated. I wouldn't take what I called blood money, so they put it into a bank account in my name in case I changed my mind."

The words rolled around in the back of Nellie's head. Luke had money? All this time? True, a thousand dollars wasn't enough to make a man rich, but for people like them, it was a small fortune. But Luke had kept it all to himself.

Nellie shook her head. No, not to himself. He'd left it in the bank, where it benefitted no one. Though she'd always told him that he was entitled to his grief, this action seemed a bit selfish somehow. Especially because she'd seen the condition of the children's clothing and shoes when she'd arrived. She stared at Luke, trying to make sense of why he'd do such a thing.

Luke glanced at Seamus and Myrna, then turned his gaze back to Nellie. "Everyone wanted me to do something with it, buy a better house, get a housekeeper and nanny for the children, and I couldn't. Every time I thought about that money, I thought about my wife in the casket, and I got sick. A woman's life is priceless, and they wanted me to accept money to replace her. I couldn't do it. Not even when things were bad, and I was desperate. I married a stranger rather than use a penny of that money."

Something inside Nellie's heart twisted in a strange way as she saw the pain in Luke's eyes. Though she understood why he'd kept the money a secret, she didn't agree with those reasons. Luke's grief had crippled him and hurt his family, and he couldn't see it. How could she be so blind as to fall in love with a man whose heart was so unavailable?

Luke turned his attention to Owen. "You said earlier that I'd already buried one wife, and you'd make sure I wouldn't have to bury another. I thank you for that, but now that I know what Big Jim really wants, a spot at that table, I can give it to him, and I can save Nellie myself."

The words were sweet, and might have been enough to turn Nellie's heart. But something in her had hardened toward him, and Nellie couldn't explain why. It was as though all of these gestures were coming too little, too late.

Owen shook his head. "We don't pay ransom, and that's exactly what this is. You pay him, and he'll be back. We're putting together a group of men to be ready when Big Jim comes for Nellie, and we'll arrest him then."

"I told you, I don't want you using my wife as bait."

There was something in the look Luke gave her that Nellie had never seen in his eyes before. Was she judging him too harshly? After all, he was willing to give up the money he'd clung to in his grief over Diana's death. But it was just money. And it seemed rash for him to suddenly be willing to give it up.

"Don't waste Diana's money on me," she told him. "Save it for the children. You may need it later."

"I don't see it as a waste." Luke walked over to her and took her by the hands. "I know I haven't loved you as I should, but I am not willing to stand idly by and lose another woman I love when I have the means to do something about it."

The spinning in Nellie's heart stopped. Everything

went still. Something prompted her to stand, to look at him, to try to figure out what exactly was going on in his head.

"What did you say?"

"I can't lose you, Nellie." Luke's eyes searched her face in a way that made her feel more vulnerable than she ever had.

"Why?" Her breath caught.

"Because I love you. Don't make me go through that again."

He sounded so sincere. He'd mentioned love twice in reference to her. And the look in his eyes nearly took her breath away.

"I'll never be Diana," she told him. "Helping me isn't going to bring her back."

"I know," he said as he bent and kissed her gently. The kiss was the briefest flutter on her lips, a tender gesture, yet it spoke of the promise of so much more.

Just as quickly as the kiss began, it ended. Luke pulled back slightly, just enough to look at her in a way that made her insides flutter.

"Which is why I can't risk losing you. Don't make me go through that pain again."

Nellie couldn't deny that she'd enjoyed the kiss. That she liked the way his touch felt, the way Luke made her feel when he looked at her like that. No man had ever made her feel so warm and safe inside.

But as she looked around the room, so much of it still a shrine to Diana, Nellie had to wonder if this was how Luke truly felt, or if it was just the desperation of not wanting to lose her that was talking. Not because he'd fallen in love with her, but because he needed her help and enjoyed her companionship. But that still wasn't love.

And yet…he had offered the money he couldn't spend because of what it had meant to him. As she searched his face, she couldn't decide if it was a gesture of love or desperation. She'd told him she wanted love in her life. Would he offer it, or at least a semblance of it, in order to get her to stay?

Though she'd never known Luke to be a liar, Nellie wasn't sure she could trust him.

"I think we need to take a step back and think about things," she said. "So much has happened in the past few days. You've had a lot of surprises sprung on you. We've both learned things about each other that have come as a shock. I had no idea you had so much money at your disposal. You had no idea about my past. It seems we were both keeping secrets from each other, so maybe we don't know each other as well as we thought."

She couldn't tell if Luke was considering her words, or if his mind was somewhere else. Nellie continued, "I don't want you to spend your money. Let's do what Will is asking us, and try it his way. If they can't capture Big Jim and his gang, then we can look at pursuing other options, such as me going with him, or you paying the ransom. But I can't think about that right now."

The words felt right coming out. Giving each other space seemed to be the best thing to do. She wanted love, and she liked how Luke made her feel. At least in this moment. But there had been other moments over the past couple of days where Luke had made her feel absolutely worthless. Which Luke was he really, on the inside? Only time would tell, and right now they didn't have the time to make any decisions about their relationship. She knew she could not think rationally, especially when it came to him.

The thought of losing Luke wasn't one she wanted to entertain. Then again, she'd never really felt like she had him to begin with. The plan hadn't been to care about him, and she should have been satisfied with their business arrangement. But now that she knew better, now that she knew she wanted more, she needed to think rationally.

It would be easy to be taken in by his sweet words and romantic gestures, to believe he loved her. But what happened a few months down the road when Luke realized that his love for a dead woman was too strong to keep his love for Nellie alive?

Though Luke knew there was wisdom in Nellie's words, they also held the sting of rejection because not once did she mention returning his feelings. That she, too, cared for him. Yes, she'd said that she wanted a marriage built on love, and he'd taken it to mean that she loved him, but what if what she really wanted was the chance to be married to someone else? Someone who loved her?

But Luke did love her, more than he could have imagined. So how did he show it to Nellie?

They continued making plans for capturing Big Jim and his men, almost as though Luke's declaration was nothing more than a minor interruption in the conversation. He supposed, as he looked at the lawmen, that to them that was all it was. Though Will and Owen had talked to Luke about his treatment of Nellie, they were probably too focused on keeping her alive.

Which Luke should be, as well.

Perhaps Nellie was right. There would be time enough to sort out their feelings for one another once they had Big Jim behind bars.

If only he could forget the feeling of her lips on his. Though it had only been the briefest of kisses, Nellie had kissed him back. Surely it meant there was hope for their future.

Once they had the final plan outlined, Luke felt slightly more comfortable about waiting for Big Jim and his men to come to them. There were dozens of saloons and places of ill repute where he could be hiding, if he was even staying in town. He'd be nearly impossible to find, and he hadn't left any direction with Nellie. The big card game wasn't until late on Christmas, which meant Big Jim would probably be by early that day.

Until then, Will had men watching both the front and back entrances of the Jeffries home, just in case Big Jim decided to come early. Christmas Day, Will would have double the amount of men on duty. When Big Jim and his men arrived, Will and his men would arrest them. Until then, Nellie and the children would remain inside the house. It seemed the safest option, even though Nellie had been hoping to attend the Christmas Eve service. But they couldn't risk endangering everyone in the church.

The plan sounded easy enough, but Luke couldn't shake the feeling that it wasn't going to be so simple.

When Luke escorted the men out, he stopped Will. "Are you sure this is going to work?"

Will nodded. "Men like Big Jim are too lazy to go to too much trouble. Not unless they know you have the money. Then it would be worth the effort."

"No." Luke shook his head. "Though George Bellingham announced that he was compensating the victims, no amount was ever publicly given. His family's financial troubles were all over the papers, so it was assumed that no one received much once the debts were settled. However, he received enough to compensate the victims, even though there was none left over for him. Several men I work with have joked about how little we must have gotten, since we still live like paupers."

Will ran his fingers down one of the sagging railings on Luke's porch. "It's well-known that you refused his money, but I don't think anyone realizes you have access to it."

Shrugging, Luke said, "I didn't want people to think I was crazy, refusing so much money. They already thought that, and I didn't want to hear any more. In my mind, doing something with that money meant that I accepted what happened to Diana, and I couldn't do that."

"What'll you do with the money now?" Will asked.

Luke hadn't thought that far ahead. Only that the money could be used to save Nellie's life. But if it wasn't needed for that purpose, then what would he do with it?

"I suppose I'll see what Nellie wants. She's right that we've had too many secrets between us, and maybe figuring out the best way to handle the money would be a good way to start fresh."

Will made an approving sound. "She's a special woman, that Nellie. I know you said some nice things in there to her, things a woman likes to hear. Be sure you follow through and live it out."

Will pulled a strip of peeling paint off the railing. "I hope that starting fresh also means giving her a decent home. You did your best with this one, using what little means you had. Nellie's a good enough woman to make the best of it, but she's right about Diana. If you're sincere about your feelings for Nellie, then it's time to finish burying your first wife, and give your whole heart to your second."

Luke took a deep breath. He hardly knew this man, who so freely seemed to be passing judgment. He meant well, which was why Luke had allowed him to continue. And it was in protection of Nellie, for which Luke could find no fault.

"You don't know what it's like to lose a beloved wife," Luke told him.

Will nodded. "You're right, I don't. But if God sees fit to bring another wonderful woman into your life, then don't you think you should be thanking Him and counting your blessings rather than continuing to wish for what you can never get back?"

Will's words echoed what Seamus, Pastor Lassiter and Owen had all told him. They spoke wisely, but none of them seemed to understand that Luke was doing his best.

"I'm trying." Luke gestured at the door. "Didn't I just tell her that in there?"

"Actions speak louder than words."

One of Will's men came running up to them.

"Will! There's a robbery in progress at the Jackson Bank. They've got hostages."

Before Will could respond, gunshots rang out from the direction of the bank, which was only a couple of blocks away.

Will turned to Luke. "I hate to ask, but do you mind running to the sheriff's office and letting them know what's happening? I'd like to take my men and get to the bank to see what we can do about the situation before it gets worse. Since it's in the opposite direction, I don't want to waste any time."

"Absolutely." Luke took a step off the porch, then stopped. "What about Nellie and the children?"

"Seamus is watching the back door. He's helped me out a couple of times on other cases, so I know he can handle whatever comes his way. Owen will remain out front. If you don't go to the sheriff, then I'll have to ask one of them to do it, and I suspect they're better with a gun than you are."

Though Luke knew the other man was right, he hated leaving Nellie and the children. But it would take him only a few minutes to get to the sheriff's office and back, so he wouldn't be gone long.

"All right," Luke said as Will turned and followed the man down the steps.

Will stopped to say something to Owen, then he ran down the street, faster than Luke would have imagined a man could run. But as he heard more shots, Luke was grateful a man like Will was on the job.

Nellie opened the door. "What's going on?"

"Robbery at Jackson's Bank. Stay inside. I'm going to get the sheriff, but you have Owen out front and Seamus in the back. I won't be gone long." Luke looked at her, wishing he could tell her something to make her realize just how much he cared about her. Though Diana hadn't been shot, something about hearing the gunshots had him thinking again about how precious life was.

"Be safe," Nellie said, giving him a tender glance. "We'll see you soon."

Something about her expression gave Luke hope. She had feelings for him, even if she was still sorting them out. And though now was not the time to discuss them, once this was all over, they'd find a way to make their marriage work.

Chapter Sixteen

Since hearing the gunshots, everything seemed eerily quiet. Though they lived in a better part of town, it wasn't uncommon for drunken miners and other miscreants to cause trouble with their guns now and again. But something about the situation felt off.

Nellie peered out the curtains of their front window. Owen was across the street, standing in the shadows as he kept watch. Myrna had gone home for a few minutes because Ellen was feeling poorly, but Nellie had heard her chat briefly with Seamus as she left.

Hopefully Luke would return soon, then perhaps things would feel normal again.

Her lips tingled, and Nellie pressed her fingertips to them. Could things feel normal after that kiss?

Amos came down the ladder, holding some mistletoe. "Look what Myrna brought us! Ours got destroyed by the bad man, and since she knew how much I love mistletoe, she brought me some."

"That's lovely." Nellie turned to the little boy and

smiled at him. "Why don't I help you hang it some-where where it will stay safe?"

Amos looked at her suspiciously. "I thought you said the bad man wasn't coming back."

"He's not."

"Then why do we need to keep my mistletoe safe?" The little boy looked at her so innocently that Nellie gathered him in her arms.

"I didn't mean it that way," Nellie said. "I just re-member that ours was getting tattered from holding it all the time, so I thought we could hang this one to keep it fresher."

Amos appeared to be deep in thought for a mo-ment. "But I want Papa to kiss you again so I can see it this time."

"How do you know about that?"

"Ruby saw." Amos grinned. "She was coming downstairs to get some more thread for the present Myrna helped us make, and she said Papa was kissing you just like he used to kiss Mama. So now I want to see it. Because then I will know that you will be our new mama forever, and never go away."

There were so many reasons for Nellie's heart to ache at this sweet child's words. How was she supposed to explain to him that she might have to go away? And that Luke's kiss might not have meant what Ruby and Amos thought it had?

"So touching." Big Jim's voice came from the back door. "Sounds like you have quite the cozy family here."

Nellie pushed Amos behind her skirts. "What do you want? You said I had until Christmas."

Big Jim gave her a nasty grin. "That was until you got the law poking around in my private affairs. Now I find that my trusted associates are a little spooked on account of not wanting the law in their business."

"There's a deputy right outside," Nellie said, looking over her shoulder. Could she signal Owen without drawing Big Jim's ire?

"You don't think I'm that stupid, do you?" Big Jim laughed. "The dummy you had out back is taking a little nap in the outhouse. And the do-gooder you had out front is a little busy."

Nellie's gut wrenched. This was why she didn't want to do things Will's way. She'd warned him that Big Jim was smart.

"What did you do to them?" Hopefully she could keep him talking long enough for Luke to return and get help.

Big Jim made a noise. "I didn't kill them, if that's what you're asking. Too many lawmen around this place. Much easier to get away if no one is killed."

He looked in Amos's direction. "Which is why you'll do what I say. I know you'd just hate for anything to happen to that sweet little boy." Big Jim glanced around the room. "Where are the girls? The big one's almost old enough to come work for me."

Nellie closed her eyes. They'd been in her room, looking at buttons for something they were making for Amos. She sent a silent prayer that Ruby would know to keep Maeve in there, away from harm.

"You leave them out of this."

He grinned again. "So you will come with me. I do like it when you cooperate."

"Why do you want me so bad?" Nellie stared at him. "I told you, we have no money. Surely you've asked around and know that I'm telling the truth."

"Yes. But I also know you have a lot of rich friends, and I'm sure they'll be willing to help your husband pay to get you back."

His words made Nellie feel even sicker. She'd worked so hard to build a life and make friends, and Big Jim was using that against her.

Nellie shook her head. "Will says that they discourage anyone from paying ransom."

The expression on Big Jim's face only made her stomach ache worse. "I'm not worried about Will Lawson. There's a bullet with his name on it, and he's walking right into it. Do you know how many people in this town hate him? Truly hate him?"

"No." The ache in her stomach moved to her throat as Nellie stared at him. "Everyone loves Will. He's well respected and has many friends."

Big Jim shrugged. "On your side of the law, maybe. But you put enough men in jail, and you find yourself with a lot of enemies. When you're in a saloon, chatting up the fellows, trying to see what your odds are against a certain lawman, you learn things. There are lots of men with scores to settle, and tonight's the reckoning. They get what they want, I get what I want, and everyone's happy."

"But I'm not!"

Nellie turned just in time to see Ruby pick up the pot of soup that had been simmering on the stove and smash it against the back of Big Jim's head. By the expression on his face, he hadn't seen it coming. His eyes widened, and he fell to the floor with a crash.

"Ruby!" Nellie stared at her, then looked down at the man on the ground, who had blood gushing from his head. It looked like he was still breathing, though.

The back door opened, and Luke ran in, breathless, holding Seamus's rifle.

"What's going on in here? I found Seamus—" He stopped when he saw Big Jim's body on the floor.

"Get out, all of you. Run to Myrna's and lock the door behind you. Stay there until I come for you."

Nellie shoved Amos in the direction of the door, then ran over to Maeve and picked her up. She took Ruby by the hand. "Come on, let's go."

She paused at the door and stared at Luke. "What about you?"

His gaze didn't leave Big Jim. "I'm staying here to make sure he doesn't leave until the law arrives."

"But he's dangerous. You don't know what he's capable of."

Luke didn't look at her. "And you don't know what I'm capable of when someone comes into my house and threatens my family. Now go."

As Nellie ran across the alley to the Fitzgeralds', pulling the children along with her, she prayed Luke would be safe. She shouldn't have left him, but she had to protect the children.

Myrna already had the back door open when Nellie crossed their yard. "Come in," she said. "Seamus is on his way to the sheriff's office. I wanted him to stay home with that knot on his head, but he said you folks were in danger. Please, tell me you're all right."

Nellie nodded as Myrna slammed the back door behind them and locked it. While the older woman made tea, Nellie relayed what had happened with Big Jim.

When Nellie got to the part about Ruby hitting him with the pot, Myrna stopped and stared at the little girl.

"What were you thinking, hitting a man like that? You could have gotten yourself killed."

Ruby stared at her defiantly. "I was thinking that I already had one mother taken from me, and I wasn't letting some mean man take this one. A girl needs a mother to guide her, and I will not be forced to find another."

Tears streamed from the little girl's face, and Nellie held her arms out to her. Ruby ran to her, sinking into Nellie's embrace.

"Please don't leave us, Nellie. I know what you told Papa, that you didn't want to be married to him anymore, but I saw you two kiss, and surely that means you've changed your mind. I promise I'll never be mean again, just stay."

Nellie held the sobbing girl close to her, then looked up to see that the other two children were also crying. Maeve probably didn't understand why she was upset, but with everyone else in such a state, she'd joined them.

Shifting her weight, Nellie moved Ruby to one side

and held out her other arm to the younger children. "Come here."

They needed no encouragement as they ran into Nellie's arms, and she held the three children as they all cried.

She didn't want to go, either. But how could she explain the difficulties of adult relationships and the fact that she would be miserable if Luke didn't truly love her?

The family, minus Luke, sat in Myrna's kitchen for quite some time, holding each other, alternating between crying and sharing their gratitude and love. And the longer they were there, the more Nellie wondered how she was ever going to leave. Could she bear to stay if Luke's declarations of love weren't real? As she kissed the tops of each of the children's heads, she prayed that God would find a way to heal the pain in both Luke's and Nellie's hearts to keep their family together.

Luke wasn't sure how long he held the gun on Big Jim. The rise and fall of the man's chest told Luke he was alive. Which meant he was still a threat. Big Jim could just be lying there, waiting for the opportunity to get up and fight Luke for the gun.

But he wasn't going to let that happen.

The front door swung open, and Owen staggered in, holding a large ball of snow to his head.

"Please tell me he didn't get them."

"They're safe at Myrna's." Luke gestured at the fallen man with Seamus's gun. "Not sure about him.

He hasn't gotten up, but that doesn't mean I trust that he won't."

"Where's Seamus?" Owen looked around the room.

"Gone to get the sheriff. He was out for a while, too, but he said he could make it."

Several lawmen entered the house, and Seamus staggered in behind them. He stopped and stared at Owen. "How'd he get you, too?"

Owen shook his head slowly. "Wasn't him. He must've had a lady friend. A fancy carriage stopped in front of me, and a lady leaned out and asked if I could help her. Of course I went over to her to see what was going on. Before I knew it, I was on the ground. Don't even know what hit me." He rubbed his head. "But it sure hurts."

The men had started dragging Big Jim out of the house. Blood was everywhere, and Luke felt sick to his stomach at the sight. How were they supposed to have Christmas in this house now?

He spied a piece of mistletoe on the ground. He'd seen Myrna give it to Amos, delighting his son. Theirs had all been destroyed with Big Jim's first visit. Luke wasn't about to let this one be lost to Amos, as well. He picked it up and shoved it in his pocket.

One of the men who'd come in turned to Owen and Seamus. "I've sent for a doctor. Why don't you two sit in the meantime?" He turned his attention to Luke. "And you can tell me what happened."

Luke stared at him. "And just who might you be?"

"US Marshal Dean Whitaker. I'm a friend of Will's. He tipped me off about Big Jim's presence in Leadville.

Our men have been chasing him across the country. You've just done us a big favor. But I still need to know what happened for my report."

As Luke relayed the events of the afternoon, including Will leaving for the bank, the man frowned. At one point, he signaled to one of the men at the door and whispered something in his ear. The other man left, and the marshal brought his attention back to Luke.

"I'd like to speak with your wife and children now. Would that be all right with you?"

Though Luke knew he needed to cooperate, he was grateful that the man had at least asked. He nodded, then guided the marshal over to Myrna's, where he found Nellie and the children holding each other.

"Papa!" The children called out his name but didn't let go of Nellie. Though he would have liked to have taken them in his arms, he also didn't want to separate them from the woman they found so much comfort in.

"Please make her stay." Ruby looked up at him with longing in her eyes. "I even got the bad guy so he can't hurt her anymore."

Luke stared at her. "You did that?"

"And I'd do it again, if it meant saving Nellie. I can't lose another mother, I just can't."

The heartbreak in his daughter's voice nearly undid him.

"Please, Papa," Amos said, tears in his eyes. "Kiss her again, so we know you love her, and she'll want to stay. I lost the mistletoe, but Nellie says you don't have to have it to kiss someone you love. And you do love her, don't you?"

Luke closed his eyes. Did his children have any idea what they were saying? Did Nellie understand that she'd not only captured his heart, but theirs, as well?

"I do," he said quietly. "But that's a grown-up matter. And right now, we have grown-up matters to discuss. This man here needs you to tell him what happened so the bad man in our house goes to jail for a very long time."

As Nellie and the children described to the marshal what happened, Luke couldn't help but admire the bravery they'd all shown. And once again, he was struck by Nellie's devotion to his children. She truly loved them, and it was clear they loved her in return. How else would Ruby have found the strength to hit Big Jim with that pot?

The back door opened, and Will entered. "Luke! Nellie! I'm so sorry. I'm glad you're all safe."

Luke turned and looked at him. "We're fine. Is everything all right at the bank?"

Will nodded, looking disgusted. "It was part of Big Jim's plan. He convinced his men to rob the bank to get their stake for the game, knowing we'd divert our men to the robbery. Stupid fools—barely old enough to shave, and Big Jim got one of them killed. The other is terrified of prison, and he's spilling his guts. Poor kid. Big Jim had him convinced it would be an easy job, but security is tighter at Jackson's than any other bank in town. I'm pretty sure he was hoping both kids would be killed so no one would know his involvement. The kid is giving us a lot of good information. Won't save him from jail, but it might spare his life."

Will turned his attention to Nellie. "You warned us he was wily. We didn't realize his reach, or how many associates he had. I'm sorry I didn't bring in more men to protect you."

The marshal clapped Will on the back. "Don't blame yourself. When Seamus arrived at the sheriff's office, I was kicking myself for not getting on an earlier train. None of us thought Big Jim would act so early. But it all worked out. We have one dead robber, two men under arrest, and by the end of the night, I'm sure the rest of Big Jim's accomplices will be in jail, as well. Go home to that pretty wife and baby of yours and get some rest."

Luke nodded. "I agree. We all did the best we could, and I'm grateful everyone is safe."

"That sounds like a good idea." Will glanced over at Nellie and the children, then back at Luke. "I'm sure we'll all be counting our blessings tonight."

He turned to the door, and the marshal followed him. "I'll walk with you. Your house is on my way to the hotel, and we can compare notes."

When the men left, Luke brought his attention back to his family. "You were all so brave. I'm so proud of you all."

Amos looked at him sternly. "We couldn't let him take our Nellie. We're not going to let her go. So fix all the grown-up things between you two and kiss her already so I know everything is going to be all right."

What could Luke tell his son to help him understand that making amends to Nellie for the way he'd treated her wasn't as simple as giving her a kiss?

"Please, Papa," Ruby said. "Don't let her go."

Luke glanced at Nellie, wondering how they were supposed to have this conversation with such insistent children around, especially when he'd agreed to give her time.

"I don't want Nellie to go," Luke said, hoping Nellie could see the sincerity in his eyes. "Please don't go." He addressed her with all the love in his heart, bestowing his full attention on her. He'd wanted to have this conversation with her alone, without an audience, but it seemed like everything important he had to say ended up being this way.

"I know I've done a terrible job being a husband to you, because I was still grieving my late wife. I'm grateful that God put so many good friends in my life to remind me that I haven't loved you as I should, and that I was ignoring a beautiful gift from God in you."

Luke swallowed as he tried to read Nellie's expression. "I tried to show you that I cared for you by letting go of my past with Diana in small ways. I built you a room, I bought you a new stove, I got the Christmas tree Ruby wanted, and I was willing to use the settlement to save you. But I never asked you what you needed from me to know that I truly love you."

Tears dotted Nellie's cheeks as he continued. "Will suggested that we get a house that doesn't hold all the memories of Diana and we start fresh using the money in the bank to build our own life. I like that idea, but I've learned my lesson. We'll decide what to do together. Because from here on out, I want our lives to be about what we choose together. Not for convenience's sake, but out of our desire to spend the rest of our lives with each other. I love you, Nellie Jeffries, and I want you to be my wife, fully, completely and for always."

Nellie kissed the top of Maeve's head as she set the little girl down and stood. "Then I guess you'd better kiss me, then."

She took a step toward him and put her arms around him, but Luke pulled away for a moment.

"Wait," he said, digging in his pocket. "Look what I found. I know we don't need it, but Amos seems to think kisses are better with mistletoe, and I'd like to see if that's true."

Luke pulled the mistletoe out of his pocket and kissed Nellie. Though he quite liked the kiss, and he would never say so to his son, he was looking forward to having Nellie alone later so he could give her an even better one.

Then again, they had the rest of their lives for that.

Epilogue

Christmas morning dawned more perfectly than Nellie could have imagined. Once again, the good women of the church had come over to help clean the mess Big Jim had made of their house, scrubbing Nellie's floor until every trace of the blood from his head wound was gone. The doctor said he would survive to stand trial, and Will was confident that they had enough evidence to put Big Jim in jail for the rest of his life.

The rest of Big Jim's men were also in jail. The man who'd been captured in the bank robbery provided a great deal of information that helped in that endeavor.

Luke came out of Nellie's room. "There seems to be a lot of packages under that tree," he said, coming behind her and wrapping his arms around her as he kissed the back of her neck.

"More than I put there," Nellie told him.

"You might have had a little help."

He spun her around and kissed her, properly. The children would be up soon, so they had to take advantage of these moments while they could. Now that Luke had finally kissed her for real, Nellie wasn't sure she ever wanted him to stop.

"I love it when you kiss," Amos said, startling them.

Luke gave Nellie a quick peck before letting her go, the promise of more to come when they were alone again.

"Good morning," Nellie said, bending down and kissing him on top of the head. "I hope you slept well."

Amos grinned. "Now that Papa's not up there snoring all night, I sleep great."

"Hey!" Luke ruffled his son's hair. "I don't snore."

Laughing, Nellie said, "You do, but I love you anyway. Now get some more wood for the fire so I can make breakfast before church."

As Luke turned for the back door, a knock sounded at the front. Amos ran to open it.

"I hope it's someone with more presents," he said.

They hadn't even opened the ones they had, and already the little boy wanted more. But how could she fault the joy of a child?

"Well," said a familiar voice, "that will depend on whether or not you've been a good boy."

Was it...?

Amos opened the door fully, and tears sprang to Nellie's eyes as she saw Mabel standing there, her husband and children behind her.

"Mabel!"

"Nellie!"

Her sister hugged her tight. "Don't ever run away again. I don't care if they burn my house to the ground or destroy everything I own. You will always be more important to me."

"I'm sorry," Nellie said. "I thought I was doing the right thing. But I'm glad you're here."

She stepped aside to admit the rest of Mabel's family. "How did you all get here so quickly?"

Mabel grinned. "Apparently your lawman friend is married to a very wealthy woman. Or at least that's what he said in his telegram. They sent the money for us to come, saying that after all you've been through, you needed your sister by your side. Which is true, but without their generosity, I would have never had the means."

Tears fell down Mabel's cheeks as she looked at Nellie. "You don't have to stay here if you don't want to. Our home is your home, and I'm so sorry you felt you had to enter into a marriage of convenience to survive."

"It's all right," Nellie said, giving her sister another quick hug, then turning to gesture toward her husband. "I fell in love with Luke, and as it turns out, he loves me, too. So, Mabel, meet my husband, Luke."

The rest of the children came down from the loft, and Nellie introduced Mabel and her family to Nellie's new family. Nellie couldn't remember a time when her heart had felt more full.

"Cousins!" Ruby's eyes lit up with excitement. "I've always wanted cousins! You never said your sister had children."

Nellie smiled at her. "It hurt too much at the time. I missed them all so much, and I couldn't bear to speak of them, knowing I'd never see them again."

"But we'll see them more now, right?" Amos asked, grinning at Mabel's son Ely. The boys were of similar ages, and Mabel's daughter Ruth was just a bit younger than Ruby. Mabel's other children, Charlie and Lydia, were between Amos and Maeve in age, but Nellie had no doubt that the children would all be friends.

"We sure will," Mabel said, looking at Nellie with such a tender expression, Nellie wasn't sure how she'd gone without her sister for so long.

Hank, Mabel's husband, nodded. "I've heard there's a lot of opportunity here in Leadville, and we've been talking about going West for a while now. Mabel wouldn't hear of it as long as she didn't know where you were. She wanted to stay put in case you found your way back. Now that you've found each other again, we're free to pursue other things."

Nellie hugged Mabel again, unable to believe that she was really here. The women quickly fell into their old routine, preparing breakfast together. Only, it wasn't the same routine, because in the background their children were playing together, a dream Nellie had never imagined would come true.

When breakfast was ready, the men came inside and Luke said grace, and his voice caught as he thanked God for their many blessings. Nellie squeezed his hand.

After they all said "Amen," Luke said, "I know I promised we'd make decisions about our future together, and I'm keeping that promise, but I wanted to see how you felt about an idea I have."

Nellie smiled at her husband. "I'd love to hear it."

"I ran into Owen at church last night, and he said

that the events of the past few days made him realize just how much his work took him from his family.
He's going to sell his house and move to a ranch he
owns just outside of town. He wanted to let me know,
because he thought his place would be good for our
family. It's not the one Diana wanted, but it has good
space for us and would suit us well. I was thinking
we should take a look. If you like it, we'll buy it, and
Mabel and her family can stay in this house until they
find a place of their own."

Nellie stared at her husband for a moment. He was
letting go of the last pieces of Diana. "Are you sure?"

"We need to build a life that's ours, not something
based on what Diana wanted. If you don't like Owen's
place, we'll keep looking until we find something that
suits you."

"That suits us," Nellie said, taking his hand.

"Yes. Us," Luke agreed, leaning over and kissing her.

* * * * *

Dear Reader,

When I was researching this story, I read newspapers printed in the same time when my story takes place. I was expecting to see something reflecting what we see in the media today about Christmas. Instead, I saw articles about activities the church planned, or, what became my favorite, commentary about how lovely the church choir sounded, and that parishioners were in for a treat come Christmas.

How I long to go back to that time! I can't imagine a better Christmas than not having all the commercialism our society associates with the holiday, and being able to truly soak in the spirit of the season.

My hope, and my prayer, for you is that during the busyness of the season upon us, you find some quiet time to soak in the gift God has given us. May God give you a reminder of His deep love for you this Christmas.

I always love hearing from my readers. Connect with me at the following places:

Website: *DanicaFavorite.com*
Twitter: *Twitter.com/danicafavorite*
Instagram: *Instagram.com/danicafavorite*
Facebook: *Facebook.com/DanicaFavoriteAuthor*

Peace to you and yours,
Danica Favorite

A LAWMAN FOR CHRISTMAS
Smoky Mountain Matches • by Karen Kirst

After lawman Ben MacGregor and avowed spinster Isabel Flores discover a four-year-old boy abandoned on her property at Christmas, they must work together to care for him. But can their temporary arrangement turn into a forever family?

MAIL-ORDER CHRISTMAS BABY
Montana Courtships • by Sherri Shackelford

When a child arrives with the Wells Fargo delivery with documents listing Heather O'Connor and Sterling Blackwell as the baby's parents, they are forced to marry to give the baby a home—and save their reputations.

THEIR MISTLETOE MATCHMAKERS
by Keli Gwyn

Lavinia Crowne heads to California planning to bring her late sister's orphaned children back east. But Henry Hawthorn, their paternal uncle, is intent on raising them in the only home they know...and three little matchmakers hope their mistletoe-filled schemes will bring their aunt and uncle together.

A CHILD'S CHRISTMAS WISH
by Erica Vetsch

After her home is destroyed in a fire, pregnant widow Kate Amaker and her in-laws take refuge with Oscar Rabb—the widowed farmer next door whose daughter has one holiday wish: a baby for Christmas.

Get 2 Free Books,
Plus 2 Free Gifts—
just for trying the Reader Service!

Love Inspired HISTORICAL

"The only way for us to clear our names is to find the real parents. If Grace's mother made the choice out of necessity," Heather said, "then she'll be missing her child terribly. Perhaps we can help."

Grace reached for her, and Heather folded her into her arms. By the looks on the gentlemen's faces, the gesture was further proof against her. But Heather was drawn to the child. The poor thing was powerless and at the mercy of strangers. Despite everything she'd been through, the baby appeared remarkably good-natured. Whatever her origins, she was a resilient child.

The reverend focused his attention on Grace with searing intensity, as though she might reveal the secret of her origins if he just looked hard enough. "Who is going to watch her for the time being?"

Sterling coughed into his fist and stared at the tips of his boots. The reverend discovered an intense fascination with the button on his sleeve.

Heather's pulse picked up speed. Surely they wouldn't leave the baby with her? "I don't think I should be seen with her. The more people connect us, the more they'll gossip."

"It's too late already," Sterling said. "There are half a dozen curious gossips milling outside the door right now."

Heather peered out the church window and immediately jerked back. Sure enough, a half dozen people were out there.

If she didn't take responsibility for the child, who would? "I'll watch her," Heather conceded.

"Thank the Lord for your kindness." The reverend clasped his hands as though in prayer. "The poor child deserves care. I'll do my best to stem the talk," he added. "But I can't make any promises."

Sterling sidled nearer. "Don't worry. I'll find the truth."

"I know you will."

A disturbing sense of intimacy left her light-headed. In the blink of an eye her painstakingly cultivated air of practicality fled. Then he turned his smile on the baby, and the moment was broken.

Heather set her lips in a grim line. His deference was practiced and meant nothing. She must always be on guard around Sterling Blackwell. She must always remember that she was no more special to him than the woman who typed out his telegrams.

He treated everyone with the same indolent consideration, and yet she'd always been susceptible to his charm.

She smoothed her hand over Grace's wild curls. They were both alone, but now they had each other.

At least for the time being.

Don't miss
MAIL-ORDER CHRISTMAS BABY by Sherri Shackelford,
available November 2017 wherever
Love Inspired® Historical books and ebooks are sold.

www.LoveInspired.com

SPECIAL EXCERPT FROM

*When Erica Lindholm and her twin babies show up at
his family farm just before Christmas, Jason Stephanidis
can tell she's hiding something. But how can he refuse
the young mother, a friend of his sister's, a place to stay
during the holidays? He never counted on wanting Erica
and the boys to be a more permanent part of his life...*

Read on for a sneak peek of
SECRET CHRISTMAS TWINS
by *Lee Tobin McClain*,
part of the **CHRISTMAS TWINS** miniseries.

Once both twins were bundled, snug between Papa
and Erica, Jason sent the horses trotting forward.
The sun was up now, making millions of diamonds
on the snow that stretched across the hills far into
the distance. He smelled pine, a sharp, resin-laden
sweetness.

When he picked up the pace, the sleigh bells jingled.

"Real sleigh bells!" Erica said, and then, as they
approached the white covered bridge decorated with a
simple wreath for Christmas, she gasped. "This is the
most beautiful place I've ever seen."

Jason glanced back, unable to resist watching her fall
in love with his home.

Papa was smiling for the first time since he'd learned
of Kimmie's death. And as they crossed the bridge and
trotted toward the church, converging with other horse-
drawn sleighs, Jason felt a sense of rightness.

Mikey started babbling to Teddy, accompanied by gestures and much repetition of his new word. Teddy tilted his head to one side and burst forth with his own stream of nonsense syllables, seeming to ask a question, batting Mikey on the arm. Mikey waved toward the horses and jabbered some more, as if he were explaining something important.

They were such personalities, even as little as they were. Jason couldn't help smiling as he watched them interact.

Once Papa had the reins set and the horses tied up, Jason jumped out of the sleigh, and then turned to help Erica down. She handed him a twin. "Can you hold Mikey?"

He caught a whiff of baby powder and pulled the little one tight against his shoulder. Then he reached out to help Erica, and she took his hand to climb down, Teddy on her hip.

When he held her hand, something electric seemed to travel right to his heart. Involuntarily he squeezed and held on.

She drew in a sharp breath as she looked at him, some mixture of puzzlement and awareness in her eyes.

What was Erica's secret?

And wasn't it curious that, after all these years, there were twins in the farmhouse again?

Don't miss
SECRET CHRISTMAS TWINS
by Lee Tobin McClain, available November 2017
wherever Love Inspired® books and ebooks are sold.

www.LoveInspired.com

LIEXP1017